Blood King

A KINGS OF VEGAS NOVEL

NATALIE KANE

&
AMPERSAND
PUBLISHING, INC.

BLOOD KING

A Kings of Vegas Novel

Natalie Kane

*This is for anyone who doesn't believe in their own strength.
You're so damn badass.
You deserve everything good. You are fucking amazing.
I'm so glad you're here.*

Prologue

JULIAN

THIS ASSHOLE THINKS he's intimidating me.

I'm sitting in Sergei Ivanov's office, across from the man himself, who's puffing away on a disgusting cigar. He's so fucking cheap, he doesn't even have the decency to smuggle Cubans in.

Sergei's refusal to part with money is the reason I'm sitting here in the first place.

"Your son is late," he says with a heavy Russian accent, as if it might be lost on me that Elliott isn't in the room.

"He'll be here," I reply. I don't bother to check my phone or my watch and show any kind of weakness in front of the head of the Bratva.

Elliott will be here.

"I'm a busy man, Mr. Stavros. If you're wasting my time—"

"I'm not wasting anyone's time, and you're not the only man in this room who has other business to attend to. Let's get started."

Sergei's eyes narrow, and then he grunts, and the man standing to his right sets a black folder on the desk.

"I took the liberty of having my attorney write a contract."

I lift an eyebrow. "A *marriage* contract?"

"That's right."

I won't be signing anything this idiot sets in front of me, but I offer him a congenial smile.

"And what are the terms in this contract?"

"Well, there's all kinds of legal speak here, but basically, your son marries my daughter, and my debt to you is forgiven."

Oh, his debt will never be forgiven.

"What else?"

"I think it's pretty standard. If Elliott cheats on her, he'll have to pay her ten million dollars—"

"You mean *you.*"

Sergei's eyes narrow. "That's right."

"And if she cheats?"

"She won't."

My lips twitch. "You seem so sure of yourself."

"My daughter has been raised to be the perfect organized crime wife. She knows what's expected of her. She'll remain faithful, she'll take her punishments, and she'll never ask for a divorce."

She'll take her punishments.

I'd like to pull the gun from the small of my back and fill his head with lead. Better than that, I'd prefer to pull my knife out and flay the skin from his pathetic, fat body.

Instead, I hold his gaze with mine.

"No."

His face turns red, but I don't give him time to argue.

"I'm not signing that or anything else you put in front of me. We've agreed to an alliance between our organizations with the marriage of my son to your daughter. That's the agreement. I won't pay you a fucking dime if one of them fucks up. You have my word that Natasha will be cared for, and while the money you owe me—all one hundred million of it—will be forgiven, it's not forgotten, Sergei. And any future money you owe me will *not* be forgiven."

His jaw is so tight, I can hear his molars grinding together.

"Papa?"

We all glance to the doorway, and I'm pretty sure one of these fuckers just shot me in the head and I'm dead because I'm looking at a literal angel.

This woman is fucking *gorgeous* in a white dress that flows just past her knees and shows off ample cleavage. Long blond hair flows in waves past her shoulders, her eyes are striking blue, the color of Kashmiri sapphires, and her glossy pink lips press in a line with uncertainty.

He's willing to sell this beautiful woman's soul away for a measly one hundred million?

I should kill him where he sits for even considering it.

"You wanted to see me?" Her voice is soft, and her eyes shift between her father and me with unease.

"Yes, come in, malyshka." Sergei hardly looks at her as he waves her in. "Sit."

"I don't want to intrude—"

"SIT!" he yells and slams his fist on his desk, and Natasha hurries to the chair near the one I'm in and takes a seat. Her back is perfectly straight, hands are folded in her lap, one ankle crossed behind the other, and she looks down at the floor obediently.

I'd really like to gut this asshole.

"This is Julian Stavros," Sergei tells his daughter, gesturing to me. "I've arranged for a marriage."

She gasps, her spine snaps even straighter, and those beautiful eyes turn to me. She blinks, looks me up and down, and her cheeks darken.

Interesting.

"I'm marrying him?" she asks timidly just as the door opens once more.

"Sorry I'm late."

I sigh and don't bother to look behind me as Elliott strolls into the room. I can smell the whiskey on him from here, and God only knows what casino he left to get here.

"Elliott," Sergei says with a nod. "This is Natasha. Your bride."

I haven't taken my eyes off her. She swallows hard, a slight frown appearing between her brows.

She wants to object.

She takes her punishments.

"My what now?" Elliott asks, and I finally look up at my son. "Since when am I getting married?"

"If you'd answered any one of my calls over the past three days, this wouldn't be news to you." My voice is calm, because I'll never give Sergei the satisfaction of seeing any emotion from me, but I'm going to have it out with my kid later.

Elliott blinks at me, then looks over at Natasha, and

when his gaze rakes over her gorgeous body, his lips spread in a smile. I want to push him out of the way and claim her for myself.

Which is fucking ridiculous.

"I'm so sorry for my manners," Elliott says as he holds a hand out for hers. "I'm Elliott."

"Natasha," she answers, eyeing his hand. She doesn't want to touch him, it's written all over her perfect face, but she holds her breath and slides her hand into his. "Hello."

"Excellent," Sergei says. "Let's have some vodka."

"No, thank you," I reply before my son can drink the man out of house and home. "The wedding will be in six weeks. We'll be in touch."

I stand and stare my son in the eyes.

"Let's go," I say, gesturing with my chin, and he smiles one more time at Natasha before he walks out of the room ahead of me.

When we're outside, he turns to talk to me, but I beat him to it.

"Not here. There are ears. Get in the car."

"But I drove my own car."

"Get in the fucking back seat, Elliott." My patience is wearing thin with my son.

He looks like he wants to argue, but finally sighs and slides into the back of the Range Rover, and I follow him. We have three other vehicles, and ten men with us, and we pull down the driveway and out onto the road.

"What the fuck, Dad?"

"We need an alliance with the Russians."

He's staring at me, his eyes suddenly sober. "I've been seeing Kitty for three months."

"And now you're not."

He shakes his head, and I lay it out for him. "You'll marry her, and you'll honor that marriage, El."

"Or?"

"Or I'm done. No more bailing you out. No more helping you. I'll cut you off and act like I've never met you in my life."

His jaw drops. "You wouldn't do that."

"Wouldn't I?"

I lift an eyebrow, and he knows this is his last chance with me. He knows what's at stake.

He sits back in the seat and stares out the window.

"I guess it's a good thing I like blonds."

One

NATASHA

MY LIFE HAS BEEN a living hell for a month.

Okay, let's be honest. It hasn't been sunshine and roses for all of my twenty-two years, which is just par for the course when you're the daughter, and only child, of the head of the Bratva. Especially when your father is . . . *horrible.* Mean. Unloving.

Yeah, my dad's an asshole.

My mom is just as bad. Maybe worse because a mother is supposed to show affection, to be the nurturing one. My mother doesn't have an unselfish bone in her body.

But I digress. It's been a month since I was summoned to my father's office and told that I'd be marrying Elliott Stavros, the son of Julian, the head of the Greek Mafia. One of the Kings of Vegas.

I don't exactly know what all of that means, except that Julian is powerful and my father wants an alliance with him. Therefore, it's up to me to be the sacrificial lamb, as if it's 1592.

Elliott has taken me out on dates, and he acts like the doting fiancé when we're around other people. So attentive and sweet. He smiles at me, opens doors, gently lays his hand on the small of my back as we walk through a room. If that were who he truly is, I wouldn't have an issue with this arrangement.

But in private?

Fuck, life is going to suck if I really have to marry this guy.

"Are you even fucking listening to me, Tash?"

I hate that nickname. No one calls me that. I've asked him to stop, but he ignores me, so I finally gave up. Because a proper Mafia wife never questions her husband.

"I'm listening." I sound like a mouse. My voice is small. I wish I had the nerve to speak up, to tell him that I'm standing six inches away from him, and *of course* I'm listening.

But I would *never.*

"I want to take you to Rapture tonight."

I barely suppress a sigh. He mentions this almost every single time I see him. The *club* isn't a dance club or a bar. No, he wants to take me to Rapture, which he's already told me about in great detail, several times. It's clearly his favorite place in the whole world, and every time he brings it up, I want to roll my eyes. It's obviously a *thing* for him.

Rapture is a high-end sex club. And I have no intention of having sex with this man until it's absolutely necessary, which I'm hoping is never, but I suspect it will happen no later than our wedding night.

Just the thought fills me with dread. I'm not attracted to Elliott. Sure, he's handsome. Tall and dark with a muscular build. But he has meanness in his eyes. His palms are always sweaty, and he reeks of whiskey.

Not sexy.

"I'm tired—"

"You're always fucking tired. Jesus, is this what it's going to be like to be married to you? Boring, frigid, and useless?"

Pretty much. Get used to it, buddy.

"I'm just . . . it makes me uncomfortable." The last word is said on a whisper.

"What does?" he asks as he slides his palm down my arm and squeezes my hand. He's trying to be comforting, but I don't like being touched by anyone, most of all my fiancé. "What makes you uncomfortable, beautiful?"

I don't want to tell him. I don't want him to hit me. Again. That seems to be his go-to when he's frustrated with me, and my cheek still aches from the last time.

"Tell me."

"Watching people have sex makes me uncomfortable."

I don't meet his eyes. I can feel my cheeks burn.

"You're going to have to get used to it because I like it there, and I go often. Unless you want me fucking other women, you'll go with me, and you'll do what I say when we're there. You'll learn to like it." He tips my chin up, leering down at me. His eyes drop to my cleavage, and then up to my mouth. "Besides, you'll be with me, and I won't let anyone else touch you. Unless we invite a third, of course."

He smirks, and I almost wince at the thought.

"But *you'll* touch me." The words are out before I can snatch them back, and he narrows his dark eyes on me.

That was the wrong thing to say.

He looks so much like his father. I've only seen Julian a few times since that first meeting. When Papa first said that a marriage had been arranged, and I thought it was to Julian, I didn't freak out. He's handsome. He seemed . . . calm. Steady. He didn't make my Spidey senses tingle with dread.

But then his son walked in, and that calm flew right out the window. Elliott is not like his father. After spending a month with my fiancé, that's plain to see.

"Yeah, Tash." His fingers slide along my neck and into the back of my hair, and it gives me the heebie-jeebies. My first instinct is to pull out of his grasp, but that'll only make things far worse for me. I manage to keep my face stoic as he moves in closer. "I'm going to touch you. I'm going to run my mouth all over you and fuck every hole you've got until you're a bloody, cum-covered mess. Because you're *mine*. I own you."

I shiver at that, and not because his words are sexy. No, they're said with a sneer, with malice, and his hand fists harder in my hair, pulling my head back.

"I can do whatever the fuck I want to you."

"And if I say no?" I hate how shaky my voice is.

"You don't get to say *no*." His nose is almost touching mine. His voice is so hard, and there's so much anger and violence in his dark eyes. "Didn't you just hear me say that I can do whatever the fuck I want?"

I swallow hard. Is this really what my life has been reduced to? Honestly, I'd rather he went out and slept with all of Vegas if it meant he'd leave me alone.

"M-maybe we can have a marriage in name only, and you can get your needs met from other women."

His eyes narrow, his jaw hardens.

"Are you telling me that you don't want me, Natasha?"

"I don't like to be touched by anyone."

He leans in even closer, until his mouth is next to my ear, making me want to gag. If being this close to the man sets off my gag reflex, how can I ever possibly have sex with him?

"Let me make myself perfectly clear. I. don't. Give a fuck if you don't like to be touched. You've got a hot-as-hell body, and I'll be using it. In private and in front of every single person at the club. You're my whore, Tash. My father paid for you and gave you to me."

I hear a door open, but I don't move. I can't. He's holding my hair so tight, if I move an inch he'll pull it out by the roots.

"I don't want to have sex with you, Elliott."

He shakes his head in frustration. "Tonight, or ever?"

"Ever."

Crack.

His open hand slaps across my face, and then he does it again, sending me crashing to the floor. My knee catches on a coffee table, cutting the skin and making me immediately start to bleed all over the tile. Pain explodes across my jaw and mouth, and blood dribbles down my chin.

"You stupid *cunt*! I don't fucking care what you want. Do you understand English?"

"What the *fuck* are you doing?"

The room goes silent, except for Elliott's fast breathing and the blood rushing through my ears. I glance toward the doorway of the penthouse and see Julian striding my way, and I flinch, cowering close to the floor.

But he doesn't hit me.

He grabs Elliott by the collar of his shirt and shakes him.

"I asked you a fucking question. I won't repeat myself."

"I'm putting her in her place."

I'm not looking at them. I can't. I'm so damn embarrassed, and all I can do is sit here on the floor, my face down, willing myself not to cry.

Don't let them see you cry, Natasha.

"That is *not* how I taught you to treat women."

There's no response. I see Elliott's feet just turn and walk away, and soon a door slams upstairs.

Oh God, I'm alone with Julian.

Two

JULIAN

FINALLY, after two days of torture, the motherfucker who tried to steal ten million dollars in diamonds from me broke and told me who the mastermind behind the heist was. All it took was me showing him his kidney.

They usually talk way before that, so I had to have respect for his endurance and pain threshold. It was impressive.

He still fucking died, of course, but he put me and my knife through our paces. I'm exhausted and covered in blood. I need a shower and a good night's sleep before I start hunting the fucking thief in the morning. Tonight, I plan to go to the penthouse that I keep in the city and crash for a solid seven hours.

I'd usually go home. I built a mansion several years ago outside of the city. It's become my sanctuary, but I'm not up for the thirty minute drive to get there tonight.

I have the penthouse for nights exactly like this.

But before I can leave my Porsche 911, the phone rings, and I recognize the number. With a sigh, I answer.

This will be about Elliott.

"Cillian, to what do I owe the pleasure?"

Cillian O'Connor is the head of the Irish mob and owns a casino here in Vegas, but his business is primarily out of New Orleans. I have no beef with the man. He runs a good casino, cleans his own money there, and doesn't interfere with my brothers and me in our city.

It's been mutually beneficial.

But I have a bad feeling about this call.

"Julian," he says smoothly. "I don't like making this call and ruining your evening."

Fuck.

"What's the problem?" I ask.

"Your son has been gambling at the Four Leaf all week and has lost more than he can cover."

I'm going to kill him.

"How much does he owe you, Cillian?"

"Just over a quarter of a million."

"Fucking hell," I mutter with a loud exhale.

"Quite," he replies, and I can hear the smile in his voice. "I have no issue with you, Julian. Your son, however, has an addiction that's starting to piss me off. So, here's what I'm going to do. I'm going to forgive this debt, and you're going to keep your kid out of my place. Permanently."

"Done. I'll pay you, Cillian."

"I don't want your money. You and I are square. Just keep him out of the Four Leaf and out of New Orleans."

"Done. Thank you."

We hang up and I drag my hand down my face in agitation. This is the third call like this in the past month.

I paid the other two debts, totaling almost half a million. Elliott is writing proverbial checks like he's already in charge, and it's going to get him killed.

He wasn't always this reckless. This . . . *stupid*. Elliott was a quiet boy, an excellent athlete, and I had high hopes for him in my organization. But a couple of years ago, he started gambling and drinking way too fucking much.

He's a liability. Not just to me personally but to our organization. To the *family*.

And I absolutely can't fucking have that. I would kill anyone else for making me look weak.

I climb out of the car and nod at my security, who followed me home, and then ride the elevator up.

At the very least, maybe I should stop protecting my son from the consequences of his actions and let someone beat him to hell and back to teach him a lesson.

Pushing through the door, I can feel that I'm not alone, which isn't a surprise. Elliott crashes here when he's not in a casino or the club. The one rule in the past was that he not bring women here, but I don't care if he stays. And now that he's engaged to Natasha, I know that he's brought her to the penthouse off and on, which doesn't really bother me, either, except that I see her more than I'd like.

Not thinking about that.

Crack!

I scowl as I turn the corner and see my son slap his fiancée across the face, twice, sending her to the floor.

"You stupid *cunt*! I don't fucking care what you want. Do you understand English?"

"What the *fuck* are you doing?" Rage roars through

me as I watch blood seep out of Natasha's leg and her lip, and I glare at my son, who's breathing hard, a look of pure malice on his face.

Christ.

He's not answering me, and the woman won't look at me, so I march to my son, fist my hand in his shirt and snarl, "I asked you a fucking question. I won't repeat myself."

"I'm putting her in her place."

Jesus fuck, this is *not* how I taught my kid to behave.

I can smell the liquor on him, and it turns my stomach, and I push him away from me.

"That is *not* how I taught you to treat women."

Elliott shakes his head and turns his back, marches to his bedroom and slams the door, and with a sigh, I turn my attention to the woman on the floor.

She's in a white dress—I've only ever seen her in white, now that I think about it—which is spattered with blood, and her blond hair is down, shielding her face from me. She's trembling, which only makes me angrier.

Has he been treating her like this the whole goddamn time? They've been seeing each other for a month.

Squatting next to Natasha, I reach over to brush her hair behind her ear, but she flinches away from me, giving the rage flowing through me a renewed energy.

"I won't hurt you," I murmur to her. "Come, let's get you cleaned up."

"I-I can just go home." Her voice is small, and she won't look me in the eyes, which annoys the shit out of me. She's too amazing to be this . . . *small.* That's the only word I have for it. Her voice, the way she's making her already petite body look tiny, as if she's trying to disappear.

This woman should stand up, take up all the space she needs and fucking roar.

"Do you want me to help you up?"

She takes a deep breath and then shakily climbs to her feet, and with my hand barely on her back, I lead her down the hall. She moves away, so I can't touch her, which I allow for now, and when we walk into my bedroom, her eyes scan the large space, the tall ceilings and wall of windows that look out to the strip, the perfectly made bed, and I guide her to my bathroom.

I have six bathrooms in this penthouse, and why I immediately brought her to mine, I don't want to think about.

"I'm going to lift you onto the vanity."

Her brows pull into a frown, but she gives me a shaky nod, granting me permission to boost her up by the waist onto the marble vanity, and then I grab a washcloth and the first aid kit from beneath the sink, ignoring the way my hands want to continue to touch her.

I turn on the water to let it warm up, and then with one finger under her chin, I lift her gaze to mine.

Christ she's fucking beautiful.

Since that day in her father's office, I've been drawn to her, which is a huge fucking problem considering she'll be marrying my son.

But who could resist these big blue eyes, the gorgeous, smooth skin, and those plump bowed lips?

And who in their right mind could possibly mistreat her?

"I'm sorry that happened." My voice is low, and my face is stoic as I take in her cut and bleeding lip and the older bruise on her jawline.

"It's not your fault," Natasha whispers. She's still shaking, and I hate it. I don't want her to be afraid of me, and she absolutely should *not* be afraid of the man she's going to be married to, and I'll be having a conversation with Elliott after I get her fixed up and headed home.

"Are you hurt too?"

I frown, following her gaze to my blood-spattered shirt.

"No. It's not mine. Does he hit you often?" I ask her as I wet a cloth and wipe it over her chin, cleaning up the blood where her lip is split. She winces but doesn't jerk away as I dab it clean.

"Only when I deserve it."

Pausing, my gaze lifts to hers, and then she looks away.

"You will never be hit like this again. Not by him."

That frown forms between her brows again, but she doesn't say anything, and resigned, I continue to clean her up.

Her knee is the worst of it. I rinse the cloth and wipe the line of blood from her shin and then wince when I see the gash over her kneecap.

"You likely need stitches."

"No." She shakes her head and rifles through my first aid kit, then comes out with butterfly strips. "These will work. I've got this."

Standing back to give her room, I watch as she opens the strips and expertly closes the gash.

"You've done that before."

She shrugs and frowns at my hand. "You have blood on your finger."

Glancing down, I see she's right. I have *her* blood on my finger. But rather than accept the cloth she offers me, I hold her gaze and lift the digit to my mouth, sucking her blood from my skin, and my heart pulses at the coppery taste on my tongue.

Her eyes dilate, and she licks her lower lip. The air between us crackles with sexual tension.

Fuck, I want to squat right here, bury my face in her pussy and eat my fill of her before I fuck her so hard, she'll never think of another man again.

She's not mine.

"Please don't make me marry him." It's whispered so softly that I almost missed it. I know, without a doubt, that she means it with her entire heart and soul.

The problem is, I also know that Elliott will be a worthless husband if he doesn't get his shit together real fast.

I don't like this part of the world I live in. But that doesn't mean that I don't have to respect it and honor the deal I made with her father.

I don't answer her. I can't. Because if I'm being brutally honest with myself, I don't want her to marry Elliott either. I'd take her for myself if I wasn't so much older than her, if I thought for a minute that I was the kind of man who could marry again.

Not replying, I simply stare into her eyes, holding her gaze until her shoulders roll forward and she looks away, making herself small again.

It grates on my goddamn nerves.

"My driver will take you home."

"Oh, I can find my own way."

Shaking my head, I help her off the vanity to her feet, steadying her, and then I back away, keeping a safe distance so I don't give in and kiss the fuck out of her.

The next fifty years or so are going to be fucking torture. I think I'd rather have my fingernails pulled out every single day for the rest of my fucking life.

"Come." I pull the phone out of my pocket and text my driver, telling him he's taking Natasha home. Then I lead her to the elevator, scooping up her purse on the way.

"I can just get a cab." I hate how fucking soft and timid her voice is. "I don't want you to go to any trouble."

"It's no trouble." I press the button for the elevator, and when it opens, I lead her inside and pass her the bag before pressing the button for the underground garage. "Never again, Natasha."

Her nod is jerky, and I back out so the elevator doors can close. Once she's out of sight, I spin on my heel and march up the stairs to Elliott's room.

Not bothering to knock, I shove the door so hard that it hits the wall, startling my son from where he's sitting by the window, drinking another fucking glass of whiskey.

"What the fuck is wrong with you?" I roar as I yank the glass from his hand, throw it against the wall, shattering it into a million pieces, and then spin to smack him across the face, making his eyes bulge in shock.

I've never hit Elliott once in his life. Not even when he was a child.

"What the fuck, Dad!"

"If you want to hit someone, you hit *me*, mother-fucker." My face is inches from his, and I'm seething as the anger I've kept on a tight leash since I saw him hit that woman finally breaks free. "You will *never* lay a hand on her in anger again."

"I'll do whatever the fuck I want." His chin juts out in defiance, and he tries to push me back, but I don't budge. "She's *mine*. I own her, thanks to you."

"She's a goddamn human being! And here I am, cleaning up your mess *again*. I pay your gambling debts, I bail your ass out of jail, and make shit go away for you, and now I have to play nursemaid to your fiancé because you can't keep your fucking hands to yourself when you're pissed off? Fuck that, Elliott. I don't even recognize you. Who the hell are you? You're risking the family, and it's going to be your fucking demise."

"You don't *have* to do any of that. I never asked you to. I can clean up my own fucking messes."

Spittle shoots out of his mouth as he yells at me, and I find my calm once more. I roll my shoulders and adjust the cuff of my shirt, and Elliott's face falls as he realizes what he just said.

"Great. From now on, you can do just that, Elliott."

"Dad, I appreciate—"

"You'll be out of here by tomorrow morning. You no longer live here. And I won't be paying off any more of your debts. You have a trust fund with plenty of money. I suggest you get control of your fucking addiction to throwing it away, so you don't end up homeless."

"*Dad*, I'm just angry, I—"

"I don't fucking care." I'm no longer yelling. I'm *tired*. The only way he's going to learn is if I give him no other choice. I haven't done him any favors by continuing to bail him out, and it stops right now. "I'm not throwing you out of the family, Elliott. I should, but not yet. However, I'm done paying your way and being your cleaning crew. Grow the fuck up. You're going to marry that girl in two weeks, honoring the alliance between our families. You're going to take care of her. You will not hurt her, and if I find out that you do, I'll cut your motherfucking hands off, and you won't be able to hit anyone ever again."

His jaw drops. He knows I'm not joking. Cutting off appendages is one of my favorite pastimes.

"I'll let my security know to escort you out of here by morning. Pack your shit, Elliott."

"Where am I supposed to go?"

I turn and lift an eyebrow. "You have contacts all over this city. Use them. Figure it the fuck out, kid. Pull yourself together and use this as the fresh start that it is. Marry the girl, get your act together. You could have a good life, Elliott."

"Fuck." He pushes his hand through his hair, and I walk out.

Looks like I'm headed to the mansion tonight after all.

When I get down to the parking garage, my security snaps to attention.

"We're going home," I say, and then turn to my driver, surprised that he's already back. "Did you get her home safely?"

His eyes slide to his colleagues and then back to me. "She, uh, refused the ride, sir."

I step to him, only inches from his face, and narrow my eyes.

He swallows hard.

"She *refused.*"

"Yes, boss. We all tried to tell her that you wouldn't be okay with that. But she said she wanted me to call her a taxi."

My blood turns to fire as I step closer and tighten his loose tie, seemingly perfectly calm on the outside.

He's not going to survive this.

"You put a Bratva princess, who didn't have any guards with her, into a fucking *cab*?"

I sense the other guys shuffling in fear. I should kill all of them for putting her at risk.

Instead, I'll make an example out of this one.

"How long have you worked for me, Johnny?"

"Three years, sir."

"And in those three years, how many times have I told you to take my orders as a *suggestion* and do whatever you want?"

He swallows hard again, sweating now. I reach into my pocket and close my hand around the switchblade I've carried on me since I was fifteen.

"N-never, boss."

"Never." I nod slowly and back away from him, and just as he takes a relieved breath, I turn back and plunge my knife in the side of his neck and watch as Johnny collapses to his knees, fighting for air, blood spurting all over my parking garage.

"If any of you even *thinks* about disobeying one of my orders, this will be a quick death compared to what I'll do to you. Do you understand?"

"Yes, boss," they all reply in unison. My eyes roam over them. All six of them are a little green. All stoic. My cousin, Jack, doesn't flinch.

Nothing makes Jack flinch.

"Have your team take him to the graveyard and pay his wife," I say to Jack, who is also my head of security. I don't have a number two. I was waiting for Elliott to pull his head out of his ass so I could groom him for the position.

That's not going to happen.

I'll have a meeting with Jack tomorrow. In the meantime, my cousin nods.

"You got it," he says. "Then I'm heading home to Alysse."

Jack's been married for five years and has a two-year-old son that I adore.

"I want to see you in my home office at nine tomorrow morning," I tell him, and he nods as I climb into the 911.

"I'll be there, boss."

Three

JULIAN

"WHY ARE you calling me at eight in the fucking morning?" I sit up in bed and scowl out the window to the backyard beyond.

"Why are you asleep this late?" Rome asks. He's one of my three best friends. The four of us run the underground of this city. We're known as the Kings of Vegas, but among the four of us, we're simply brothers. There isn't anything I wouldn't do for them, and vice versa. We work well together, we help each other, and it's been that way since we were teenagers.

"Because I didn't get to sleep until about four hours ago." I turn to the side of the bed and scratch my nails over my scalp. "What do you want?"

"Why is your son calling me, asking if he can have one of the apartments in my building?"

My eyes narrow. Rome owns Rapture and the high-rise building it's housed in, just off the strip. Some of his staff lives in the apartments. Other apartments are used as luxury rentals for the members of the club that travel to Vegas to experience the opulent hedonism that it offers.

In other words, it's fancy as fuck.

Of course my kid is asking to live there.

"I hope to Christ you told him no."

"I don't have any availability right now," Rome replies. "But I could open something up if you want me to."

"No. I kicked him out last night, and he needs to figure it out for himself. I told him to use his contacts, and I guess that's what he's doing, but this is still too close to home. Also, if he's still in arrears in his membership dues, kick him out."

Rome whistles in my ear. "The kid pissed you off."

"He beat up his fiancé last night," I reply, and I can just imagine Rome's face on the other end of the line. Hard. Pissed. "Then he claimed that he owns her, so he can do whatever he wants to her."

"Fuck."

"He's about to learn what being an adult is all about."

"Good. It's probably time for that, if I'm being honest."

"I know." I stand and pad into the bathroom to relieve myself.

"Are you pissing on the phone with me?"

"You're the one who woke me up." Another call beeps through, and checking the screen, I say, "I have to go. Sergei's calling me."

"Go piss in *his* ear," Rome says before hanging up.

I flush and start to wash my hands as I answer Sergei's call.

"Yes?"

"And good morning to you too."

I roll my eyes and dry my hands. Looks like I'm up for the day.

"What can I do for you, Sergei?"

"Your son called me this morning." *Motherfucking shit.* "He tells me that he's now homeless, turned out by his own father."

"That's none of your business."

"It *is* my business when he's marrying my daughter. I won't allow Natasha to be homeless the minute she marries your son, Julian. He also tells me," he continues before I can reply, "that he was kicked out *because* of Natasha."

"That's not true," I interrupt. "He fucked up, and now he gets to clean up his own messes. It had nothing at all to do with your daughter."

"The wedding needs to happen in three days," Sergei says. "And there had better be a decent home for my daughter to live in once they say 'I do.'"

"Or what, Sergei?"

He's quiet for a moment, but I continue.

"You'll pull out of the agreement? Fine. Then you owe me a hundred and fifty million dollars."

"The debt was one hundred million."

"And if you pull out of the deal, I add on interest and fees for wasting my fucking time."

He's fuming on the other end.

"You're the one with a fortune to lose."

"And you're the one who will have a war at his doorstep if you don't take care of my daughter."

"Elliott is the one marrying her, it's his responsibility to care for her, but I'm telling you that she will be fine. If you don't believe me, wire me the money and the deal is off, and we can go to war. You don't scare me, Sergei."

"Three days."

"Why are you moving the timeline up?"

"Because I have business in two weeks, and I'll be out of the country."

He hangs up and I sigh, then dress in the usual black slacks and dress shirt and suit coat, and once I've fastened my Patek Philippe watch, I walk to the kitchen and pour a cup of coffee before I make my way to my office.

Thirty minutes later, Jack walks in, dressed the same as me, but with a white shirt rather than black, and sits across from me.

"Did you sleep at all?" he asks, eyeing me.

"Not much," I admit. "Did you pay Johnny's wife?"

"Yeah. She didn't shed many tears. Sounds like he kicked her around a lot."

I lean back in my chair. *What the fuck is up with these assholes? My son included.*

"Well, at least she's taken care of now. Jack, we need to talk."

He narrows his eyes and folds his hands over his lap. This man has been by my side since we were kids. A close friend to me since we were sixteen and he kicked my ass in a boxing ring. He's quiet. He's fucking badass, and there's no one I trust more to have my back. This conversation is a long time coming.

"I was hoping that Elliott would get his shit together and become worthy of being my number two, but it's plain to see that's not going to happen. You know this business inside and out. Shit, you grew up in it with me, and you're the one person in my organization that I trust implicitly. You're being promoted."

His eyebrows climb. That's a huge fucking display of emotion for this man. He's more stoic than me, and that's saying a lot. "I pretty much already do the job, boss."

"And now you have the title to go with it, along with the pay raise."

"I don't need more money." He's also incredibly stubborn.

I tilt my head. "Are you passing up an additional five million a year?"

"Fuck no. I'm not stupid. I'm telling you that I'm your number two whether it's official or not. I don't need the title." His face hasn't softened at all, but his eyes hold emotion as he stares back at me.

This should have been his position from the beginning, and we both know it.

"And that's why you're my number two. Effective immediately. Now, we need to plan a wedding for three days from now."

"I thought it was in two weeks."

"The timeline has changed."

Four

❧

NATASHA

MY FATHER WOULD HAVE BEATEN the shit out of me if I'd let Julian's men drive me home last night and he saw me get out of the car without Elliott there. Elliott always sends me home in a cab. Every time. I would think that it would bother my father, but it doesn't seem to.

And honestly, I'm okay with that.

I'm always surrounded by the men my father assigns to me, and being in the taxi is the only time that I'm alone. I mean, aside from the driver, but they don't care about me. They don't even know who I am.

The fact that my father is okay with Elliott sending me home in a cab is insane to me, but he allows it.

No one was around when I got home, and I was able to sneak up to my room without being noticed.

I've managed to cover the bruises on my jaw with makeup, but there's no hiding a split lip. My father prefers for me to wear dresses, but I put on a pair of white wide-leg slacks and a cream sleeveless blouse so I can hide my knee. I've managed to avoid my father all day long. I'm not sure where he is, but he's not home, so I've spent most of the day in the library, alternating between reading in a cozy chair and sitting with my one true love: the piano.

Movement at the entrance of the library catches my eye as I finish a song, and I smile at my mother, but that pulls on the split lip, and I wince.

"What happened to your face?" she asks. There's no warmth there. No concern. Just curiosity.

"Elliott." I shrug a shoulder, and her eyes narrow.

"If you fuck this up for your father, he won't be happy."

"I haven't fucked anything up," I reply. My mother is the one person in this world that I feel comfortable speaking my mind to. I'm never disrespectful, but I do stand up for myself. She hates me almost as much as Papa does, but she's never laid a hand on me. "He got mad, that's all. Mama, I don't want to marry him."

She smirks and sits on the couch nearby. She's dressed impeccably in a red dress, her blond hair styled in a fierce bun at the nape of her neck, makeup painted perfectly. The Botox she gets regularly hides any of the lines that show her age.

"I didn't want to marry your father, but here we are." She tilts her head, watching me. "This is the life we live, Natasha."

"I know. I just don't like it."

"You don't have to like it, you just have to follow orders." She examines her perfect red-tipped nails. "Your father needs this alliance."

"I know."

She checks the time, and a little smile tugs at her lips. "It's time for my tennis lesson."

That's code for *I'll be fucking my tennis coach for the next two hours in the guest house.*

"Enjoy," I reply and start to play again, but then my phone pings with a text.

> Elliott: I apologize for last night. I'd like
> to take you out for dinner tonight to
> make it up to you.

I close my eyes on a deep sigh. He always apologizes. Doesn't mean that anything's going to change. But my father needs this, so I'll suck it up and play nice.

> Me: What time should I be ready?

> Elliott: Thank you, baby. I'll pick you
> up at 7.

I wince. *Baby.* Ugh, I hate it when he calls me that. Or anything at all. The man gives me the serious creeps, and I have to marry him?

Suddenly, heavy footsteps stomp down the hallway, and my father barrels into the library, his face masked in rage. Viktor, his number two, is right behind him, with fucking *excitement* on his ugly face.

"What did you do?"

Frowning, I stand from the piano and back away from him. "What do you mean?"

"What the fuck did you do to earn that beating?" He points to my lip. "Your mother just told me that Elliott hit you last night, and I want to know what you did to earn it."

My mother just threw me under the bus so my dad would be occupied with me and she could flit away to fuck her tennis coach.

That's pretty on brand for her.

"Papa, it was a misunderstanding."

"That's bullshit."

My back hits the bookcase, and I don't have anywhere to go, so when Papa reaches me, he slaps me, reopening the wound on my lip and making me see stars.

"What. Did. You. Do."

"I didn't do anything." My voice is so quiet, it's almost nonexistent. "I promise."

"A man only punishes when it's necessary."

If I wasn't so good at keeping a straight face, I would laugh at that. Men hit women all the time, whether they deserve it or not.

"He's already apologized," I tell him. "He's taking me to dinner tonight."

"If you ruin this for me," he threatens, getting so close I can smell his rancid breath, a mixture of cigars and vodka, "I'll kill you. You're only good for one thing, and that's this alliance. Without it, I'll put you in the ground and not think twice about it."

I believe him.

"Yes, Papa."

He slaps me again, on a roll now, and then punches me in the ribs, making me cry out before I can stop myself. Crying only makes it worse.

It feels like the beating goes on forever, until finally

I'm on the ground, and he kicks me one last time in the stomach and spits on me.

"If you wear slacks in this house again, I'll break your fucking legs. You're getting married in three days. We've moved the wedding up."

He leaves, and when I hear the footsteps disappear down the hallway, I curl in on myself and let the tears come.

I watch movies and read books, and I see men being kind to women in them, but that's just fiction. People don't really act like that.

Except Julian, who actually helped you last night.

He was kind. His touch was gentle. His eyes are hard, and he never smiles, never has a tender expression on his face, but I believed him when he said he wouldn't hurt me.

No one has ever told me that they wouldn't hurt me before. They haven't even tried to lie and say they wouldn't.

Because hurting me is inevitable.

Slowly, I pick myself up off the floor and make my way to my rooms. I have a bedroom, sitting room, and bathroom on the second floor, on the opposite side of the house from my parents. It's quiet over here, and the only place in the mansion where I feel somewhat safe.

Of course, they wouldn't let me have a piano here. No, that would have been too generous.

Stripping down, I stand in front of the mirror and take stock of my injuries.

It's bad this time.

Bruises run up and down my ribs on both sides. My

lip is bleeding again, and I have new bruises, including next to my eye. The strips on my knee broke open and ruined my pants.

I'm a mess.

It's not even the pain that bothers me. Not anymore. I've gotten used to ignoring it.

It's the fact that the people in my life think that this is okay. How long am I supposed to endure this before I go out of my mind?

I have only three hours before Elliott will be here to pick me up, so I get into the shower and let the hot water soothe my injuries. Once I'm out, I take some pain medicine and then get to work trying to cover the worst of it with makeup.

I choose a floor-length white sleeveless dress, and dry and curl my hair, and once I'm ready to go, I walk down to the foyer to wait for Elliott.

I don't have to wait long.

He and my father are laughing at something, and when they see me walk in, they both smile at me, like they have a secret.

This can only be bad for me.

"There she is," Elliott says and holds his hand out for mine. Papa knows that I don't like to be touched, and he glares at me, willing me to ignore the offered hand so he can beat me some more.

So, I take a breath and slide my hand into Elliott's, ignoring how sweaty his palm is.

"Hello," I say, and keep my face blank when he leans over to kiss my cheek.

"You're fucking gorgeous," he whispers in my ear.

"Thank you." I offer him a small smile, ignoring the pain in my lip, and then before I know it, we're in his Range Rover, headed into town.

"You really do look great," he says, offering me a smile.

"Thank you." I swallow and glance his way. He's sober tonight, and he looks handsome in a dark suit. Deciding to be kind and make the most of the calm, I reply, "You look nice too."

Elliott offers me a grin that's just this side of smarmy. It's like he can't help but be a pervert.

How is he Julian's son? They look similar, but their personalities couldn't be more different.

"I'm glad you think so. I have plans for us tonight, Tash."

Fuck. This doesn't bode well for me at all.

SOBRIETY ONLY LASTED HALFWAY INTO DINNER before the fourth glass of wine caught up with him.

Elliott takes a bite of his steak, and then he leans over to act like he's my lover, whispering sweet nothings in my ear.

Gross.

"Your tits are fucking *amazing* in that dress."

I sigh and take a sip of water. "Thanks."

"After this, we're going to Rapture."

No.

"Oh, I don't—"

"We're going," he says, his voice harder now, and he narrows his eyes, practically daring me to argue.

I've already been beaten twice in the past twenty-four hours. I'd rather avoid a third time. I don't think my ribs can take it. I'm so damn sore, now that my meds are wearing off, and I realize that I forgot to put some in my handbag.

"You'll like it." His voice is calmer now, and he smirks as he sips his wine. "And don't worry, there will be other girls there to show you the ropes."

"Uh, what?"

"You'll see." He winks at me, and my stomach sinks to my toes.

I hurt everywhere, and I'm *not* in the mood to have to fight off Elliott's advances tonight, least of all at a sex club in front of strangers. I don't care how fancy it is, I don't want to go.

Dinner passes too quickly, and then we're back at his car, and he should *not* be driving after all the wine he consumed with his meal.

"Do you want me to drive?" I ask, and I immediately realize that I said the wrong thing when he rounds on me and cages me against the side of the vehicle.

"What are you saying, Tash?"

I swallow hard, tying to keep my face expressionless. "I just haven't had anything to drink, that's all."

"Get. In. The motherfucking car."

He pushes away from me, and I do as I'm told, even though I know that this is absolutely *not safe*. I spend the entire twenty-minute trip fighting off a panic attack as

Elliott weaves through the lanes, cutting off other drivers and laughing like a lunatic because I'm scared.

I hate how much he loves to frighten me.

"You need to lighten up, babe," he says when he parks in front of the valet, and I immediately get out of the car, ignoring the way my ribs are singing. My jaw aches. My eye socket throbs.

Fuck, I hurt.

"Come on." He takes my hand and drags me through the front doors where there's a reception area. "Hey, Beth."

The tiniest woman I've ever seen gives Elliott a cautious smile. "Hello, Mr. Stavros. Is this your guest tonight?"

"My fiancé," he confirms. "Natasha."

"Welcome to Rapture," Beth says with a genuine smile for me. "If you have any questions—"

"She doesn't."

Elliott's acting almost manic, with jerky movements as he pulls me down a dark hallway and then into what looks like an opulent lounge. People are sitting at tables or at the bar, chatting and drinking. It looks like any high-end cocktail lounge, and it puts me at ease.

This I can do.

There are no naked bodies, no one is having sex. It seems normal. And even better, everyone here is dressed to the nines, in designer clothes and beautiful jewelry. There's nothing seedy about this place.

"I'll take an old-fashioned," Elliott says to the bartender, a stunning brunette with curves for days. Her pretty smile turns to me.

"What can I get you?" she asks.

"Just water, please."

"A dirty martini," Elliott replies, shaking his head. "You'll need the liquid courage."

The bartender eyes me. "What do *you* want?" she asks me.

"Just water."

"An old-fashioned and a water, coming up." She bustles away, and Elliott squeezes my hip, where he's holding onto me.

"Keep pissing me off and see where it gets you, Tash."

Julian said he wouldn't hurt me again.

But I should have known that was a lie.

Elliott knocks back two drinks in fast succession and then takes my hand and leads me to a set of doors.

"It's time for something a little more . . . *fun*," he says, wiggling his eyebrows.

My stomach sinks again, and I hold my breath as we walk inside.

The room is beautiful, draped in white and awash in soft colors. Sensual music tinkles in the air, and there are people having sex, kissing, laughing.

A woman is bent over a bench, and a man is using a leather whip to hit her, and I feel like I'm shrinking in on myself.

I don't want to be here. There is nothing about this that excites or entices me.

I also don't want to be hit anymore today.

"Come on. I'll give you a tour later," Elliott says as he drags me through the room to another hallway lined with doors. He pushes one open, and we step inside, and I freeze.

It's not empty.

There's a king bed, and a woman, beautiful with long dark hair and a slim body, is already lying there, naked, and grins at Elliott as he drops my hand and approaches her.

"Hey there, handsome," she says as she moves onto all fours and crawls over to him.

He frames her face and kisses her hard, and I want to turn around and *run*.

"Come here," he says, gesturing to me. "This is Miranda, and she's going to play with us tonight."

"*Us*?" I ask, feeling all the blood drain from my face.

"I'll be careful," Miranda says with a smile. "Since it's your first time and all."

My eyes shoot to Elliott, who's smirking at me.

"Take your clothes off, Tash."

I shake my head, and that pisses him off, so he slips his hand into my cleavage and rips the dress in two. It's still hanging on my body, and I try to cover myself, but he slaps my hands out of the way.

"The sooner you realize that you're mine, the better. We can make this fun, or we can make this painful. It's really up to you. But either way, I'm fucking you tonight. After everything I went through last night, you owe me this, and I'm collecting."

"Let's make it fun," Miranda suggests with a wink. "Babe, why don't you and I get started, so Tash can see how good it's going to be."

He watches my face, and then he smirks. "Good idea.

You sit right here. If you make a move for that door, I'll break your fingers."

I gasp, and he smiles, pleased with my fear.

I can't do this.

But he jerks me into the chair, then turns to Miranda, and as he strips out of his clothes, he kisses her.

I close my eyes.

"You'll watch this," he says. "Open your eyes, Tash."

I follow his orders and watch the horror unfold.

Five

JULIAN

I NEED TO GET LAID.

For the past twenty-four hours, all I've thought about is Natasha, and that's a big problem, considering she's about to marry my son in just a matter of days.

Lusting after my future daughter-in-law is not something I'm proud of, and not something I'd admit to anyone else.

The issue is, I haven't gotten my dick wet in too long. I've been busy with work, getting Elliott out of trouble, and helping my brothers with their businesses. It's time to make a visit to Rapture.

I never walk in through the front door. My brothers and I come and go through Rome's private entrance. Tonight is no different. I nod at security and then make my way to the bar, where Rome's wife, Eloise—Lulu for short—is busy mixing drinks. She's a beautiful woman, with long dark hair and pretty brown eyes and a curvy body that Rome's obsessed with. Let's be honest, he's obsessed with every little thing about her.

I'm happy for him.

"Hey, Julian," Lulu says with a grin. "Your usual?"

"Please."

She nods and grabs a glass, then pours two fingers of Macallan into it before sliding it over to me.

"How's it going?" she asks me. "You missed family dinner on Sunday."

"I'm sorry, I was out of the country."

She lifts an eyebrow. "Fancy."

With a smirk, I take a sip of the whisky.

Sunday dinner is something Lulu started just after she and Rome got together. She's an excellent cook, and she loves using her talent for large groups of people. So, each week, she invites me, Mateo, and Carson to dinner, along with our number twos and her friend Scarlett. Nothing brings this woman more joy than feeding us. And we all adore her and her cooking.

It's not a hardship by any means.

And I try not to miss it, but this past Sunday couldn't be helped.

"What did you cook?" I ask her.

"Do you really want to torture yourself with that question?" she counters, resting her hand on her hip with a knowing smile.

"I can handle it."

"I made chicken parm with fettuccini alfredo and—"

"Okay, I really don't want to know." My stomach growls at the thought, and she sends me a knowing smile.

Chicken parm is my favorite.

"I'll make it again soon. Don't miss this coming Sunday, okay?"

"Yes, ma'am."

I haven't quite finished my drink when Rome is suddenly at my side.

"With me," he mutters quietly, and I know that whatever he has to tell or show me isn't good. Before we walk away, he turns to his wife. "You good, Firefly?"

"I'm great."

He nods and then leads me to the elevator.

"What's up?" I ask when we're in the car.

"I need to show you," he replies, shaking his head, and when the doors open, he leads me to the control room, where monitors are set up with live feeds from all over the club. "You know that we have cameras in every room, even the private rooms, for security purposes."

"Sure."

He taps some keys, and suddenly the screen changes to one of the privacy rooms. I can clearly see that my son is fucking some woman—Miranda, if I remember correctly—and he smacks her breast hard, making her flinch.

"Sound?" I ask, and Rome hits another key.

"You see this, you stupid bitch? Look at how much she loves my cock. I'm going to fuck her ass next, and make her bleed good. This is what I expect out of you. This is what I'm going to do to you, every day for the rest of your fucking life," Elliott spits out. "This is how you satisfy your husband."

"Who's he talking to?" Rome asks.

"Is there another camera? She's off—fuck, he's got Natasha in there. Which room?"

"Six," he says, and then I'm running with Rome on my heels.

"Call the men," I tell him. "I want six of them."

He nods, already tapping his screen. Not bothering to wait for the elevator, I take the stairs two at a time, then race down the hallway to the private rooms and try the knob for room six, but it's locked.

"I have a key," Rome says, pulling a master key card out of his wallet, and when the light turns green, I rush inside and see nothing but red at the scene before me.

Natasha is in a chair, her dress torn and body bared, shaking, her eyes glassy and staring off in the distance like she's in shock.

Elliott is fucking the shit out of Miranda, who has a black eye and is weeping, murmuring her safe word over and over again.

"You piece of shit." I'm on him in a flash, yanking him off the woman, and punch him in the face, making him cry out. "What the fuck have you done?"

His eyes are manic and full of glee at the destruction he's caused as our men file in.

"Get him in the cell," I instruct them, and Elliott's eyes turn to me.

"What the fuck, Dad?"

"In the cell," I repeat.

Rome already has Miranda wrapped in a blanket, and I ignore my kid, who's yelling and throwing a fit as he's dragged away, and immediately squat in front of Natasha.

"Hey." I reach up to brush her hair off her cheek, but she flinches, and I have to work to keep the rage down, so

I don't scare her, curling my hands into fists. "Natasha, it's Julian. I'm not Elliott. He's not going to hurt you."

"You said that before," she whispers, still not looking at me. She's rocking back and forth and doesn't even try to close her ripped dress to cover herself, as if she's forgotten the state she's in.

Fucking fuck.

I promised her he wouldn't touch her again, and he did it the very next day. *The next motherfucking day.*

"I'm getting Scarlett and Eloise," Rome says. "Then we'll go to the basement."

I nod but don't take my eyes off Natasha.

"I know, I did. I'm so sorry. I didn't know he'd do this." I shake my head and let myself look down at her body so I can cover her, but then I notice the bruises that run up and down her ribs. They're fresh.

When I look back up at her face, I can see new marks on her, the lip is reopened.

She's been worked over something awful, and I see fucking *black*.

"Natasha. Look at me." My voice is harder than I'd like, but I'm so damn pissed that I want to *roar*.

"Here's a blanket." I glance up at Scarlett, the manager of the playroom and Eloise's best friend, as she offers me the blanket for Natasha. "I'm right here, and Lulu's on the way."

"Thanks. Natasha, I'm going to cover you. Is that okay?"

Her nod is shaky, and she's still not looking me in the eyes as I drape the warm blanket around her. She gathers it to her, nuzzling into it.

"Who bruised your ribs, sweetheart?"

She frowns at me, like she doesn't understand what I'm saying.

"Who hurt you today, Natasha? You have new bruises that weren't there last night."

"My f-father," she whispers. "Got in trouble for making Elliott mad."

I'm going to kill them all.

"And your face?"

"Papa," she replies.

"Did Elliott hit you today?"

Slowly, Natasha shakes her head, and her lower lip trembles. Christ, I want to scoop her against me and comfort her, but from what I've gathered, Natasha doesn't like to be touched.

And who can blame her?

"He made me watch." She swallows hard. "And he hurt her. He said I have to do that."

Her blue eyes are wide and pleading as they finally turn to me.

"Please don't make me."

"You don't have to do anything you don't want to. And I know that I fucked up my promise from last night, but I'm telling you right now that *no one* is going to hurt you again. Not your father, not Elliott. No one."

"You can't promise that," she says softly, eyeing Lulu as she walks into the room. "Because that's just what they do."

"Never again," I repeat. "You're going to go with Scarlett and Lulu. They're going to take care of you while I go to work."

Natasha frowns, confused.

"Why would they do that? I can just go home."

"Nah, you should come hang out with us," Scarlett says, her voice soothing. "Lulu's penthouse is ridiculously gorgeous, and you can borrow some comfies from us. Relax and feel better."

"But *why*?" Natasha asks.

"Because you've had a shitty night, and we're here to help you feel better," Lulu replies.

Natasha's shaking is gone, but her eyes are still glassy.

"Take her up to the penthouse," I tell the girls. "I'll check on her when we're done downstairs."

"You got it," Lulu replies. "Come on, honey. We've got you."

It takes everything in me to leave Natasha with Lulu and Scarlett, but I know they'll take good care of her, and I need to get in that room with my son.

It's time he learns a lesson.

Rome's waiting for me in the basement of Rapture, outside the cell we use to torture information out of people.

"What the fuck, Julian?"

I stop and rub my hand over the back of my neck.

"You've met Natasha, his fiancé."

"Yeah, but why the fuck was he making her watch him torture Miranda? She was saying her safe word, and he ignored her. You *know* what I do to assholes who do that in my club."

It's not tolerated, and they typically end up dead.

And honestly, Elliott deserves that for what he did in that room.

For hurting those women.

For once again showing the goddamn world what a weak asshole he is, thus putting my entire *empire* on the line. Every move my son makes is absolutely unacceptable. *No one* threatens my family and lives to tell about it.

"Oh, he's going to pay for it. For what he did to Miranda, and what he's been doing to Natasha."

"Did he put those bruises on her ribs?" Rome asks me.

"No, she says her father did that."

Rome shakes his head. The Kings of Vegas aren't good men. We do a lot of shady shit, but we don't hurt women, and we're working on dismantling the flesh trade in this city, which is taking longer than any of us are happy about.

"Sergei's also going to pay," I say, eyeing the door to the cell. "I'm not going to kill my son, but he's not leaving here whole."

Rome's face is grim.

"Look, if you want me to handle it, I can. Or if you want to call in Mateo and Carson, we can do this for you. You don't have to torture your own son, Julian."

All I can see is Natasha's beautiful face, so fucking scared and bruised, and the anger still pulses through me. I know that if I walk in there right now, I'll end him.

I'll kill my child. Because he's grown into a monster, and I won't tolerate that.

"Call the others," I reply, letting out a breath. "And maybe I'll calm down a bit while we wait for them."

Rome nods and pulls out his phone, and I do the same, calling Jack so I can fill him in.

"I'm on my way," Jack says grimly. "Julian, this can't keep happening. You can't keep him in the family. It's a disgrace, a weakness. Your enemies will think you're an easy target."

I blow out another breath, pacing the hallway as Jack tells me exactly what I already know.

"I'm aware."

"Which means the alliance with the Russians—"

"You leave that to me," I growl into the phone. "I'll take care of her."

Jack pauses. "Do you have feelings for the girl?"

"Just get here."

I hang up and Rome turns to me. "They're on the way."

"Jack is as well."

The door opens and Rome's number two, Luke, steps out.

"He's pissed himself," Luke says with disgust.

A slow smile spreads over my lips. "Good."

Six

NATASHA

"I'M MAKING TEA," the one named Lulu says as Scarlett sits next to me on a couch in the most beautiful penthouse I've ever seen.

"Do you want me to get you some comfortable clothes?" Scarlett asks. She's very sweet. They both are. Both beautiful and kind, and I'm not sure why they're being so nice to me.

Because Julian told them to.

Julian found me. He stopped Elliott, and he found me before my fiancé could rape me and hurt me the way he was hurting that woman.

"Where's Julian?" I ask softly.

"He's with the other guys taking care of Elliott," Lulu says as she passes me the hot cup of tea.

"Was Elliott hurt?" I ask with a frown.

That doesn't sound right. Everything in my head feels jumbled. I tried to block out what my fiancé was doing to that poor woman, to pull inside myself and disassociate. It was horrifying.

"Not yet," Scarlett adds. "But he will be when they're done with him."

My gaze bounces between the two women. "What do you mean?"

"Rome and Julian won't let him get away with treating you and Miranda like that," Lulu says. "Rome has a strict policy about consent, and if a person says their safe word, it's honored, *or else.*"

"Is that why she kept saying 'cucumber'?"

"Yes," Scarlett says and reaches over to pat my knee, but I flinch out of the way.

"I'm sorry, I don't like to be touched."

"No problem at all," the other woman assures me, holding her hands up and keeping a safe distance away. "Your body, your choice."

I scoff at that before sipping my tea, which is perfectly sweet, and then setting it on a nearby table.

"I know that you're only being nice because Julian made you, so if you don't mind, I'll get a cab and go home."

"I don't do anything that Julian *makes* me do," Lulu says, tilting her head to the side. "He's not the boss of any of us."

"He's a man."

Both of them blink fast, as if they can't believe what I just said.

Let's be clear, even *I* don't necessarily believe that it's right to always do the man's bidding, but it was drilled into me for *years.*

Obviously, not all Mafia families are trained the same.

"And?" Scarlett asks. "Look, we respect him, and the other three, because they're the crime bosses, and let's be honest, they can get a little scary, but they're also fair and have earned our respect."

"Rome is my husband," Lulu adds. "And yeah, he can be intense, but I don't blindly do what he says just because he's a *man*."

"Who are the *other three*?" I ask.

"There are four Kings of Vegas. Have you heard of them?" Lulu asks.

I nod. "I know that Julian is one of them because I've heard my father talk about it."

"Yep, Julian, Rome, Mateo and Carson. They're all best friends, pretty much brothers," Lulu says. "And they each have their own things going, but they also work together."

"Kind of like a Mafia gang?" I ask, and they both smile at me.

"Totally like that," Scarlett says with a laugh. "My man, Luke, is Rome's number two."

I nod. "I know what that means. My father is the head of the Bratva. I just didn't know who exactly all of the players are. I'm on a nccd-to-know basis, and according to my father, I don't need to know much."

Lulu wrinkles her nose. "My dad was the head of the Italian Mafia. It's such a patriarchal thing. So misogynistic."

"Very," I agree, loosening up just a bit. I have things in common with these women. It's the first time in my life that I've been around women who understand my world. I've never been allowed to socialize before, and this feels . . . nice. "What happened to your father?"

"Rome killed him." She shrugs a shoulder. "It's a longer story than that, but that's what it boils down to. My father tried to sell me in an arranged marriage, and I was having none of it. That's how I met my husband."

I shake my head mournfully. "I wish I could get out of my arranged marriage. I have to marry Elliott."

"Julian's son?" Scarlett asks. "The idiot who abused you and hurt Miranda?"

Wordlessly, I nod.

"Oh, hell no." Lulu shakes her head. "Absolutely not. There's no way Julian will let that happen."

"He's the one who made the agreement with my father. There's a lot of money involved. It's an alliance thing, and I have to do it, or my papa will kill me."

They're both silent as they stare at me.

"I'll talk to Rome," Lulu begins, but I shake my head adamantly.

"No, you won't. This is business. You understand that. I've known since I was a child that this was my fate. I wish it wasn't Elliott. He's not a good man, and it's going to suck, but it is what it is."

"It is what it is?" Scarlett demands. "I think we need something stronger than tea."

"Do you have any chocolate?" I ask. "Sugar is actually my drug of choice."

"You've come to the right place. I just made cannoli," Lulu says and stands, gesturing for us to follow her. "Come on, let's eat them all and discuss how we're getting you out of this marriage."

I appreciate that they want to help, but there is no getting out of it.

However, I won't turn down sweets.

Seven

JULIAN

"NO KILLING, JUST MAKE IT HURT," Carson says with a nod. "Got it."

Carson is the scariest of the group, and that's saying something because we're all powerful, mean men. I wouldn't want to fuck with any of them.

But in addition to the casino he runs, Carson is an assassin. That's his favorite thing to do. He's the biggest of us, and I've seen him tear men apart with his bare hands, without breaking a sweat.

Scary motherfucker.

Mateo, the fourth of us, nods solemnly. He runs weapons and drugs and cleans his money through our legitimate businesses.

He also has the shortest temper, which again, is saying a lot.

I push into the cell, leading the group, and find my son strung up by his wrists to the ceiling. He's in handcuffs, which are attached to hooks.

And he's a blubbering mess.

I love my son, but I hate the man he's become.

Slowly, I shove my hands in my pockets and stride over to where Elliott hangs. No one has dared touch him, so there are no wounds, no bruises.

"Dad, there's been a mistake."

I slap him across the face with an open hand, humiliating him more than hurting him.

"Do you think I'm stupid?"

Elliott sniffles, and when he turns his gaze at me, his eyes are full of hate and malice.

The blubbering was a show, which I knew. I know my kid.

"I think you're going soft," he replies coldly. "And I can't wait to take over the organization and run this city the way it should be run."

Carson growls behind me, and as Elliott's gaze flicks to him, a little fear slips through.

"You're under the impression that you'll be inheriting my empire," I say as I calmly stroll away from him to the tool bench. There are knives, shears, pliers, saws, drills, tire irons, and many other tools that we use to hurt men much stronger than my boy.

Mateo prefers fire.

Carson? Well, whatever's handy is fine with him.

Rome is similar to Carson, but has a thing for an axe.

Me? I like knives.

So, I grab a little paring knife. It's small, but sharp as hell, and Elliott will think that I'm going easy on him.

And I am.

But not nearly as easy as he thinks.

"He thinks I'm soft," I say to Mateo as I walk past him.

"I suspect he's about to learn differently," Mateo says with a sinister smile.

"For fuck's sake, I'm your *son*." There's still so much confidence in his voice. "You're not going to kill me."

"There are so many things that can happen to you worse than death," I inform him. "Maybe it's my fault that I didn't show you more of this side of the business."

"You haven't shown me *shit*," Elliott spits out.

"That's the thing. If you want to be a part of the business, you fucking earn it. You don't strut all over *my fucking city* and put the family in danger. You do *not* make it seem like the Kings of Vegas are weak. I will protect my organization, my brothers, and my fucking livelihood at all costs, even if that means disinheriting and punishing my own son. You're not an exception, Elliott."

I slash a short line down his outer thigh, just enough to hurt like fuck, but not make him bleed out, and listen to him scream in pain.

Carson grins.

Crazy fucker.

"You'll never be the next in line, Elliott. Jack will take over if anything happens to me."

"It's *mine*," Elliott hisses, and I take the knife to his arm this time. Just a small two inch cut, but the blood beads up and runs down into his armpit and over his ribs.

"Your behavior makes me look weak to my enemies,

and you've tested my patience for the last fucking time." I toss the knife aside, take off my suit coat and roll my sleeves. "You've hurt Natasha after I gave you the order to leave her alone."

Elliott snarls, and I turn and land a punch in his gut, sending him swinging on the chains.

"I GAVE YOU A FUCKING ORDER!"

I hit him again and again, seeing Natasha, so perfect and scared, and I throw punches until my hands are sore and my arms sing from the exertion. Until his face is swollen and he's sweaty, and Mateo grabs my arm.

"No killing him," he reminds me.

"Stop," Elliott wheezes out through his swollen jaw. "Please."

"Take him to the cell in my building," I instruct Jack, who nods once, always so stoic. But I can see the anger and disappointment in his eyes as he stares at my son. Jack was there the day Elliott was born. He's known him all his life. "He'll stay there for at least a week. One meal a day."

"No," Elliott says.

"Yes." I stand eye to eye with him. "You're going to learn that *I'm* the one in control, Elliott. I'm the only one with the power, and I'm a scary motherfucker. Eventually, you'll yield to me. I'll see you in a week."

With that, I turn and grab my coat and follow the others out of the room.

"I need some whiskey," I mutter to Rome.

"I've got you," he says. "What about your alliance with Ivanov? Isn't Elliott supposed to marry the Bratva daughter in three days?"

Two days now.

"Leave that to me."

"I have to go hunt a guy down," Carson says. "Call me if you need me."

"Thanks for coming. Sorry I did all the work myself."

Carson grins. "I wouldn't have missed it. Elliott's needed a beating for a while."

"Everyone thinks my kid's an asshole. Good to know."

Mateo claps his hand on my shoulder. "Elliott *is* an asshole. I have to go too."

He leaves right behind Carson, and Rome and I get into the elevator and ride it up to Rome's penthouse.

"He is no longer welcome in my club," Rome says simply.

"Obviously. I'll pay Miranda well as an apology."

When we walk inside, we stutter to a stop and take in the scene before us.

All three women are in the kitchen, eating a platter of cannoli—fuck, those look good—and laughing.

Natasha is laughing.

Her face is lit up, and fuck me, it's stunning. I've hardly seen her smile before this. Listening to her laugh is like music.

But when she spots me, she sobers and lowers the cannoli to a plate as she casts her eyes to the floor.

No. I want her smile back.

"I'm glad you three are having fun," I say as Rome walks around the island to hug his wife.

"I should go home," Natasha says. She's still wrapped in the blanket. "All of my things are at home."

I don't want her going back there. I don't want to risk that her asshole father will lay hands on her again.

"I have clothes for you," Lulu says, and dashes up the stairs to the primary bedroom. "I'll be right back!"

"Oh, I can just use this blanket."

"I think your family will ask questions if you do that," Rome reminds her, and her face drains of color.

"Why don't you come to my penthouse with me for the night," I offer.

"No." She shakes her head, and her hands tremble as she pushes her hair over her shoulder. She looks like she's on the verge of a panic attack. "My father would—"

"Okay, we'll get you home. Wear Lulu's clothes, and if anyone asks, you fell into the pool, and your dress got ruined."

She blinks in surprise. "Oh, that could work."

"It'll work."

Just a few more days, and then she'll never have to go back there.

Lulu shows Natasha to the bathroom where she can change her clothes, and Rome watches me from the other side of the kitchen.

"You're going to marry her."

"I didn't say that."

The fucker smirks. "You didn't have to. I hope you know what you're doing."

"It's a business transaction." And I'll keep telling myself that.

"Right."

"I'm ready."

I turn at the sound of her voice and almost swallow

my tongue. Lulu's clothes are just a little big on Natasha, but she looks adorable in the leggings and oversize T-shirt.

"That's better," I reply. "Come on. I'll take you home."

Eight

NATASHA

I WAS NEVER one of those girls who dreamed of what her special day would look like. I didn't have vision boards with pretty dresses and color swatches and flower arrangements. When you're told from the time you can walk that you'll be used as a bargaining chip and *given* to a man to further the success of your father's organization, the romance of a wedding is stripped away from you.

I have to admit, as I stand here in the bridal room of the church and stare at the dress hanging on the mirror, it's . . . horrible. I don't know who chose it. I certainly didn't. I never set foot in a dress shop, so I have no idea if this monstrosity will fit or how it'll look on my hourglass frame. I have boobs and hips, so sometimes things don't fit quite right.

Mostly, as I stare at the lace and crystals before me, I'm wondering if there's something in this room I can use to kill myself.

Yeah, I said it.

The hair and makeup people have left me alone, and

63

despair overwhelms me. I barely left my rooms at my father's house since Julian dropped me off there the other night after the fiasco at Rapture. I kept to myself, sneaking down for meals, and then right back upstairs because my poor body needed time to heal. In an *unexpected* turn of events, my father did come to me this morning and gifted me my grandmother's necklace. I finger the pendant as I stare at my dress, caught in memories of the only person who's ever shown me any kind of affection.

She was a wonderful woman, and I remember her wearing this little emerald pendant. There are tiny diamonds around the substantially sized emerald, and I love it so much. I'll wear it all the time.

I have no idea what to expect tonight, and I spent the past few days coming to terms with the fact that I'm marrying a monster.

That my body is no longer my own.

I haven't heard from Elliott since that night. No apology texts, no flowers, nothing. Which is actually good because all I've done is have panic attacks at the thought of marrying that . . . devil.

Elliott Stavros is evil.

I know that Julian assured me that Elliott wouldn't hurt me again, but he can't make that promise because he won't live with us. He won't be there 24-7 to protect me.

And the thought of living with Elliott makes me feel hollow. I'd honestly rather die than have to live with being raped and brutalized every day for the rest of my life.

There's a knock on the door, and then Lulu pokes her head in, but she's not smiling.

"Why are you alone?" she asks me as she steps inside and closes the door behind her.

"They finished my hair and makeup," I tell her, watching her warily. "Is everyone here?"

"I haven't seen Elliott yet, but everyone else is, yeah. Your father looks . . . angry."

"He always looks angry."

She nods and then gestures to the dress. "Want help?"

I pause.

"Or do you want me to get you the fuck out of here?" she offers. "Because I will. Rome won't let anyone hurt me."

I can't help the little humorless chuckle at the offer. "I wish it was that simple. They'd just find me and make me do it anyway. And my father would punish me, and I'd rather not."

She nods, as if she understands, and it makes me feel a *little* better.

Suddenly, there's another knock, much harsher than Lulu's, and the door is flung open, revealing my father.

"Why aren't you ready? It's time."

"We were just talking," I tell him, and he glares at Lulu, putting my back up.

She's my friend.

"Did you know that arranged marriages are from the Dark Ages?" Lulu asks him, not afraid of him at all.

I wish I had her confidence.

"This is none of your fucking business," Papa replies,

narrowing his eyes, and he moves to take a step toward her, but I shield her with my own body.

"No." His eyes widen in surprise. I've *never* stood up to my father. "You won't hurt her for speaking up for me. She's my friend, Papa."

"I'll do—"

"Finish that sentence." We all turn at the sound of Rome's voice. His hands are balled in fists, his face a mask of fury as he stares Papa down. "And make one move toward my wife, so I can skin you alive."

"She's trying to interfere—"

"I don't give a fuck what she's doing," Rome says, and strides over to take Lulu in his arms. "You'll never look at her or speak to her in anger again."

Papa glares at me.

"Get dressed and get your ass out there."

With that, he spins on his heel and walks away, and I let out the breath I was holding.

"I'm sorry," I say softly.

"Not your fault," Lulu says with a smile. "Now, I'll help you put your dress on."

"Oh, you don't have to—"

"Rome, can I have your knife, please?"

Rome's eyebrow climbs, but he pushes his tattoo-covered hand into his pocket and comes out with a switchblade, then passes it to his wife.

"Be careful," he says to her.

Lulu grins. "Thanks. I have some dress surgery to do."

"I'll wait outside for you," Rome says, and kisses

Lulu softly on the forehead before nodding at me and walking out, closing the door behind him.

"He's really nice to you."

Lulu nods, watching me with somber eyes. "He loves me. He would *never* hurt me."

"I love that for you." And it's the truth, I do love it for her. Everyone should have that security.

I don't know what it feels like to be loved.

Aside from my babushka, no one has ever loved me before, and she died when I was just five. I don't have many memories of her.

"We have work to do with this. Tell me you didn't choose it yourself," Lulu says, gesturing to the puffy shoulders on the dress.

"I've never seen it before."

"Well, good, because now I can say this without hurting your feelings. It sucks. I mean, it's not cheap materials, so we can work with it, but it's so not your style."

"You hardly know me."

She turns and smiles at me. "And yet, I know that *this* is not the dress for you. Let's get you in it, and then I'll start cutting. I promise, I won't hurt you."

I believe her. Lulu is absolutely someone that I could be friends with. So, with her help, we manage to get the dress on me.

It fits well, but I look like a big, puffy marshmallow in this thing.

"Why did they think these shoulders and sleeves were a good idea?" She takes her knife and carefully cuts through the seam, then yanks the sleeve off me, and now I can see that as a tank-style dress, it's much better.

"Okay, this is an improvement."

"Right? I think so too. Let me do the other side."

Ten minutes later, I'm staring at my reflection, the dress completely different from before.

The bow at the top of my ass is gone, thank God. My hair is curled and flows over my shoulders. I didn't want to wear it up today. I like having it down.

My makeup is flawless, showing off my eyes and lips. The artist managed a precise eyeliner wing, which is something I've never been able to master. My breasts are high and perfect in the dress, and it's even cinched at the waist, then molds around my hips, showing off my figure just right.

I feel like a movie star from the 1950s or something.

"You're a freaking *bombshell*," Lulu says with a wide smile. "Holy shit, you're beautiful, Natasha."

"I actually feel beautiful."

For the first time in my life.

Too bad it's also on the *worst* day of my life.

Taking a deep breath, I turn to Lulu and offer her my hand. I don't like to be touched, but I feel safe with her.

She takes my hand and gives it a squeeze.

"Thank you. So much."

"You're welcome. I know this isn't what you want, but I just need you to know that I'm your friend, and if you ever need anything, all you have to do is call me. I'll make sure you have my number before we leave today."

"Thank you." Giving her one more squeeze, I pull away, and she steps out of the room ahead of me.

Rome is waiting for her, takes his knife from her and slips it in his pocket before wrapping his arm around her waist.

"You're a lovely bride," he says to me with a soft smile.

He's such a big, scary man, but his smile is kind.

"Thanks," I murmur and drop my gaze.

"Your father isn't walking you down the aisle?" Rome asks me.

"No. I'm fine."

After a silent moment, Lulu and Rome walk into the sanctuary to take their seats, and I follow. Music starts, and of course it's a song that I hate. I wouldn't have chosen it. I'm holding flowers that were waiting for me in the room.

A bouquet of funeral lilies.

Appropriate, I guess.

I can't look up as I walk down the aisle. I don't want to see Elliott and his mean face. I don't want to see my parents. I don't want to be here.

I don't want to be here.

Swallowing hard, I try to keep my panic at bay, and when I reach the front of the church, I take my place next to black dress shoes.

But then I take a breath, and I don't smell Elliott at all.

I smell *cedarwood*. With a touch of leather.

I smell *Julian*.

My gaze travels up the tall, broad body before me, and I'm stunned to find *Julian* standing before me in a black suit, looking so unbearably handsome, and his lips twitch at the corners as he holds my gaze and reaches for my hand.

I'm too surprised to pull away or flinch at the warmth of his hand.

Julian is standing here.

"You can start," Julian tells the pastor, or priest, or whatever he is.

"Dearly beloved . . ."

I don't even pay attention to the words because I'm standing next to Julian.

Not Elliott.

What is going on?

Suddenly, Julian is making vows to me in his deep voice.

"—to honor and cherish as long as we both shall live."

And then it's my turn, and with a shaky voice, I manage to repeat the vows.

We exchange rings.

We say *I do*.

And then I hear the words "You may kiss your bride."

Oh God.

But Julian doesn't flinch, and doesn't ignore the suggestion either. With his hand still in mine, he leans down and gently places a ghost of a kiss over my lips, sending tingles down my spine.

Holy shit.

He barely touched me and I'm tingling.

Nine

JULIAN

I CAN'T LOOK AWAY from my wife.

My fucking wife.

We're in the back of my armored SUV, headed to the mansion, and she's buckled in next to me but hasn't said a word since *I do.*

Her parents didn't congratulate her before we got in the car to leave.

In fact, aside from shaking my hand before the ceremony, Sergei didn't say much to me at all. He didn't even balk at the fact that it was me marrying her instead of Elliott.

Not one word was said about it, and I don't trust that.

When Natasha got down the aisle and looked up at me, her blue eyes were wide and . . . *relieved.* Shocked, certainly, but I could almost touch the relief that surrounded her, and I knew that I was doing the right thing.

Of course, this is just a business arrangement.

When I said those words to Rome, Carson, and Mateo earlier, they all laughed in my face, and I almost pulled my gun on them.

Assholes.

Natasha clears her throat next to me, and I turn to her, then reach for her hand. She doesn't flinch or shy away, and I take that as a good sign.

"You look absolutely gorgeous, Angel."

Her eyelashes flutter, and then she glances over at me. "Thank you."

"We're going to the mansion. You've been there before."

"Once," she says with a nod. "Briefly."

"It's your new home. I want you to be comfortable there, Natasha."

She bites her lip and then nods timidly, and I keep her hand in mine for the rest of the drive. When my driver pulls up to the house, I turn to her.

"Wait for me here."

"Okay."

I climb out and fasten the button on my suit, then walk around the vehicle to open her door. Reaching across her, I unclip the belt and offer her my hand, helping her out and onto the pavement.

Before she can pull away, I sweep her up into my arms, and she lets out the cutest little yelp.

"What are you doing?" She wraps her arms around my neck, holding on.

"Carrying you over the threshold. It's tradition." I

smile at her, and then open the door and walk through and set her back on her feet in the foyer. "Welcome home, Mrs. Stavros."

She mouths the words *Mrs. Stavros*, as if she's giving them a try, and I take her hand again.

Natasha doesn't pull away. *Another win.*

"Like I said, this is your home. You can change anything you don't like. I got you your own credit card, but it isn't here yet."

"I get money?" she asks in surprise.

"Yes, you'll have my card, and you can spend whatever you want. There's no limit." I keep my stride short so she doesn't fall behind in the heels she's wearing under that incredible dress, and lead her past the formal living room, dining room, and farther to my favorite parts of the house. "I don't think you've been back here."

"No," she says, shaking her head, her eyes wide as she takes it all in.

"I spend most of my time back here. It's more casual and comfortable."

There's a less formal living area with expansive windows that look out at the gardens and the pool. Yes, we live in the desert, but I wanted gardens, so I pay a shit ton to have them maintained.

The furniture is comfortable, and the room looks into the gourmet kitchen.

But Natasha only has eyes for my Steinway.

She drops my hand and makes a beeline for the baby grand piano, and immediately runs her fingers over the keys.

"This is incredible," she breathes.

"Do you play?"

She nods and then bites her lip. "Can I use it?"

"Any time you want. Come, I'll show you the rest, and then you can get settled."

Reluctantly, she leaves the piano, and then to my surprise, she slips her hand in mine again, as if it's the most natural thing, and I smile in response.

"Help yourself in the kitchen." I gesture to the fridge. "It's well stocked, but if you want or need anything specific, just tell me, and I'll make sure it's brought in."

"Thank you," she whispers softly.

Leading her to the stairs, we then climb to the second floor, and I gesture to the doors that line the hallway.

"These are guest rooms," I tell her. "They rarely get used. The primary suite is at the end of the hall, and you're always welcome there. You don't have to knock."

She glances up at me and frowns. "Where is my room, then?"

Opening the door next to mine, I gesture inside, and she walks in.

"This is your private space. Your things were brought over this morning and have been put away. I also hired Lulu's personal shoppers to fill the closet with anything you could want. If you don't like anything, we can send it back."

"You shopped for me?" she asks, raising her eyebrows. "*Today?*"

"Honestly, no. Lulu and the personal shoppers

Rome hires for her did. You didn't have much, and I thought you should have options."

She peeks her head in the closet, and a smile tickles her lips. "There's so much color."

"I know you usually wear white, so if you don't like color—"

"I do." She swallows hard and glances back at me. "I wasn't allowed to wear it before."

She wasn't allowed.

Christ.

"You can wear whatever you want here. And if what's in your closet isn't satisfactory, by all means, take my card and go shopping. I'm sure Lulu and Scarlett would love to join you."

"Oh, that sounds like fun."

I nod and shove my hands in my pockets, suddenly nervous that she hates this house and everything in it.

"What are the rules?" she asks, turning to face me. "I know what's expected of me, but you must have household rules."

I tip my head to the side, taking her in. *Fuck*, she's beautiful. "If you leave the mansion, you take two guards with you. Jack, my number two, will assign a detail to you. I don't want you leaving without them."

"Of course," she whispers, as if she's disappointed.

"That's for your safety, not because I feel the need to control you."

She frowns. "No one cares about hurting me."

"You're my wife, and I'm the head of the Greek Mafia, one of the Kings of Vegas, and there are plenty of assholes out there who want to hurt *me*. The best and most expedient way for them to do that is to hurt you. So, you'll always have the detail with you."

She nods slowly. "I promise. What else?"

"That's pretty much it."

"So, this is a marriage in name only? We can—"

"No." I close the gap between us and tip her face up so I can see her gorgeous eyes. "This isn't in name only. If I find out that anyone else has touched you, I'll cut off their dick and feed it to them before I slice their throat."

She swallows thickly and narrows her eyes at me.

"Say what you want to say, Natasha."

"No one else touches you either."

With a smile, I lean into her. "I like that you're possessive, Angel. And just so we understand each other, I take my vows seriously. I'm not interested in other women. You don't have to worry about that."

"Okay."

"I want to kiss you," I murmur, staring down at her delectable lips.

"Okay," she says again, and my eyes fly back to hers.

"You don't like to be touched, and I'm respecting that boundary. Or trying to. I don't want to make you uncomfortable."

Her brows pull together for just a heartbeat, and then she lifts her chin a half an inch more.

"You're not making me uncomfortable."

My thumb skims over that plump bottom lip, so soft and sweet and everything I'm aching for. I want to push my hands in her thick, gorgeous blond hair and kiss the fuck out of her until she can't breathe.

Baby steps.

Instead, I lower my mouth to hers and sweep my lips back and forth before sinking in and kissing her chastely.

She moans in the back of her throat, encouraging me to deepen the kiss. I lick over the seam of her mouth, and she opens for me. Her hands settle on my chest, and I can't resist tasting her, nipping that lip, brushing my tongue over hers.

When I back away, her eyes are glassy, and she glides her tongue over her bottom lip, as if she's seeking the taste of me.

Oh, Angel, there's much more where that came from.

"Get comfortable," I tell her. "I'll be in my office downstairs if you need anything."

"Julian?"

Fuck, I love the sound of my name on her lips.

"Yes?"

"Can I have your phone number? I mean, I don't have it, and if something happened and I needed you—"

"Of course. I'm sorry that I didn't think of it. Where's your phone?"

She frowns and looks around for her bag, finds it on the bed, and reaches for it. When she pulls the phone out, she passes it to me, and I open a new text field, type in my number, and send a message.

We both hear my phone ping in my pocket.

"There you go."

"Thank you." She takes the phone back and bites her lower lip. "For everything. Is, um, is Elliott alive?"

She's staring at the floor, not even looking me in the face with the question.

"Yeah, Angel, he's alive."

She nods. "Okay. I'm going to change now."

"I'll be downstairs."

My fingers itch to help her with her zipper, but instead, I walk out the door and close it behind me, then head into my own room to change my clothes before I go to the office.

NATASHA

TODAY HAS *NOT* BEEN what I expected. Not at all.

First of all, I married Julian, and although I'm terrified of him, he's been kind to me so far. Of course, we've only been married for a matter of hours, but he welcomed me into his home and even gave me my own room. I don't have to share his bed. If he's to be believed, I don't have to do anything I don't want to.

My room has windows that look out to the gorgeous gardens, the likes of which I've only seen in magazines or online, a huge bed that looks so soft and cozy with sage green and cream linens, and a massive closet stuffed to the brim with brand-new, colorful clothes.

Color. I get to wear color.

Last month, Elliott took me to a gala, and I chose a blue dress to wear because I thought it made my eyes pop and I felt pretty in it, but when I got home that night, my father beat me for choosing it.

You only wear white.

But not anymore. Don't get me wrong, I like white, and I look good in it, but I can't wait to try so many other colors.

After I manage to wiggle my way out of the dress, practically dislocating my shoulder to reach the zipper, I lay it carefully over the chair that sits in front of a small desk and then cross to the attached bathroom.

I don't know who designed this house, but they should win some sort of an award because everything is just so . . . *stunning*. But it's not over the top. It's not in your face like the opulence of my father's house, where he's all about showing off how rich he is.

That's not this house.

It's . . . lovely. And although enormous, it's also homey.

There's a deep freestanding soaking tub that I'll be taking a dip in later. The double vanity is marble, the shower is big enough for a party of six, and all my toiletries are already here.

Opening drawers, I discover that my makeup, my skin care, *everything* has been transferred to this house and put away, as if I've lived here for years. As if little elves went into my bedroom at my father's house and magically moved it all here.

How in the world did he manage to do all of this?

I lift my gaze to the woman in the mirror and take stock. The bruises on my ribs have faded to a sickly green and thankfully aren't as sore as they were a few days ago. Hopefully, Julian isn't repulsed by them, since there's nothing I can do about them. My lip has finally healed enough that it doesn't split every time I talk or smile and is easily coverable by makeup.

After I strip out of my underwear and pin my hair up, I take a quick shower, careful not to ruin said makeup, and take my time soaking in the hot water. When I get out, I slather on my lotion and then pad into the closet to pull on clothes.

But when I open the top drawer, I'm surprised to discover not just underwear and bras but lingerie too.

New, sexy things.

Lace and satin, with bows and clasps, and I can only deduce that this must be what Julian prefers. My stomach jitters at the thought of having sex with my new husband, but not in a horrifying way. Yes, the thought of sex terrifies me, but Julian has only touched me with gentle hands so far. I don't think he'd be rough with me. He actually smiled at me earlier, and Julian is always so serious. So somber. His smile took my breath away.

And when he carried me over that threshold, I didn't want him to put me down.

That's new for me.

Not to mention, he held my hand during the entire tour of the house, and both times that he's kissed me, he was gentle. So no, I don't think he would be mean with me during sex. Honestly, I'm curious to experience it with him. Julian's scent calms me and stirs something in my belly, makes my core ache in a way that it hasn't before.

Perhaps I'm naive, and behind closed doors, Julian is into the whips and chains and all of the scary things I saw in the club that night. Because when it comes down to it,

I don't really know Julian Stavros at all. But I know how I feel when I'm around him, and I actually *want* my husband to touch me.

With a nervous sigh, I pull from the drawer the white lace lingerie, a matching bra and pantie set with a garter belt and thigh-high stockings. Once I have them on, I look at myself in the mirror and have to admit, I look damn hot, bruises and all.

Grabbing the heels I wore for the wedding, I slide my feet in them because they match the outfit, turn to see my backside, which is not covered at *all* thanks to the white thong I have on, and my ass is on full display. And then I wrinkle my nose.

Because although I look like a woman who's ready to get it on after her wedding, I feel like I might throw up from nerves.

I'm finally not panicked at the idea of a man touching me. I get to touch *him*. I have to do things to him to satisfy him and make sure he doesn't want to punish me.

The perfect wife is always available to service her husband's needs.

And it's our wedding day. I'd rather get this over with now so I can get on with it and not be afraid anymore.

So, dressed in my sexy bridal outfit, and trying my best to gather all of the self-confidence I have in me so I don't embarrass the hell out of myself, I open the door of my bedroom and step out, listening. The house is quiet as I walk to the stairs.

If he has guards in the house, and they were to see me, I'd die from mortification.

But I don't hear any voices, so I walk downstairs to

Julian's office. The door is open, and when I stop at the threshold, Julian's eyes come up from his computer and then widen as he takes me in from head to toe.

My husband is stupidly handsome.

He's changed into a black button-down, with the top two buttons undone and his sleeves rolled up just below his elbows, showing off muscles and thick veins that snake down his forearms. I can see tattoos on his right arm but can't tell from here what they are. They're . . . *sexy.* His thick, dark hair is styled, and for the first time in my life, I want to push my fingers through someone else's strands, just to see what it feels like.

Julian swallows hard before meeting my gaze with his dark one.

"I don't think I've ever seen anyone more beautiful than you, Angel."

His voice is rough, and it moves through me like warm honey. I can see from the look in his eyes that he means every word. It gives me the confidence I need to walk toward him. His eyes never leave mine as I cross the room, and yeah, nerves have settled into my stomach.

"You don't have to do this," he says as he scoots his chair back, making room for me.

The comment makes me pause. "I'm sorry, do you not want—"

"Come here, Angel."

His voice is still rough, but it's firmer, too, and I like it.

I want him to tell me what to do because I'm at a total loss here. I'm no seductress.

When I step in front of him, his eyes narrow as he takes in the bruises over my ribs.

"They don't hurt anymore," I whisper. "They just look bad. I'm sorry, I couldn't cover them—"

"You don't ever need to apologize to me for that," he replies as his gaze travels up my torso to my eyes. "What do you plan to do right now, Natasha?"

I lick my lips because I didn't really plan for anything. I put on the underwear and then came to find him, without any other thought. I have no experience with this. For fuck's sake, I'm a virgin.

"Um, well, I found the pretty underwear in my drawer, and I assumed you wanted me to wear it."

His eyes narrow and he tilts his head to the side. "I didn't choose it, but whoever did is getting a raise."

My lips tip up into a smile. "You like it."

"Very much. I had no idea I was a lingerie man, but it seems I am when it comes to you." His hands grip onto the armrests of his chair, as if he's doing everything in his power not to touch me.

You don't like to be touched, and I'm respecting that boundary.

Knowing that he won't touch me first, and that as his wife, I have obligations, I sink down to my knees and move between his spread thighs, watching him as I reach for the buckle on his belt. His jaw flexes as I unfasten it. I can feel that he's already hard. *So hard.*

In the past, this would have sent me running for the hills.

But with Julian, I'm . . . *fascinated.* Did I do that? I

don't know how that's possible. I haven't even touched him.

"You can take me out," he says with a low voice. "But look at me while you do it."

My eyes fly up to his, and my breath catches at the fire I see in his gaze. He wants me. I can see it written all over his handsome face.

But he's letting me take the lead, and that's the sexiest thing about this whole moment. I don't feel forced or coerced or shamed.

I feel desired.

And I get to be the one in charge. Or, at least, have a say in how this goes down. Even if it's only this first time, I appreciate it.

"Is this okay?" I ask him as I wrap my hand around his warm, velvety shaft and nudge his pants and boxers out of the way. He growls and tips his head back, swallows thickly as if he's gathering himself, and then he pins me in his gaze once more.

"Having your hands on me is every daydream I've ever had. Do you want me to give you instructions, or do you want to play?" His jaw is tight, and he sounds almost like he's in pain.

My eyes drift down to the hardness in my hands, and my mouth goes dry. He's big. There's no way I can get all of this in my mouth without choking, but I'd like to try to please him.

"Direct me, please."

He growls low in his throat, and it sends a shiver through me. His eyes are so dark, so *hot*, that it makes me bite my lip and squeeze my thighs together. "Good girl. You're so beautiful on your knees for me."

Oh, I like that. I like being praised by him, so I offer him a small smile and then lean forward to swipe my tongue over the tip of him, over that little bead of moisture that tastes salty and a little musky, and Julian closes his eyes as his dick flexes in my hands.

"Fuck, you're going to destroy me."

That doesn't sound like a bad thing, and I can't resist licking him again, then running my tongue along the edge of his crown.

"Open your mouth."

Eleven

JULIAN

I KNOW I haven't done anything good enough in this life to earn having this perfect woman on her knees with my cock in her hands, but I won't question it. I want her, just like this, every single fucking day for the rest of my life.

At my order, Natasha's jaw drops, and I guide myself between her lips. When she clamps them around me, I moan and tip my head back as heat rushes through me.

I'm going to embarrass myself. Her mouth feels too good. Christ, I'm forty-three years old, have fucked my way through this city, and this inexperienced woman's mouth makes me feel sixteen again.

"Fuck, your mouth is perfect." I keep my hands firmly on the chair, not wanting to scare her. I don't know what prompted this whole thing, but I'll be damned if I'll do anything to stop it.

My wife is a walking wet dream, and I would have sworn this is *not* the way today would have gone. I thought for sure that I wouldn't see her for the rest of the day.

I've never been so happy to be wrong in my life.

Her big blue eyes are on me as she tries to sink down lower, her inexperience obvious, and *so fucking sexy*. I stop her and smile down at her.

"Hold on, sweetheart. Take a breath for me. Good girl. Now, relax your jaw a little." Watching me, she does as she's told, and then she starts to move, and *holy fuck, I think I just saw heaven*. "God, baby, that's so good."

I want with everything in me to push my hands into her hair, but instead I let her have this. I'll eventually touch her all over, and take my time with it, but first I have to build trust between us.

Her hands move up and down my shaft where she can't fit me in her mouth, and she hums in the back of her throat because, if I'm not mistaken, my wife is enjoying giving me the best blow job of my fucking life.

"Goddamn, you were made for me," I murmur, and her eyes drift closed with pleasure. Her cheeks darken. She moans in the back of her throat, sending electricity through me.

My angel has a praise kink.

I can work with this.

"Look at those gorgeous lips wrapped around my cock, so damn perfectly." She whimpers and sucks harder, and my vision goes dark. "You're trying to make me come, aren't you, beautiful girl?"

She nods, those sapphire eyes full of desire.

"If you don't want me to come in your pretty little

mouth, you need to back off now, Natasha, because I'm about to lose control."

But she doesn't move away.

She picks up the pace, her hands tighten, she sucks even *harder*, and there's no way I can hold back as the climax moves through me. My balls tighten as I lift my hips off the chair and come hard down her throat, and she sucks every drop down.

I can't help it, my hands move from the chair to her hair, and I see her wince, so I pull back.

Christ, I can't catch my breath. "Fuck, you're incredible, Angel. I'm going to touch you now."

She nods, and I reach down to lift her off her knees and into my lap, where I wrap my arms around her and just hold her.

"Is this okay?" I murmur before kissing her temple.

"This is nice," she says, but frowns up at me. "Don't you want to—"

"Fuck yes, I want to bend you over my desk and fuck you six ways to Sunday, but I don't think you're ready for that. What brought this on? Not that I'm complaining. That was the best blow job I've ever had."

She doesn't look like she believes me. "I'm quite sure that's not true, but thanks for saying it."

"One, I don't lie. And two, your mouth is every damn fantasy I've ever had."

Her cheeks darken again with the praise, and I can't resist brushing my finger down her soft skin.

She doesn't flinch away.

"So, with that established, and at the risk of sounding ungrateful, which I'm not, what brought this on?"

Natasha nibbles her lip, and I nudge her chin up so she's looking at me as I tug the lip free with my thumb.

"What is it, Angel. You can tell me."

"It's what I'm supposed to do." The words are whispered, making me frown.

"I told you earlier, you'll do what you *want*. If that's not your thing, you don't ever have to do it again." I push her hair behind her ear and smile down at her. "But now that I know how good you are at it, I hope to Christ it's your thing."

She laughs, and I feel like I won the fucking lottery. God, she has the most magical, musical laugh.

"I liked it," she says shyly. "I don't mind doing that."

"It's on the table, then. We'll figure the rest out as we go. I'm sorry to have to tell you this, but I'm short on time. I have to leave for a while."

"Oh, I'm sorry for keeping you." Suddenly, all playfulness is gone from her face, and before I can stop her, Natasha squirms out of my lap and backs out of reach. "How many days will you be gone?"

"Days?" I shake my head as I stand. "No, I won't be gone for more than a few hours."

Her shoulders fall with relief.

"I have some business to see to, but I'll be back this evening. Just make yourself at home. Get settled. I mean that, there's nowhere in the house or on the grounds that are off limits to you."

"Do you have guards inside the house?" She pushes her hair over her shoulder, and I want to kiss her there on that smooth skin and then ghost my lips up her neck to her ear and get lost in her for about a week. Fuck, I'm already hard again. "Julian?"

"No. Guards are never in our home, they're stationed outside. Unless there's a threat or a problem."

"Okay." She nods. "Where is your household staff?"

Lifting a brow, I reach out and take her hand.

I can't keep my hands off my wife.

"I have a housekeeper, Ruth, who comes in once a week, on Fridays. She's here all day. That's the only staff I have."

"No cook."

"No cook," I confirm. "But if you want me to hire one—"

"No." She shakes her head. "I can do it. Well, I hope your business is good today."

She looks like she feels awkward as she smiles at me, and I won't fucking have that.

"Natasha. Come here." I crook my finger at her.

Obeying, she walks even closer to me, so close that I can smell the jasmine on her, and I lean in to kiss her forehead, breathing her in.

"Get comfortable here," I tell her softly. I'm enjoying this private and intimate moment with her, and I'm a little fucking pissed that I have to leave her. "I'll see you later. I won't be too late."

She nods, offers me another smile, and then walks out of my office. The white lace does *nothing* to cover her ass, and she has perfect dimples above each cheek.

I can't wait to nibble on them.

Fuck. For the first time in *years*, I don't want to go to work.

"Why are you here?" Mateo asks with a scowl. He's just arrived at the same time as me. "It's your fucking wedding day."

"We have work to do," I reply, walking next to him into the King of Spades, Carson's casino that just happens to be next door to Rapture. "Even on wedding days."

"Pretty sure you could have stayed home for this."

I shake my head. "It's not like I'm on a fucking honeymoon. This isn't exactly a love match, you know."

Definitely not a love match, but damn if I don't fucking like her.

Mateo lifts a brow. "She's fucking hot, man. If it's not a love match, you won't mind if—"

"I'll cut your liver out and feed it to you," I reply before he can finish the thought, and the asshole smirks at me.

"That's what I thought. You keep telling yourself that it's not a real marriage." He claps me on the shoulder as we walk into Carson's office, and we both stop short.

Because sitting across the desk from our brother is Sergei.

As in, my new father-in-law.

Rome's leaning against the window, his arms crossed over his chest, and he lifts his chin at me.

I'm not going to like this.

"You left my daughter alone already?" he asks but doesn't look angry. No, this motherfucker looks like the cat that ate the proverbial canary. "We taught her to be a better wife than that. She should still be on her knees—"

"Finish that sentence," I say as I pull my gun from the small of my back. "I fucking dare you."

Sergei laughs and waves me off.

"I'm not here to start a fight. Quite the contrary."

Moving into the room, I close the door behind us, and Mateo stands behind Carson. I join Rome at the window.

None of us wants to sit.

Fuck that.

"What do you want, Sergei?" This comes from Carson, who's glaring at the older man.

"Well, it's not so much about what I want as it is what I'm entitled to. You see, you threw me for a loop today when you decided to cast off your son and marry my daughter yourself."

I knew this was going to come back to bite me in the fucking ass.

"You should have said something before the ceremony if you object. Not that it would have changed the outcome."

The asshole shakes his head. "On the contrary. I don't object at all, because now that my daughter has married one of the Kings of Vegas, I'm in the perfect position."

The four of us don't reply, just continue staring at him, and then Carson starts to laugh.

"Fuck you," Carson growls. "You don't marry into this organization like you do a family."

"Either you accept me as an equal, or I take all four of you down."

"Or," Rome suggests, "we take you downstairs and simply kill you. That would solve a lot of problems."

"Works for me." I push off the glass, and Sergei holds up his hand, stopping us.

"I have information," he says, getting our attention, but his eyes are pinned to Carson. "On Adam Damien."

"The fuck did you just say?" Carson stands, leaning over his desk toward the older man. "Choose your next words carefully, or I'll pull your trachea out of your goddamn ugly-ass nose."

I hate it when he does that. It's so damn messy.

"You heard me." Sergei sits back smugly in his chair, examining his nails. "I have information that you're going to want. But I won't give it to you unless you make me a king."

"Murder it is," Mateo says, clapping his hands and then rubbing them together with anticipation. "Can I play with the blowtorch this time? You assholes always get all the fun."

"If you kill me, my daughter will die."

Now, his eyes find mine.

"You can't hide her away in your mansion forever. My men will find her, torture and rape her, and then kill her painfully. Is that what you want for your new wife, Julian?"

"He's bluffing," Rome says.

"I guess that's the chance you take," Sergei replies as

he stands. "I understand these decisions take a little time. So you think on it and call me."

He turns to walk out the door, and everything in me screams to take his fucking head off.

But if he's not lying, I can't risk Natasha's life.

So, we watch him walk out the door, and then we all turn to Carson.

"You know as well as I do that any information that sack of shit has on Damien is intel that we can get ourselves," Mateo says, shaking his head.

Now everyone turns to eye me.

"I'll start digging tonight." I'm the hacker of our organization, and there isn't much that I can't find out. If there's new chatter about the man that sent Carson to prison and killed the love of his life, I'll find it. "I'll report back in the morning."

Twelve

∼≈∽

NATASHA

"SHIT, DAMN, FUCK," I mutter as I consult my phone, and the lovely photo of the salad on the website, and then the mess in the bowl in front of me.

It's supposed to be a Greek salad, but it looks like slop. I swear, I followed the recipe to the *letter*, but it doesn't look great at all.

"Maybe it's one of those situations where it might not look pretty, but it's actually delicious." I prop my hands on my hips and stare into the bowl, then shrug and cover it and set it in the fridge. "Or, it has to set up in the fridge. I bet that's it."

I also found a recipe for a Greek chicken casserole. Yes, there's a theme for this dinner. My new husband is the head of the Greek Mafia. I want to cook Mediterranean food for him. I've never cooked a day in my life, because we always had a chef on staff, but it was drilled into me ad nauseam that this is one of my many jobs as Julian's wife.

I have to have dinner waiting for him every single day.

I'm the one who is supposed to plan the menu, and if we don't have a chef, that means that I'm in charge of preparing the meal. I can read a recipe. I'm an intelligent woman.

"I can do this," I say for the hundredth time and pull the cooked chicken out of the oven. The recipe called for it to be pan fried, but I've never used a gas stovetop before, and this behemoth is scary.

Don't get me wrong. I would bet that the whole set up cost well into the five figures and that every chef in the world would give it a gold star.

But it's intimidating as hell.

So, instead, I googled how to bake chicken because the oven isn't quite as intimidating, and I did that instead. Now, I have to cut up the chicken and mix it with the other ingredients for the casserole. Cutting and stirring I can do. In fact, I have a Taylor Swift song blaring through my phone as I stir and wiggle my hips.

This part is fun.

Once the mixture is poured into the dish and I've covered it with cheese, I skim the directions again. Bake for thirty minutes. Then broil.

I examine the oven and see that there is a setting for Bake but also a setting for Broil.

"Well, which is it?" I tap my finger on my lips and then shrug. "Must be a typo. I'll broil for thirty minutes."

After turning the oven to the right setting, I slip the glass dish inside and then survey the kitchen.

"Whoa."

Okay, so I'm not a tidy cook. I have a heaping sink of

dirty dishes, knives, and utensils, some not even used, strewn about the countertop, and is that *flour* on the floor?

I didn't use flour. At all.

It's fine, I'll get it all cleaned up while the casserole bakes. I bebop my way to the closet where I found cleaning supplies earlier and pull out a broom and some sponges.

Taylor and I are singing about being the man, elbow deep in dish water, when I start to smell something . . . not right.

Blinking, I frown and glance over my shoulder toward the oven, and *holy fucking shit*.

The oven is on fire.

I squeal and splash soapy water everywhere as I spin and grab a towel to quickly dry my hands, then open the oven, and a plume of smoke fills the kitchen.

"Shit!"

The alarms start to go off, and I race for the doors that lead to a stunning courtyard and pool area, open them wide, and do the same with the windows around the breakfast nook, hoping the smoke will drift outdoors.

Grabbing the oven mitts, I reach inside and pull out the dish, set it on the stove, and feel my shoulders sag.

"It's not supposed to be black."

Thirteen

JULIAN

THE CLOSER I get to home, the more my blood simmers with rage.

That son of a bitch just threatened to kill *my wife*.

And for that, he's going to suffer. He's going to suffer for a long, long time, until he begs for me to kill him.

Even then, I'll keep him alive to make him suffer some more.

I'm itching to get to my office, to fire up the computers and start digging into what Sergei could possibly have on Damien. I'll be surprised if I find anything at all.

Damien is a ghost. We hear murmurs here and there, but that's all they are. He's not stupid enough to come to Vegas.

He'd be dead within ten minutes of stepping foot in our city.

But I'll do my due diligence and search for anything that might give Carson a lead to bring his nemesis to justice. And by *justice*, I mean torn into pieces and left in the desert for the critters.

Once I'm home, I walk inside and immediately realize that something is . . . very wrong.

The smoke alarm is going off, and I can smell something burning. Running for the kitchen, I come to a halt and then feel a smile spread over my face as I watch my angel flutter around, opening windows and cursing, her music playing on her phone.

She's pulled her long hair up into a messy bun on the top of her head. She's wearing a red tank top that molds over her flawless breasts, along with denim shorts that showcase her perfect ass and legs.

Legs that I want to prop over my shoulders as soon as humanly possible so I can feast on her delectable pussy.

Natasha rushes back to the oven, and with huge black mitts on her hands, pulls a baking dish out and sets it on the stove, then closes the oven, cutting off some of the smoke.

"It's not supposed to be black," she mutters, her shoulders drooping with defeat, and I can't stay away any longer.

"What's happened?" I ask, startling her.

"I'm sorry." She shrinks away from me, her eyes widening. "I didn't mean to. I'm so sorry."

I reach out to run my hand down her arm to soothe her, and she flinches, as if I'm going to hit her.

"Hey, look at me." She presses her lips together and lifts her pretty blue gaze to mine. "I want you to hear every word I'm about to say. Are you listening?"

She nods sharply.

"I'm *never* going to lift my hand to you in anger. I will never hit you, punch you, or strike you in any way. You don't have to be afraid of that when it comes to me."

"Okay," she whispers, and then takes a deep, shaky breath. "I tried to make you dinner."

"I see that." My lips twitch as I glance over at the dish on the stove and feel something in my chest shift. *She was cooking for me.* "What was it?"

"Greek casserole." Her voice is so small again, and I can't wait for the day that she's not afraid to speak up to me.

We'll get there.

"Wait, I made a salad too," she says with hope springing to life in her eyes. She spins and opens the fridge, then pulls out a bowl and uncovers it.

She wrinkles her nose when she peers inside.

"I don't know about this."

Without looking at it, I grab a fork and dig in.

This could kill me.

First of all, it looks like soup. It's clearly overdressed and incredibly soggy. It tastes like . . . paper.

How my perfect wife managed that, I'll never know.

"Wait!" She turns to me after cleaning up something off the floor. "You don't have to eat that."

"You made it." I shrug and reach for a big spoon and a plate. "I'll eat the casserole too."

"No!" She shakes her head and grabs the spoon and plate from my hands. "You will *not* eat that."

I smirk, take the tools from her, and scoop out a big helping of the . . . mess on the stove.

"No, Julian." She's staring at my plate in horror. "Please don't eat it."

"But you made it for me."

"And I failed. Horribly. I don't want you to get sick." She shakes her head and takes the plate from me, setting it aside. "I'll learn, I promise."

Her lower lip trembles, and I pull her into my arms, where she immediately goes stiff as a board.

"What are you doing?" she asks.

"I'm hugging you, Angel." She frowns up at me, and I swear to Christ, a crack the size of Nevada spears through my chest. "Hasn't anyone ever hugged you?"

Her mouth opens, but she doesn't say anything, and then she leans into me, her cheek on my chest, and I loop my arms around her and hold her to me.

"It's our wedding day," I remind her.

"And I ruined it."

"No, sweetheart, you didn't." I can't help but smile and run my hand down her back. I think I've smiled more today than in the past ten years combined. "I should be taking you out to dinner."

"I'd like to stay here."

"You like it here?" I tip her chin up so I can see her face.

"Yeah, I like it."

"Good. Okay, we'll stay in. What would you like me to order for you? Anything you want."

Natasha leans back into me, clinging to me, and I want to burn the fucking world down.

No one has ever hugged my wife.

"Chinese food, please."

"You got it." Reluctantly, I let her go so I can pull my phone out and text my men. "What would you like?"

"Sweet-and-sour chicken, combination rice, beef with broccoli, two orders of egg rolls, hot and sour soup" —she narrows her eyes and looks at the ceiling—"I think that's it."

"Can I share yours, or should I get my own?"

She smirks at me. "I think it's plenty for both of us, unless you want something different."

Shaking my head, I text out the order to Jack, and then I add one last message.

Me: This is for my wife. If it's not hot and in perfect condition when it arrives, you won't like my wrath.

Jack: Yes, boss. Should be here in less than an hour.

"There. It's on the way. Are you okay?"

Natasha sighs and looks over the kitchen. "I'm fine, I'm just sorry that my first try at dinner was such a raging failure."

"You know, I think we'll be laughing about this in about twenty years."

Her lips twitch into a reluctant smile. "You're right."

"I have to do some work in my office, but you're welcome to come in there any time."

I know that I've repeated myself with regard to telling her that she's welcome wherever I am, but I want her to understand that this is her *home*. She can go anywhere she wants.

I don't want her to feel like a guest.

"Okay, I'll finish cleaning this up, and then I'll bring dinner into the office, if that's okay?"

With a smile, I lean in and press my lips to hers. "Perfect. Thank you."

"I didn't do anything." I love it when she whispers like that. It makes my cock harden and my blood simmer.

"Not true." I don't ask for permission when I push my hands over her hips and sink into her lips, and she doesn't flinch away from me. She makes that sexy-as-fuck whimpering noise in the back of her throat as she opens to me, inviting me in for more, and I take it.

I'll take anything this amazing woman is willing to give me.

Fourteen

NATASHA

I'M SO EMBARRASSED.

I love that Julian didn't punish me or even make me feel bad for the epic failure that was dinner, but still.

Ugh.

"Way to make a first impression, Natasha."

Rolling my eyes, I finish drying the last dish. The casserole dish had to be thrown away. There was no saving it. I tried.

It died an honorable death.

There's a short knock on the front door, and then it opens, and a man roughly the size of a car strolls in carrying the takeout food.

"Uh, hi." I feel uncomfortable because I'm not exactly dressed for company. I don't usually show much skin. I've always been a little self-conscious of my curves, and I prefer to not show too much, especially to Julian's men.

"Mrs. Stavros," he says with a nod. "I'm Jack, Julian's number two."

"Jack, can you do me a favor?"

He lifts an eyebrow. "Sure."

"Do you mind if, in the future, you just text me to let me know the food's here and leave it by the front door?"

"Like DoorDash?" he asks as if he can't believe what he's hearing. His face is so . . . *cold*. Shit, I've pissed him off.

"Yes, please. It would make me feel safer." Who am I right now? I've *never* been this outspoken, but Julian insists that this is my home, and damn it, I want to be comfortable here.

"You heard her," Julian says, surprising me as he walks into the room. "Unless it's an emergency, or I ask you to come inside, you don't."

Jack looks over at me, and for a second, I think he's going to argue, but I lift my chin.

"This is *my* home now, too, Jack."

"You're right," he says with a nod. "May I please have your number, so I can text you in situations like these?"

"I'll text it to you," Julian says. "Thanks, Jack."

The other man nods, and then he leaves, and I let out the breath I'd been holding.

"Don't apologize," Julian says before I can do just that. "I'm so fucking proud of you."

I blink rapidly, taken aback. "What? Why?"

"Because you spoke up for yourself, and that's sexy as fuck, Angel. I want you to do that all the damn time. Tell all of us exactly what you need."

I feel my cheeks heat. "I wasn't comfortable with him here when I'm dressed like this, but I thought you'd get mad at me for giving your man orders. Also, I think I pissed him off. He looks so grumpy."

Julian's gaze travels down my body, and I flush even more. At this point, I probably look like a lobster.

"First of all, you were respectful in how you asked, Natasha. Your request wasn't unreasonable. Second, Jack isn't mad at you. That's just how he looks. Also, we're in agreement. You can wear whatever you want, but I like that you don't want to show this spectacular body to anyone but me."

He smirks as I bite my lip and lifts the bags of food, then offers me his free hand. I immediately slide mine in his, and he gives it a squeeze.

"Let's go eat this in the office," he suggests, and I nod, walking with him.

"Did you build this house?" I ask him.

"About five years ago, yes. I inherited the land from my father and never bothered building out here before that because it was thirty minutes from any of my businesses in the city, so it wasn't exactly convenient."

He doesn't walk around to sit behind his desk. Instead, he sits in one of the two visitor's chairs, and I sit next to him, helping him dig into boxes, and once everything is open, we each take a set of chopsticks and dig in.

"Oh my God, it's so good," I say around a bite of egg roll. "I was hungry. Okay, what changed? Why did you build it five years ago?"

I glance over and find him watching me with somber eyes.

"What's wrong?"

"You're gorgeous when you eat."

I cover my mouth with a paper napkin and shake my head. "I eat like a linebacker. I like food. Tell me more. I'm trying to get to know my husband."

His eyes heat at that word, and he takes a bite of beef with broccoli. "I needed a sanctuary out of the city. I kept my building with the penthouse, so I could crash there when I had late nights at work, but this is home. Elliott always hated it out here. He prefers the city."

I nod, chewing slowly. "Where *is* Elliott, Julian?"

He doesn't even look my way. "You don't need to worry about that."

"I just—"

"Are you disappointed?" he counters, his voice calm as can be, but his eyes are *not* calm.

"That I didn't marry him?" I ask, and he simply holds my gaze. "Fuck no. I don't want to insult you, but your son is . . . horrible."

He winces and then nods. "I'm aware. He didn't used to be. Since he's become addicted to gambling and alcohol, he's gotten worse. He's learning his lesson."

"What does that mean?" I whisper.

"Exactly how it sounds. Now, tell me about you. Did you go to college?"

The subject of Elliott is obviously closed, so I take a deep breath and reach for the beef with broccoli and pop a bite in my mouth.

"Yes, I graduated from high school at sixteen and immediately started college. I have an MBA."

Julian stares at me for a full ten seconds. "You're twenty-two, and you're telling me you already finished your bachelor's and then got an MBA?"

"Yes. All from UNLV. I wasn't allowed to go away for school. In fact, I've never left the state of Nevada."

Now he scowls. "Your father just kept you here? No vacations, no sightseeing?"

Shaking my head, I reach for the box of sweet-and-sour chicken and take a bite.

"No. Here's the thing with my father: Children, *girls* in particular, are pawns. I was never under the illusion that my life is my own. I knew that one day I'd get married off to someone for the betterment of my father's business. I went to business school so that if I never did marry, I'd be an asset to him."

"Is that what you wanted to do?"

I scowl and reach for another egg roll. *I really am hungry.* "Of course not. It's boring as hell. But I'm smart, and I'm good at it, and that was the only option I was given."

Shrugging a shoulder, I take a sip of my water.

"What would you *like* to do?"

"What do you mean?"

Julian lets out a humorless chuckle. "Angel, if you could choose *anything* to do, what would it be?"

"Like, for money?"

"No, for fulfillment. You don't need money. I have more than we'll ever use. I want to know what you're passionate about. What do you enjoy?"

"It's not cooking." I cringe, and he laughs out loud, making my whole body come alive.

He has the best laugh.

"Playing the piano." I look down in embarrassment. "I'd like to teach children how to play."

"Done. I'll buy you a building tomorrow."

I scoff and shake my head. "Yeah, right."

"Why wouldn't I? You're not a prisoner here, Natasha. If you want to teach music, that's what you'll do."

"I don't need a building. Most music teachers go to the client's home to teach."

He's already shaking his head. "I can't have that. It's too risky. Puts you in dangerous situations. But I'd love to arrange for your own space. The clients will have to come to you, and you'll have guards with you at all times. That's my compromise."

My jaw drops and then closes again.

"Nothing to say?"

"I—you'd do that for me?"

"Without hesitation."

I search his face, but he's not bluffing.

"Can I have some time first? I've had a lot of changes, and I'd like to settle into this new life before I add on a music school."

"That sounds fair." Julian reaches over to wipe something off the corner of my mouth, and I don't flinch.

Progress.

He sucks the sauce from his finger and then takes another bite of beef and points at my necklace.

"That's beautiful."

I fiddle with the pendant and smile softly. "It was my babushka's. My grandmother. Papa gave it to me the other day, told me she'd want me to have it. I was kind of shocked because he's not typically the sentimental type, but I didn't ask questions because I loved my babushka, and now I have something of hers."

Julian nods thoughtfully.

"Can I ask a personal question?" I set the Chinese container down and lean back in the chair, stuffed from the delicious food.

Julian does the same, and then we're just sitting in this big, masculine office, facing each other in these soft brown leather chairs, as if we've known each other for a long time.

"There's nothing you can't ask me, Angel."

"I have two, actually."

He reaches over to take my hand and threads his fingers through mine, and it sends a thrill up my arm.

I love his touch. It's been one day, and I already really love the way he touches me. It's the biggest surprise of all.

"Only two?" His lips tip up into a wry smile, and I can't help but smile back at him.

"Okay, to be fair, I'll likely have way more than that as time goes on, but for now, it's two."

"Shoot."

"Oh, wait, three."

Julian laughs and nods. "Okay, let's hear them."

"Well, when you said *shoot*, it reminded me. Can I learn? To shoot, that is."

His smile fades and he narrows his eyes. "Why?"

I blow out a breath and squeeze his fingers. "Because I'm married to Julian Stavros. My father is the head of the Bratva. I'm a smart girl, Julian. At any given moment, I could be in a scary situation and need to know how to get out of it. I don't know how to shoot; my father wouldn't let me. But I think it's a good skill to have."

"Agreed. Lulu and Scarlett work with all of us learning the same thing you're talking about. You can join them if you want."

"Oh." That makes me nervous. My stomach turns at that, and Julian frowns because apparently I don't have a poker face around this man.

"You don't like Lulu?"

"No, I do. She's very sweet and was so good to me today."

Did the wedding really happen *today*? It feels like so long ago.

"But I'm not great with people, and making friends is hard. I don't mind learning by myself."

"Why don't you give it a try, and if you're still uncomfortable, we'll work something out."

I nod in agreement. "We're good at the compromise thing."

He smiles softly, and it hits me in the feels. "Okay, next question."

"Does our age difference bother you?"

My husband goes very still, and the muscle in his jaw twitches. "No. Does it bother *you*?"

"Not at all. You're what, fifty?" I press my lips together because I know he's not fifty, and he barks out a laugh.

"Sometimes I feel fifty. I'm forty-three. Elliott's twenty-five."

"You were a young dad." My voice is quiet but not judgmental.

"I was a fucking baby."

"And that leads to the last question of the night." I lick my lips and try to pull my hand out of Julian's, but he holds on tight and frowns at me. "Where's his mom?"

"She died about a year after Elliott was born. I met her in school when I was seventeen, and we were *not* planning to get pregnant. Sienna was a nice girl. I liked her a lot, and we had fun together. Maybe too much fun for our age. And then she was pregnant, and I married her. She died in a car accident."

"I'm sorry," I whisper.

"She died before you were born, Angel. There's nothing to be sorry for. It was a long time ago, and while I never would have wished her dead, our marriage wasn't likely to survive. We were far too young. Now, I have a question for you."

"Oh geez. Okay. I'm an open book."

He covers his mouth with his free hand and laughs. "You look scared out of your mind."

"I guess I didn't take into account that the questions worked both ways." I clear my throat. "I'm ready."

"How are you?"

I blink at him. "That's it?"

"Yes. I want to know how you're doing with everything that happened today. Don't sugarcoat it for my benefit."

"You actually care." I can't believe I voiced the words out loud. "Made men rarely do. You get what you want, and everyone else can fuck off."

"I'm not going to lie to you, Natasha. I'm a shit human. I have exactly that attitude, except when it comes to my family. My brothers, my men, and now, you. I don't give a shit about anyone else. So yeah, I care. I want to know how you're holding up."

Biting my lower lip, I take a deep breath and think about it.

"I was so scared this morning," I admit. "Terrified. Elliott was *never* kind to me unless we were around other people. Then he was the doting fiancé. But the second we were alone, he tormented me relentlessly."

Julian growls next to me, and I jerk my gaze to his.

"Keep going, Angel."

"I shouldn't say bad things about your son."

"You should always tell me the truth. Go on."

"I thought about killing myself—"

He reaches for me then and pulls me into his lap, his arms wrapped around me like earlier, and he kisses the top of my head.

"I didn't want to live a life where I was afraid all of the time. Not anymore. Not ever again." I let myself lean into him and swallow the tears that want to come. "But then Lulu came in and helped me rip apart that horrible dress."

He leans back and frowns down at me. "What do you mean?"

"It had poofy sleeves and a big stupid bow over the ass. It looked like something from the 1980s. So, we did surgery on it."

"It was beautiful on you." He ghosts his knuckles down my cheek. "Don't ever say those words again, about not wanting to be alive. Do you hear me?"

"It was bad," I whisper. "You've seen the bruises."

"I don't ever want you to feel that way again, and I'll do everything in my power to make sure you have a life that you enjoy." He presses his lips to my forehead.

"When I got to the front of the church, I could smell you, and when I looked up and saw you standing there, it was like all of the terror and horror was just . . . *calm*. Like I could finally breathe. And don't get me wrong, you still make me nervous because I don't know you well, but you've never hurt me."

"And I never will." It sounds like a solemn vow, and it fills me with warmth just as much as leaning against his hard chest does.

"It's been a busy day," I say softly.

"And I still have work to do," he murmurs. "But I want to make sure you're okay first."

"I'm great." I grin up at him, realizing that it's the truth. "I'll clean up this food and put the leftovers in the fridge for tomorrow."

"You like leftovers?"

"Duh. Chinese is better the next day. It's science." Grinning, I lean in and press my lips to his cheek, startling him, and then he yanks me back to him and crashes his mouth to mine, kissing me so desperately, as if he's wanted to do it all his life.

And I love it.

I wrap my arms around his neck and press close to him as I push my fingers into the softest hair I've ever felt.

And then I back away.

"You have to work," I remind him. My lips are buzzing from that spectacular kiss.

"I'll probably be here all night," he agrees. "Just let me know if you need me."

I nod, and then climb off his lap and gather the food cartons, closing them and stacking them back in the bags, and then I offer my husband a smile before I walk out of the room.

It only takes a moment to put the food away before I make my way up to my bedroom.

Just let me know if you need me.

I wonder if he would think I was coming on too strong if I told him I'd like to sleep in his bed? There's just something about his warm scent that soothes me, and I bet his bed smells like heaven.

But he's working, and I want to leave him be, so I close the door of my room and get ready for sleep.

JULIAN

"THERE'S NOTHING AT ALL?" Carson asks. We're back at his office at the casino. All four of us, plus our number twos.

"Nothing," I reply, shaking my head. "I was up all night, looking through chat after chat on the dark web, in all the usual places where his name is mentioned, and then I dug deeper."

I blow out a breath and push my hand through my hair. I'm fucking exhausted. I managed to grab a couple of hours of sleep this afternoon, before I came to the city for this meeting, and what I have to do after.

I've hardly seen my wife at all today. But I *did* hear her playing the piano this afternoon before I left, and everything in me wanted to go sit with her. She's fucking talented.

"There are the usual hits out on his life," I add and see the hate gleam in Carson's blue eyes. "Sixteen as of this morning, to be exact. I see that you've contracted for all of them."

"If anyone's going to kill him, it's going to be me," he replies, his voice laced with hate and revenge. "What else?"

"The last known information on Damien was when everything went down with Lulu and her father."

Rome stands and paces the room. He came close to losing his wife that day, at the hands of her corrupted piece-of-shit father, and it still fucks with him.

"Since then, he's gone underground again. No known location. No sightings, and we've been monitoring traffic cams as well, looking for his face. He's not in Vegas, that we know for sure, but it's a big fucking world, Carson. I'm telling you, there's no intel. Sergei is lying out of his fat ass, trying to get a rise out of us."

"Figured as much," Mateo mutters. "Sergei couldn't find information with a map and a GPS. He's an idiot."

"An idiot with an army," Rome reminds us. "We don't respect or like him, but we shouldn't underestimate him."

"I don't like that he lives in our city," I mutter.

"As long as he keeps his business dealings in Russia and LA, I don't give a fuck where he lives," Carson replies. "Now, we need to go down to the cell."

Mateo and Carson share a look while Rome and I come to attention.

"Who's down there?" I ask.

"The motherfucking mayor of our fine city."

Rome growls. It seems the conversation is going to center around the assholes who've fucked with his wife today.

The last time any of us saw Aaron Pierce was right

after he put his hands on Lulu at the bar and then was kicked out of the club permanently. We roughed him up that night.

If he'd been anyone else, he'd be at the graveyard right now.

Instead, he was given a warning, a beating, and a lesson about putting his hands where they're not supposed to be.

"What did he do now?" I ask.

"He owes my casino about a million," Carson says. "And he cornered one of my waitresses in a hallway and tried to fucking rape her."

"Let's go," Rome says, marching to the door. "He's done. No more mercy for this piece of shit."

I roll my shoulders and follow the others. I do have other business to see to tonight, but I wouldn't miss this for the world.

Each of us owns many businesses in the city, but each of us also chose a building here on the strip to buy and use as our home base. Rome's and Carson's buildings are attached by a skybridge, and they share many of the same clientele between Carson's high-end casino and Rome's luxury adult club. Mateo's building is on the other end of the strip, and mine is in the middle.

I'll get over there after we take care of this handsy piece of garbage.

"I'll keep a look out for him," I tell Carson, and he knows that I mean Damien. "I've put feelers out and set up trigger words to ping me whenever anyone searches for them on the dark web. Nothing will happen where he's concerned without us hearing about it."

"I appreciate it," he says, clapping me on the shoulder. "Now, let's go see to this fucker."

The eight of us—our number twos are silent but never leave our side—walk out of the elevator and down a cement hallway to where Carson has four cells. Three are used for holding, and one is for torture.

I'll give you one guess which room we walk into.

"Oh, this is fun," Spider, Carson's number two, says as he rubs his hands together. "I hate this guy."

"You can't kill me," Pierce announces as we stroll inside. He's sweaty, his red hair plastered to his forehead. He's wearing black slacks and an orange golf shirt, which makes him look like a pumpkin. Or an idiot.

"Is it casual Saturday?" I ask the others, eyeing the mayor's stupid outfit.

"Seems so," Mateo says with a shrug. "Or, lame-ass outfit Saturday. I would have played along, but I don't shop at Walmart."

"Fuck you," Pierce snarls, and Mateo smirks. "I'm going home."

The man is chained to the floor, sitting in a metal chair.

He's not going anywhere.

"No, you're not," Rome says, shaking his head. "It seems you just can't keep your disgusting fucking hands off of women who don't want you to touch them."

"Lies."

"Not to mention all of the money you owe me," Carson growls. "You see, that pisses me off. You come into my establishment, my *house*, and not only do you take advantage of me by racking up the kind of debt that an idiot like you can't pay off, but then you go and harass my employees on top of it."

"I didn't harass anyone. She fucking wanted it."

"That's why she kneed him in the balls and called her manager," Spider says to Rome. "Because she wanted this limp-dicked asshole to fuck with her. Makes sense."

"You're a problem," Carson continues as he walks over to his workbench.

Carson doesn't keep as many tools around as the rest of us because the scary-as-fuck assassin prefers to kill men with his bare hands.

But today, he grabs a sledgehammer off the bench and casually strolls toward Pierce.

"I have the money to square the debt," Pierce says, eyeing the hammer. He keeps his voice even, but the man is scared out of his mind right now.

And he should be.

I cross my arms over my chest and grin. *This is going to be fun to watch.*

"Sure you do," Carson says with a nod, then pulls back and swings, taking out Pierce's knee, splitting his pants and the skin, and making him bleed all over the fucking place.

"Fuck, that's gotta hurt," Luke says to Spider, who nods in agreement.

Pierce howls in pain, writhing against the chains holding him down.

"You keep touching things that don't fucking belong to you," Carson says in Pierce's face, and then his hand jabs out so fast, I would have missed it if I'd blinked, and he rips the other man's throat out.

Pierce's eyes go wide, and he gurgles for about three seconds before the life leaves them, and he slumps over dead.

"Graveyard," Carson growls at Spider, who nods and pulls his phone out of his pocket to take care of the body.

"That was fast," Mateo says. "You could have used the sledgehammer a little more."

"He annoyed the fuck out of me," Carson replies, pulling his hand down his face. "And I want to go home."

"Fair enough," Rome says as we turn to file out. "You're all coming for dinner tomorrow. Eloise is making . . . well, I forget what she's making, but it'll be delicious, and it'll crush her if you don't show up."

"We'll be there," I reply with a nod. "I have other business, unless you have anything else?"

"We're good," Mateo says. "I'm headed over to Rapture."

Once we've all gone our separate ways, Jack and I climb into the back of my SUV.

"To the office," I tell my driver, meaning the building down the street, and turn to Jack. "It's time for me to check on Elliott."

"He's not happy with you," Jack replies, shaking his head.

"I'm sure he's pissed as fuck. I don't fucking care."

When we get inside, I hit the button for the penthouse first, and Jack and I ride in silence. When we reach the top floor, I take a look around.

I haven't been up here in a few days. Not since the night that I found Elliott at the club with Natasha.

Knowing that he hurt her in here makes me want to burn it to the ground.

"I want a crew in here to demo the whole fucking thing," I tell Jack, who stares at me, stunned. "And then I need to hire a decorator to come in and start from scratch. Have them consult with my wife. It should be the way she wants it."

"But why?"

"Because I can't tear the whole building down without walking through too much red tape. This is getting an overhaul as soon as possible. Arrange for the demo."

"You got it, boss. Do you want me to donate the furniture?"

"That's fine. And have my personal things taken to the mansion. Elliott's can go in the fucking trash. Speaking of, let's go downstairs."

Once down in the basement, we walk to the cell where my son is being held. I haven't been here since I ordered that he be brought here, and I haven't asked any questions. Jack gives me daily reports that Elliott's alive, but that's it.

Pausing outside the door, I turn to my second.

"Report."

"He's eating one meal a day. Refused to eat at all for the first two days, but then hunger got the better of him. We're feeding him shit."

"Good."

"I didn't want him to freeze to death at night, so he's wearing a T-shirt and sweats that I got from his room upstairs."

"Fine. Anything else?"

"I suspect that the cuts you gave him are infected, but he won't let me look at them."

With a sigh, I turn and unlock the door, then step inside and feel my stomach roll over.

My son should not be in here.

He's lost some weight already. His skin is gray, his lips are chapped, and his dark hair is a mess.

He looks up at me, firms his chin, and then looks away.

None of my cells are meant to be luxury accommodations. Most of the men brought here don't make it out alive. I certainly don't want my son to sit in his own filth, on a dirt floor, in the cold. But my kid needs a huge helping of humble pie, so here we are.

"Are you ready to talk to me?"

Elliott turns his head away like an insolent child.

"I'm prepared to give you options, Elliott."

Still nothing in response.

"Fine. Another week it is."

I turn to walk away, and Elliott starts to yell.

"Wait, what are the options. Dad!" I don't stop walking. "You're such a piece of shit! Just wait until I'm out of here, and how I'll make you wish you were never born!"

I slam the door closed behind me and stare at Jack, who just sighs.

"Food every other day. Water once a day. I'll be back in a week."

He nods grimly and I walk away.

IT'S LATE, PAST MIDNIGHT, WHEN I WALK INTO the mansion. I ended up going up to the office in the penthouse to get some last minute work done, including going over the shipment I'm expecting in my port in LA tomorrow, before I decided to head home.

I hate that I haven't seen Natasha today, and now she's probably in bed. Unless she's a night owl.

I don't even know whether my wife prefers morning or night.

Walking through the house, I grin to myself. I can smell her soft jasmine scent in the air. The mansion already feels more like a home because she's in it. I tug off my tie and jacket and am rolling my sleeves when the kitchen comes into view, and I stumble to a stop.

My angel is sitting on a stool at the island, slumped over, sleeping.

There are two bowls of food sitting there, uneaten.

She didn't eat?

When I approach, I see that it's not leftover Chinese either. This is soup that she must have heated in the microwave, but it's gone cold now.

Shit.

I didn't call or text to let her know that I'd be late. I haven't had anyone to answer to in *years.*

Natasha shifts on the stool and opens her eyes, and then they grow wide when she sees me, and she sits up.

"Oh, I'll heat this up. I'm so sorry, I didn't mean to fall asleep."

"You should have gone to bed, sweetheart." I stride to her and cup her cheek. She doesn't flinch, and it warms my chest. "Why are you still up?"

"It's my job."

I frown down at her. "What's your job?"

"As a wife, it's my job to make sure dinner is ready for whenever you get home, and I'm not allowed to leave the kitchen until after you've eaten."

What in the actual fuck is she talking about?

"Who taught you that, Natasha?"

She yawns, and I lift her into my arms, carrying her to the stairs.

"My mom. It's part of being an organized crime wife."

Shaking my head, I press my lips to her temple. "We're going to talk about these rules in the morning, but I want to make it clear that I don't expect you to have dinner ready for me ever, Angel. I'm hiring a chef."

"You don't have to. I figured out the microwave."

Fuck, she's the sweetest thing.

"Yeah, I do. No more cooking for you."

Her eyes blink open, and she stares up at me. "I just want to be a good wife, so you don't send me back."

"You're staying here, with me, forever."

"Promise?"

"Yeah, baby. That's what the wedding vows were for, remember?"

She nods and looks around and then frowns. "This isn't my room."

"It's where you belong. This is *our* room now."

"Oh, good." It's a whisper. "I almost asked to sleep in here last night."

Surprised, I set her on the bed and squat in front of her. "You should have said something."

"You were busy working."

Unable to stop myself, I reach up and hook her soft hair behind her ear. "I'm never too busy for you. I want you to tell me what you need or want. Always."

She's in a loose tank and sleep shorts, so I help her under the covers and kiss her head.

"Are you working all night again?" she asks around a yawn.

"No. I just need a quick shower, and then I'll be back."

"Okay." She nuzzles down into the pillow and takes a deep breath. "You smell so good."

I hurry through the shower, anxious to be with her, and when I finally crawl into bed, I wrap myself around her from behind and tug her against my chest. She wiggles against me, making my cock hard as fuck, but I don't do anything more than pepper kisses on her cheek and neck and then, with her safe in my arms, fall asleep.

Sixteen

NATASHA

KISSES.

Someone is kissing my neck and chest and tugging my shirt up my torso, and I lift my arms so it can slide off because this feels fucking *amazing*.

"Fucking Christ, you're gorgeous." That's Julian's rough voice in my ear, just before he sinks his teeth into my neck, making my back bow up off the bed. His hand roams over to my breast and pinches the nipple.

"Hmm," I moan, arching into his touch.

"So damn sweet," he murmurs, leaving open-mouthed kisses along my jawline. "I'm fucking starving, Angel."

"I can make breakfast. Or, you know, try."

I feel him grin against my skin, and it sends another tingle through me.

"You have what I want right here. You're so damn warm and soft and *perfect*." His mouth slants over mine, and he sinks into me, kissing me so slowly and deeply, pulling me further out of sleep.

God, I've never wanted anyone the way I want this man. This is the best way to wake up *ever*.

Sign me up for this every day of my life.

I'm starting to *crave* his touch. Not just tolerate it, but I need it like I need air. I had the best night's sleep of my life in his arms.

And now, my body is on *fire* for him.

"Open your eyes, angelos mou, I want you to look at me."

I manage to get my eyes open and then sigh in happiness because my husband is gloriously naked, braced above me, his arms flexed under the pressure of keeping his weight over me, and *holy shit*, he's something glorious to behold.

"You're so fucking beautiful," he says against my lips, his dark eyes pinned to mine.

"I was just thinking the same about you."

Pleasure moves through those eyes, and I can't stop touching his tattoos. He has so many, all down his right arm, and I *love* them.

But before I can ask any questions, his magical lips start to journey down my body. He pauses at my breasts, laving them with his tongue, before he moves farther south.

"Julian, you don't have to—"

"No, I don't have to do a fucking thing, but I get to eat this gorgeous pussy for breakfast." He bites me, right where my leg meets my hip, and I groan in pure, unadulterated lust. "I'm going to consume every fucking inch of you, wife."

Oh, hell yes. Please consume me.

Before I can voice those thoughts, he spreads my legs, and then his mouth is on me, making me see stars. I swear, the world explodes around me when he licks me from my entrance to my clit, and then back down again.

"So fucking sweet," he growls. "And all fucking mine."

"Yours." I can't resist reaching down to fist my hand in his hair, and when my hips come up off the bed and electricity shoots up my spine, I don't know if I'm holding him to me or trying to push him away. "Oh God."

"So responsive," he murmurs, and brushes his fingertip over my lips before pressing inside, and we both groan. "Fuck, you're tight, baby. Even with just one finger."

Of course, I am. I'm a virgin.

But I can't voice that thought out loud because I'm fairly sure my soul just left my body.

"Julian!"

"Oh, I like that. Good fucking girl. I want my name coming out of your mouth when I'm eating this cunt. Say it again."

He sucks on my clit and adds another finger inside me, and I scream his name.

"Julian!"

"Mm, that's my dirty little angel." He nibbles on my inner thigh. "We're not close to being done. You can make a bigger mess than this."

Panting, I stare down at him. His mouth is glistening with my climax, and he's grinning up at me.

This is the sexiest moment of my life.

"We're doing this again," he says and presses a wet kiss to my pubis, just above my clit. "Fuck."

I moan and circle my hips. "I can return the favor, you know."

"There's no favor here. That implies that I didn't want to do this in the first place. When in reality"—he brushes his knuckles up and down my slit, so gently that it sends little sparks through me—"I've been *craving* this for a long fucking time. Longer than I want to admit. Now, I'm going to eat you, and you're going to soak this bed. Got it?"

"Soak the bed?" I frown down at him. "I don't want to . . . *pee on you*. I'm not into that."

He chuckles and kisses my other thigh, as if he thinks I'm adorable. "That's not what this is. You have to trust me. Can you do that?"

I blink at him and then nod slowly, and he presses the sweetest kiss right over my clit.

"Good girl."

God, I really love it when he praises me.

"I love how wet you are," he murmurs as he brushes his lips back and forth over my slit. Every move he makes sends nothing but pure, euphoric sensation through me. "I might hang out here all day."

"I don't have plans," I reply before he bites my thigh, making me chuckle.

"Look at how swollen you are already." He laps at me, all over my center, from my ass now to my clit, and my face flames in embarrassment. No one has *ever* touched me there.

No one has ever touched me anywhere down there, but definitely not my ass.

"Eyes on me," he reminds me.

"I'm embarrassed," I whisper and cover my face with one hand.

"Not acceptable. I won't have it. You're fucking gorgeous, Natasha."

"You just had your mouth on my . . ." I shake my head, my cheeks flaming.

"On this?" He swirls his tongue over the tight muscle, and I roll my lips inward, enjoying the way it feels, but knowing that it should be so *wrong*. "I'm going to have more than my mouth on it, eventually."

I gasp and stare down at him.

"That got your eyes on me. Yes, Angel, I plan to fuck this ass, but not today. Right now, I'm going to make you lose your fucking mind and soak my face."

I wrinkle my nose, and he chuckles again.

"Stop making fun of me."

He shakes his head and pushes up, covering me with his broad, muscled body so he can kiss me, and I can taste myself on his lips and smell my musky essence all over his skin. His hard, gorgeous cock slides against my slit, and I *want him*.

"Taste how delicious you are, *angelos mou*. Fucking amazing. I'm not making fun of you, I'm having fun *with* you, and that's the second new experience for me today."

"What was the first?" My voice is a whisper.

"Waking up with a woman in my bed. That hasn't happened since—in a long time."

Since his first wife died.

He doesn't let me respond before he kisses his way down again and nudges his shoulders between my thighs.

"Now, where was I? Ah yes, making you squirt all over my face." He grins, and then his fingers are inside me and his tongue is working magic on my clit, and my body ignites all over again.

"Holy shit."

"Mm," he replies. He turns his fingers and makes a *come here* motion, and holy fucking shit, the world falls out from under me.

"Oh my fucking God!" I'm thrashing my head back and forth, my hips are bucking, and I think I might have just died for about a millisecond. "Holy shit, Julian."

"Mm-hmm." He's lapping at me again, and when I can look down at him, I feel my eyes widen in horror.

The bed is *soaked*.

"Oh God, I'm so sorry, I didn't mean to do that."

"*I* meant to do that," he says as he kisses his way back up to me. "And you have nothing to be sorry for. That's the sexiest fucking thing I've seen, and we'll be doing it again. Often."

"But maybe not in the bed, because now we have to clean this up."

He chuckles and nuzzles my neck. "I'll clean it up, Angel."

"Did you call me that in Greek? Angel?" I ask him, suddenly feeling shy.

"I called you *my* angel."

I like that.

"Now—" But before he can complete that thought, his phone starts to ring at the side of the bed. "I'll fucking kill whoever that is."

"Just ignore it."

The phone stops ringing, and Julian shrugs a shoulder and goes back to kissing me, but then it starts to ring again.

"Fuck," he growls, and rolls to the side of the bed, scooping up the phone on his way. "What?"

I can't hear what they're saying on the other end of the line, but his whole body goes tight.

"When?"

I reach out and drag my hand down his back, from his neck to his ass. I like having free rein to touch this sexy man.

The tattoos on his right arm move up to his shoulder and over his shoulder blade. They're all different images. Flowers, knives—a *lot* of different knives—and a clock.

"The shipment arrives this evening, you know that. I want everything in place, with extra men. No fucking this up. Yeah, I'll make those calls now. Keep me informed."

He hangs up and then pushes his hands through his hair before turning to look down at me.

He cups my face, his thumb dusting over my cheek so gently, it makes me want to purr.

"You don't flinch when I touch you anymore," he says, watching me carefully.

"I love it when you touch me," I admit, and his lips curve.

"Good. Because I plan to have my hands on you at

every opportunity. I have to cut this short, but I'm taking a rain check on what comes next."

"I need coffee," I inform him.

"Me too." He leans over to kiss me softly, and *holy shit*, this man can kiss. His lips should come with a warning label.

Seventeen

NATASHA

TODAY HAS BEEN the best day that I've had in a long while. After waking up to the spiciest sexual experience of my life—and we haven't even actually had sex yet—I had some coffee and sat out by the pool to read for a while. Julian spent a long time in his office. Every once in a while, I'd hear him yell at someone on the phone.

My husband is intense when he's in work mode.

But he's only ever good to me.

Part of me wonders if I'm giving him too much trust too soon. We've only been married for a few days, and although he's never threatened me in the past, I should keep my guard up and my eyes open. Because men can be unpredictable in our world.

I should know that better than anyone.

With a sigh, I fiddle with my necklace and close my eyes, enjoying the sunshine. I was in the shade for a while, but it feels good in the sun. With it being fall, the days have been getting cooler and cooler, so it's not too horribly hot today.

Not like the oppressive heat over the summer.

"You're going to burn."

Blinking my eyes open, I turn my head toward that familiar deep voice and smile. "I haven't been in the sun long. Are you okay?"

"I'm fine, why do you ask?"

He sits in the chair next to me and reaches for my hand.

"I heard you yell a couple of times."

"I'm having issues with a shipment that's coming into my LA port tonight. I don't want to have to go there, so I've been trying to manage it from my office."

"Why don't you want to go to California?"

He squeezes my fingers before bringing them to his lips. "Because I have a sexy wife at home, and I'd rather not leave her."

Okay, that might be the sweetest thing anyone's ever said to me.

"I'd be okay," I whisper, and then yelp when he tugs me into his lap and buries his face in my neck, giving it a little nibble. "Okay, fine, I like it better when you're here."

"That's what I wanted to hear. We have to go in a few minutes."

I can't resist dragging my fingers down his cheek as I ask, "Go where?"

"We're going into the city for dinner," he replies. "Nothing fancy."

"Oh, I'll go change. I don't know if you're aware, but my super over-the-top husband bought me all kinds of pretty new clothes, and I've hardly had the chance to wear them."

Julian smirks and then pats me on the ass as I stand up to go inside and get ready.

"I like this sassy side of you, Angel."

Me too.

I WONDER WHERE HE'S TAKING ME.

Staring out the window of the SUV, I see the lights of the city come into view. I know that Las Vegas can be a dangerous, seedy place for a lot of people, but I've always thought it was beautiful. I love all the lights, the people shuffling around. Some of them make me laugh, like that Elvis impersonator who's currently thrusting his hips back and forth, drawing a crowd.

"I love this city," I find myself saying out loud. "I always have. Even the tourist traps."

"I'm glad you do because you're married to a man who owns most of it," he says, bringing my hand to his lips. "Before we get where we're going, I want to take a minute to talk about what you said when I got home last night."

"What did I say?" I ask him.

"That having food ready for me, and not leaving the kitchen until I've eaten, is your job."

"It is—"

"No. It isn't, Natasha. I want you to throw pretty much every rule you've been taught out the fucking window. You and I are figuring this out as we go. There aren't any rules until we make them for ourselves. I don't want you to go without eating or to exhaust yourself like that again. Eat when you're hungry, especially if I'm not home. And I'll do better at communicating with you. I should have let you know that I'd be home late, and I'll do better."

"Okay. Thank you." I lick my lips. "I have a rule."

His eyebrow kicks up with amusement. "I can't wait to hear this."

"No other women."

"I already told you that I'm not interested in other women."

"I know." I nod and squeeze his hand in mine, trying to reassure myself more than him. "And I believe you. But in our world, most men don't honor that for long. If you're ever with someone else, you won't be with *me* ever again. I can't handle that, Julian."

He nods and reaches out to cup my cheek.

"If you're ever with anyone else, I'll fillet him with my dullest knife over the course of a year, taking a little at a time."

"Well, that sounds delightful. I'm changing my answer to that."

Julian barks out a laugh, and then we're parked, and I look out the window.

My body goes ice cold.

Every muscle seizes.

Oh no. Not this. Anything but this.

Suddenly, my door is opened, and Julian is helping me out of the vehicle.

"I th-thought you said you were taking me to dinner." I can't take my eyes off the Rapture sign.

I don't want to be here.

"I am," he replies, and with his arm around my shoulders, he leads me into the building.

I can't do it.

I'm going to fuck you so hard, and for so long, your entire body will be a mangled, disgusting mess. You'll be begging me for mercy, but no one will hear you.

"Angel?"

I shake my head jerkily as we board the elevator. My teeth are chattering, and I can't pull in a breath.

"Natasha, look at me." The elevator jerks to a stop, and then his hands are on my face and his forehead is resting on mine. "Take a breath. Like this, take a breath in, baby."

"Can't. Can't be here. Please."

"No, Christ, we're not going to Rapture."

I shiver at the word.

"We're going to the penthouse. To Rome and Lulu's for family dinner. I'm not taking you to the club."

I want to cry. God, I want to cry and beg him to take me out of here.

"I h-hate this building."

"You have nothing to be afraid of," he assures me, his voice so hard and sure. "I'm right here, and I'm never leaving you alone. Nothing can hurt you, *angelos mou.* Lulu invites all of us for dinner every week. Food is her thing."

I swallow hard as my lungs finally fill with air, and then the elevator is moving again. When we reach the top, Julian walks me out into the hallway and then tugs me against him.

"We'll stay out here until you settle," he murmurs against the top of my head. He presses kisses there, and it makes me calm down more. I've never found comfort in anyone's arms before, but this I could become accustomed to. "I'm sorry, I thought it would be a fun surprise to see everyone. I didn't even think to warn you that we were coming here."

Taking a deep breath, I pull back and try to smile up at him. "I'm okay."

"Are you sure?"

I nod, not wanting to embarrass him by keeping him out here in the hallway any longer. Rome's guards are watching us, and I don't want to give him a reason to be angry.

He hooks his finger under my chin and tilts my face up to his.

"Look at me, not them. I want you to tell me if you're not okay, Natasha. Nothing is more important than you, so say the word, and we'll leave."

I shake my head and pat Julian's chest. "No, I don't want to leave. As long as we don't go down to the club, I'll be fine."

"Someday, I'll take you there and show you how good it can be. What you experienced is not at all what the club is about. But no, for tonight, we're going to enjoy some time with family."

Julian leads me to the door and places his palm on the reader and then opens the door when it unlocks.

"You have access to Rome's home?"

"We all do," he replies. "For all of our homes. We're brothers in every sense of the word. But I don't walk in without knocking unless he's expecting me."

He smiles down at me and leads me inside, and the scene before me is *not* what I was expecting.

The made men I grew up around are stoic. Hard. Angry. They don't laugh or smile or joke around.

But that's exactly what this group of people is doing.

I don't know some of them. I recognize Lulu and Scarlett, and Rome of course. The others were at our wedding, but I don't think we've met.

"They're here," Lulu says with a bright smile. "Come in, you guys. Natasha, do you know everyone?"

"I don't think—"

"I'm Spider," a man with a bald head and a spiderweb tattooed on his scalp, says with a remarkably kind smile for someone so scary. He doesn't make a move to touch me. "Carson's second."

"Who's Carson?" I ask.

"Me." The scariest man I've ever seen in my life, and that's saying a lot, crosses over to me. He's so damn *big*. Well over six and a half feet tall, with tattoos down his fingers, his dark blond hair brushed back off his face. He reminds me of a bigger version of Jax from *Sons of Anarchy*. I'm pretty sure he was at the wedding, but I was too upset to pay attention to the guests that day.

"You're a scary man." *Did I just say that out loud?*

Carson's lips twitch, and he winks at me. Should a

man be this scary *and* handsome at the same time? It doesn't seem fair.

"Not to you," he replies easily. "You have nothing to be afraid of. Welcome to the family, little one."

I'm introduced to Mateo, who's tall, dark, and handsome. All these men are sexy in their own way. Of course, my husband outshines them all.

But I'm biased.

"You know Jack," Julian says, gesturing to his second in command. "That's Diego, Mateo's second, and you've met Luke."

"I'm with him," Luke reminds me, gesturing to Rome. "And we'll get you a spreadsheet so you can remember everyone."

"That might be helpful," I reply with a grin and look around the room. There's a lot of power here. So much that it practically has its own heartbeat. "Thanks for inviting me."

"Come help me," Lulu says, waving for me to follow her, but I'm reluctant to let go of Julian's hand.

He kisses my knuckles and leans down to whisper in my ear.

"Go chat with them. I won't be far away."

With a nod, I follow Scarlett and Lulu into the kitchen, where there's already the beginnings of a huge feast spread out on the countertop. Platters of food are laid out, and I can see that Lulu's still assembling some of it.

"Did you make all of this?" I ask as I climb on a stool on the other side of the island, right next to Scarlett.

"Food is Lulu's love language," Scarlett informs me. "And the best part is, we get all the benefits."

"I wish I knew how to cook," I say as Lulu offers me a dish full of olives, and I take one, pop it into my mouth. "But I'm hopeless at it. I almost burned the house down the other day. The appliances are too fancy for me to figure out."

"I can teach you some basics," Lulu says with a shrug. "It's not hard once you get the hang of it. How is everything going? Are you and Julian getting along?"

"And how are you after that night at the club?" Scarlett adds. "We want to know *everything*. And don't worry, the guys will be busy until we call them to dinner, so it's just us girls."

Just us girls.

I like these two. I want to fit in with Julian's family, and if I'm going to be here every week with them, I need to trust that I can open up to them.

"Julian and I are . . . *great,* actually. I have no complaints so far."

Lulu wiggles her eyebrows as she stirs something in a bowl. "I like the sound of that."

"And as far as the other, I was doing fine until we got to this building, and then I had a panic attack."

"Makes sense," Scarlett says with a nod. "You had something traumatic happen to you here. But I can *promise* you, it'll never happen again."

"That's what Julian said too."

"Never," Lulu agrees. "It's a fun place."

I shudder at the thought. "I'll take your word for it."

I bite my lip, and I reach for another olive but don't eat it. "Can I ask you guys some questions?"

"You can ask us anything," Lulu replies with a smile. "We're your friends, Natasha. Hell, your husband and mine are brothers in every way that counts, which means that you're my sister."

Sister. That makes my throat want to close up.

"You're safe here," Scarlett adds, and reaches out to pat my hand.

I don't flinch away from her touch, and I'm filled with pride in myself.

I'm getting better.

"You two are both with powerful, dangerous men."

They nod, watching me with open expressions on their gorgeous faces, giving me the confidence to continue.

"Do you feel . . . *safe* with them?"

"Personally, I've never felt safer," Scarlett says and looks to Lulu, who nods.

"I'm the same. I also grew up in an organized crime household with a father who was ruthless and abusive, and well, it was *bad*. I didn't, and still don't, trust easy. Rome would *never* hurt me."

"Luke is so protective, I think if someone just thought about saying something unkind to me, he'd take out their tongue."

The two of them laugh, but I don't join them. Because this is important to me.

"What about cheating?"

Their smiles fall, and then they shake their heads adamantly.

"No," Scarlett says. "Not a chance. When would they have time?"

"You'd be surprised," I mutter, staring at the olive in my fingers that I keep rolling back and forth. "I grew up in this life, and I don't know anyone who stayed faithful, including my own parents."

"Our guys are a different breed," Lulu says. "They may live in the morally gray side of life, but when it comes to us, they are next-level obsessed."

"But they have access to a whole sex club. The *whole* club. They could hook up with anyone, anytime."

"I have no need for that," Rome says from behind me, startling me, and I feel my cheeks burn in embarrassment as he walks around to pull Lulu in his arms. She smiles up at him so brightly, the love is written all over her. "The club is my business, but Eloise is my *life*."

Okay, that was swoony as fuck.

"I'm sorry, I shouldn't have—"

"You absolutely *should* ask questions," Rome interjects. "You're new to us, Natasha. And this is a safe space for you to do that. I apologize for interrupting, but I'm hungry."

Lulu chuckles and tips her head back, inviting a kiss, and Rome grabs her throat as he kisses her deeply. When he looks at her, it's as if she hung the moon.

There's no malice or hate anywhere in this home.

It's so amazing. And so different from what I know.

It's not long before we're all seated around a huge table in the dining room, passing around bowls of spaghetti and meatballs, salad, and fresh bread. Luke sits next to Scarlett and scoots her closer to him, leans in and kisses her temple, and then continues his conversation with Spider.

I glance next to me, where Julian sits, talking with Rome, and I can't resist reaching over to rest my hand on his thigh.

Without hesitation or breaking his train of thought, his hand covers mine, and he gives it a squeeze. When there's a break in the conversation, he glances down at me and lifts an eyebrow.

"You okay, angelos mou?"

I nod and offer him a smile, and then I glance at his brothers.

"So, who's going to tell me embarrassing stories about my husband from when he was a kid?"

The conversation stops around us, and all three of them, along with Jack and Luke, grin at me.

"I like her," Mateo says. "I'll tell you everything you want to know. So, this one time when we were in high school, Julian thought it would be a good idea to steal the principal's classic Mustang and take it for a ride."

"To be fair," Rome adds, "he'd been stealing cars for a while by then. So, the 'Stang shouldn't have been an issue."

"It wasn't an issue," Julian insists, and I'm riveted.

"Did you get caught?"

"He never took the car," Mateo continues. "Because when he got to the staff parking lot that morning to take it, he found the principal and his secretary fucking on it."

"On it?" My eyes bug out, and I blink up at my husband. "*On it?*"

"It was early. He always got there early. Now I know

why. And let me just say, I never needed to see his old naked ass fucking her against the hood of that sweet car. I should have stolen it later, just out of spite."

"Aww, you were traumatized." I rub his back soothingly, and the guys all laugh. "Poor guy."

Julian catches my gaze and winks.

"He hacked into the high school system and changed all of our grades to A's," Luke says with a grin. "Remember that? Good times."

"You're welcome," Julian says smoothly. "Is this walk down memory lane about over?"

"You can hack into stuff?" I nod, impressed, and Julian smirks down at me. "Me too. My father finally took my computer away because I kept getting into his financials so I could tell him where he was messing up. That's why I'm computerless right now."

"You hacked into your father's *banking information*?" Carson asks, clearly impressed.

"Well, he made me get an MBA, and then he wouldn't let me use it. He broke my ribs, though, when he discovered I'd been in his—"

"What the fuck did you just say?" Julian growls next to me, and I look up in surprise, noticing that all of the men are glaring at me.

Eight scary-as-hell men are super pissed off right now.

"Oh, um, nothing. I'm sorry, my mouth was running away from me, and . . . I'll stop."

I press my lips together, cursing myself for not knowing when to shut up. But then suddenly, Julian turns my face to his, and he kisses my forehead.

"He's going to pay for that," is all he says, and we drop the subject.

"Kind of cool that you both have computer skills," Scarlett says, and smiles at me. "It's always good to have hobbies in common."

"I'm not *that* good at it—"

"Banking institutions aren't easy to get into," Julian says easily. "Not to mention, you have an MBA at twenty-fucking-two. You're the brains in this relationship, Angel."

"I hate to break it to you," Carson says, "but she's also the beauty."

"You're not telling me anything I don't know," Julian replies.

"Okay, you're just trying to butter me up, so I like you." I laugh and lift my wineglass. "It worked. I like you. Now we need to talk about someone else."

"I love that sound," Julian murmurs in my ear as he passes me a platter of bread.

"What sound?"

"Your laugh, Angel." He kisses my temple, and when I glance up, I find Mateo watching us with a smirk on his lips.

Dinner is delicious. The rest of the conversation flows effortlessly through the meal, and they include me in it. They ask me questions. They make me feel like I belong here, with them.

Did I mention how good the food is? Because holy shit, I could eat a third plate, but then I would literally explode, and no one wants that.

"I have homemade ice cream sundaes for dessert," Lulu says, making me groan.

"Uncle. I can't get anything else in my stomach." I pat my belly and lean back in the chair. "I'm going to explode."

"We'll wait a few minutes to serve it, because you're going to want it, my friend."

I lean on Julian's shoulder, so content with how this evening has gone. His hand comes up to my cheek, and he brushes my hair behind my ear as he continues to hold a conversation. I love that he does that. He acknowledges that I'm next to him, even when he's talking with someone else.

"I should be getting word from the port in the next fifteen minutes," Julian says to Jack, who's sitting across from him.

"Our guys have it handled, boss."

"This is the first major shipment since *before*." I don't know what he's referring to, but I can tell that my husband is on edge. "And if it blows up in my face, heads will roll."

"It's going to be fine," Jack insists, and then their phones both start to ring.

Eighteen

JULIAN

I GRIN and feel some of the tension leave my shoulders as I read my wife's words. I fucking *hate* that I was pulled away from the rest of the evening with her, and someone is going to die for it tonight. They're going to suffer for the fact that I'm not nine inches deep inside of my perfect Angel right now.

Instead, I'm on my plane, headed to LA with my brothers and our men. Because something went very wrong at my port, even though the entire operation was planned meticulously. It should have been a flawless transaction.

> Me: It's your super fancy kitchen too,
> Angel. Lulu's always welcome at our
> house. You don't have to ask for
> permission to spend time with your
> friends. However, if you ever invite a
> man to our home, my men will be
> instructed to kill him on sight.

I lean back in the seat and grin when I see the dancing bubble appear on the screen, and I wait for her response.

> Wife: So murderous tonight! Someone
> pissed you off. I'm sorry. Please stay
> safe, okay? Also, I don't know any
> men to invite to our house. I haven't
> gone home yet. Scarlett, Lulu and I
> are eating too much ice cream,
> drinking wine, and talking about you.

I smirk and ignore Mateo when he says, "Someone is smitten with his new wife."

> Me: I hope you're saying good things
> about me. Just tell Benji when you're
> ready to go home, and he'll escort
> you. You'll have a team of four
> with you.

"You're grinning at your phone, man."

I glance up at Rome and then flip him the bird. "Like I haven't caught you with a stupid-ass smile on your face when you're talking to your wife."

"I'm just pointing out the glaring fact that you've

been insisting to anyone who will listen that this is just a business arrangement.”

“It is.”

It's not.

“Right.” Rome smirks, and I return my attention to my phone.

> Wife: Four men feels excessive, Julian. I'm sure one will be fine. I just need a ride.

> Me: Four men, Angel. Don't argue with me. Text me when you get home.

> Wife: Is it too needy of me to ask you to text me when you land in LA?

> Me: You can never be too needy. I'll keep you posted. Don't worry about me, just have fun tonight. I should be home tomorrow.

> Wife: *kissy face emoji*

“Fuck.”

I'm too fucking pissed off to agree with Carson as we stand in my building. My empty motherfucking building.

Empty aside from ten of my men who are all dead, all gutted. I know every single one of the men who works for me. I know their families. I visit them on holidays and invite them to my home for cookouts. These men were *my family*.

And someone slaughtered them and took my product.

"Jesus Christ," Jack says, his usually stoic face haggard as he kneels next to Theo, one of the men who's been with us the longest. Theo was in charge, and when shit went down, he had time to press Call on his phone, so we could hear what was happening.

"I found something," Diego calls out, and I turn in surprise.

"How? The place is fucking empty."

Millions worth of stones are gone.

Rage fuels me as I stride to where Diego's holding an envelope in his gloved hand, and he passes it to me.

My name is written on the back.

Thanks for the heads up.

"The fuck does this mean?" I ask, showing it to the others. "This doesn't make any fucking sense."

"No one knew about this shipment but our people," Jack says, shaking his head. "There's no way that word got out to any of our enemies."

"We're going to scour this fucking city, and I'm going to kill every single person who knows about this. It's about to be a long fucking night."

"Just the way I like it," Carson says with a gleam in his eye. "Let's go hunting, boys."

MORE THAN FORTY-EIGHT HOURS LATER, WELL past midnight, I stride into my house. I'm ready to fall into bed with my wife and sleep for a solid six hours before I fuck her for a week straight.

We've been married for almost a week, and I haven't been inside her yet.

I should be fucking tortured for that.

Music fills the air as I close the door behind me, and all the tension that I've been carrying since I received that call at Rome's place slowly eases out of me. Natasha is sitting at the piano, playing a song I know well, and fuck if it isn't the best homecoming I've ever had.

Before I reach her, I shed my jacket and tie and roll my sleeves on my forearms, then slip out of my shoes, making myself comfortable and giving myself a moment to listen, to take in every note as my girl plays.

This woman is fucking *talented*.

She pours her heart out into the music. I can feel it in my soul as I stride into the room and spot her in the darkness. The only light comes from above the stove in the kitchen. I can see Natasha's refection in the dark windows next to the piano. Her eyes are closed as her hands move over the keys, not missing a note.

Not wanting to startle her, I stand back, hands in my pockets, and listen to her play. Finally, after the final note disappears, she folds her hands in her lap and opens her eyes, seeing me in the window.

She doesn't jump.

She smiles.

And I can't stay away from her for another second.

I cross to her, and she slides over on the bench, making room for me to join her. When I sit, she tips her head onto my shoulder and exhales, as if in relief.

"You're home."

"I'm home, Angel. I texted you when I landed."

"I must have left my phone in the bedroom after my shower." She turns her face and kisses my biceps, and the fact that she's touching me so freely is not lost on me. "Are you okay?"

"Just tired."

The truth is, I'm fucking exhausted. I haven't slept in two days. We tracked down eight men that we know for sure were there the other night but didn't get much information out of them.

It was frustrating as fuck.

And I missed being here, with my wife.

She lays her fingers on the keys but doesn't play, and I kiss the top of her head.

"Play for me," I whisper to her as I breathe her in. "Whatever you want."

She takes a breath, and then her hands move again, this time playing an Adele song that I recognize, and after a few moments, I join her.

Her eyes are wide when they shoot up to mine, and then a smile transforms her beautiful face, and we play the song together.

It's sexy, sitting here with her on this bench, playing a

song so in sync with each other. This might be the most intimate I've ever been with anyone in my life.

And when the song is over, I lift her onto my lap, cup her cheek, and cover her mouth with mine. Her lips are so fucking sweet, I don't know how I lived without them for the last forty-eight hours.

Definitely not a business arrangement for me anymore.

I'm not sure if it ever really was.

"I missed you," she whispers against my lips as my hands glide over her ass, pulling her closer. "This big house is lonely without you in it."

"You're the sweetest thing," I murmur, brushing a few strands of hair off her cheek and hooking them behind her ear. "I don't deserve your goodness, Natasha. But I'm never letting you go."

I crush my mouth to hers and lick over the seam of her lips, and when she whimpers and opens for me, my immediate thought is *now I'm home.*

Her arms wrap around my neck, and she pushes her hot pussy against my already hard cock, and that's all the invitation I need.

"I'm not waiting one more fucking minute," I growl against her lips. "I need to sink inside your perfect pussy and live there for the immediate future."

She lifts an eyebrow.

"Good because you've been torturing me with your amazing, muscled forearms playing this piano, and I'm all kinds of turned on right now."

Without another word, I lift her, wrap her legs

around my waist, and carry her back to our bed. My first instinct was to spread her out on the piano and eat her, but I want her in our bed.

All fucking night.

Nineteen

NATASHA

GOD, I missed him. And now that I'm in his arms, I don't ever want him to leave again. Julian has quickly become my safe place. The house was so quiet without him in it, but the second he walked through the front door, the entire energy of the house shifted. It finally felt like a home again.

Julian is my home.

"I need you naked, Angel," he growls and sets me on my feet before he lifts my shirt over my head, tossing it aside. I was dressed for bed, so I'm not wearing anything under it, and his eyes fall to my breasts, making my nipples harden. *God, I love the way he looks at me.* Like he wants to devour me. "Your body is perfect."

"I don't—"

"Perfect," he insists as his fingers slip into the elastic of my shorts, and he nudges them down until they pool around my feet, and I kick them aside.

"You're way overdressed, Mr. Stavros."

His lips twitch with amusement, and his fingertips

drag over my hips and up my sides, making me shiver, and goose bumps break out over my skin.

"If I take my clothes off, I'll be inside you in about two seconds." His lips are next to my ear, his hands skimming over my skin, and *holy God*, I want him.

"Great. Sounds like a solid plan."

His hot eyes find mine, and his mouth kicks up in a grin. "You like that idea?"

"Best idea I've ever heard." My hands dive for his shirt, unfastening the buttons as quickly as I can, and when he's finally standing before me, gloriously naked, I bite my lip and take a deep breath. "Wow."

Julian laughs and backs me up against the bed, kissing me as I scoot back toward the pillows, and then I wrap my arms around his shoulders and hold on as he devours me. His tongue is bold, but not too much, as it slides against my own, and his hand glides down my body, over my breast and stomach, until his fingers drift through my slit, making me gasp.

"Fuck, you're so damn ready for me." He drags his nose over mine. "So fucking soft and wet and *ready*. I'm so sorry that it's taken us so long to get here, but there will be no interruptions tonight. I promise you that."

"I've been wet from the second I saw you." I've never been this bold with my words before, but my husband seems to enjoy it when I tell him how I feel. What I want. What I like.

And I'm not even sure what I like, exactly.

But Julian's amazing mouth all over my body is *fantastic*.

"You're delicious," he mutters as he nibbles his way

down my neck. "So fucking irresistible. I was going to spread you out and bury my face in your pussy for about an hour, but I don't have any patience left, Angel, so that's going to have to wait."

"Great. I can't wait for you either." I reach down between us and grip onto his hard, velvety shaft, and Julian groans against my neck. "Please, I need you, Julian."

"Christ, I can't deny you anything."

He leans up and watches as I guide him to my entrance, and when he starts to push in, I bite my lip, bracing myself for the pain.

Oh God.

He's so damn big, I'm not sure how he's supposed to fit, but I'm so turned on, I can't stop him. *I don't ever want him to stop.* I need this powerful, amazing man inside me like I need air.

"You're taking me so well, baby." That makes me purr, and he grits his teeth as he pushes further. "God, you're so fucking tight."

And when he meets resistance, his eyes fly open, and he stares down at me with a combination of wonder and concern.

"Jesus, are you—?"

I nod and bite my lip. "Please don't stop."

"Baby, I . . . *Christ.*" He closes his eyes and rests his forehead on mine. "This is going to hurt, sweetheart."

I lift my hips, and squeeze around him, making him swear under his breath, and then he pushes all the way in, until his hips meet my body, and we both gasp, our eyes pinned to each other.

"I'm sorry. Shit, this is the best thing I've ever felt in my goddamn life." He peppers kisses on my cheek and neck, soothing me. "Breathe for me, Angel."

I take a deep breath and shiver when his lips ghost over that spot on my neck that makes me crazy.

"Fuck, keep squeezing me like that and I won't be able to hold back."

"Don't hold back." My nails dig into his ass, pulling him closer. "Never. Fuck me, Julian."

He growls and pulls out, until just the tip is still inside, and then he pushes back in, and my muscles relax, and a pleasure that I've never felt before takes over.

"Oh God."

"You're so damn amazing," he murmurs before pulling my nipple into his mouth and tugging on it with his teeth. His body is just incredible, his abs flexing as he rolls his hips, fucking me so well, this must be what heaven is like.

He looks down between us and stops moving altogether.

My eyes follow his, and for a minute, seeing my blood on him makes me want to hide my face again, but then he swipes his thumb over his shaft, wiping up the blood, and he licks it off, his black gaze holding mine.

"Holy shit," I whisper.

"Your virgin blood on my cock is the sexiest fucking thing I've ever seen in my life."

He starts to pound into me, as if his restraint has snapped, he covers my mouth, and I can taste the coppery essence of my blood on his tongue.

It doesn't disgust me.

It makes me . . . *lose my damn mind.*

I rake my fingernails down his back, and he bites my lower lip, and then he's fucking me hard and fast, one hand on my throat and the other planted on the bed just above my head, staring down at me like I'm his whole world.

"You're so fucking *beautiful*. And you're mine, Natasha. Do you understand? This virgin pussy is mine."

"I'm all yours," I manage to say before my core tightens and I feel an orgasm building that might just make me pass out. "Julian."

"That's right, baby. Fucking hell." I squeeze around him and his jaw clenches, and then he's coming with me, his hips jerking against me as he comes apart, and then he curls around me, holding me so tenderly, so *lovingly*, that it brings tears to my eyes.

This is how it's supposed to be, and I'm so relieved that my first time was here, with Julian.

Breathing hard, he pulls out of me, and then brushes his finger through my slit, gathering our cum and my blood, and he looks so damn pleased with himself, I can't help but chuckle.

"You find this funny?"

"I think I'm delirious, and you look incredibly pleased with yourself."

His face softens, and he paints our mess over my lower lip.

Without being asked, I sweep my tongue over that lip, and his eyes dilate.

"You're fucking perfect for me."

"Good because you're stuck with me."

Suddenly, Julian rolls off me and pulls me from the bed, leading me to the bathroom.

"I'm going to clean you up," he says as he turns on the shower. "And then I'm going to fuck you against that tile."

"That's the second-best idea I've heard all night."

Twenty

NATASHA

"THAT'S IT?"

I stare dubiously into the pot on the stove and then look over at Lulu, who's grinning widely at me. It's been just under a week since we were all at Lulu's home for dinner, and I love that she came over to spend the day with me. I've already learned so much from my new friend.

"That's it, friend. You're doing great. Mac and cheese is my favorite thing to make because it's *so good* and easy."

"Except when you shred your finger instead of the cheese." I hold up my bandaged hand, and we both laugh.

"Eh, what's a little blood?" Lulu waves me off and then turns to the mixer on the island. I didn't know we even had a mixer until the two of us went scavenging through the huge butler's pantry to see what kind of supplies we have on hand. "Okay, we're going to mix the cookie dough and then use the ice cream scoop to measure out the perfect amount for each cookie."

"Right." I watch carefully as Lulu turns the mixer on and starts to add ingredients.

"You can wait to do this at the end, but it's just easier to start it up and add stuff."

"Easy. Gotcha."

This doesn't look easy at all. Ask me to invest your stock portfolio, and I can do that with my eyes closed.

But make a batch of peanut butter cookies? I'm lost.

Thanks to my friend, I now know how to work the gas stove, and the difference between Bake and Broil, so there's been some progress today.

"I'm glad you know what Julian's favorite cookies are," I say as we roll out balls of dough and place them on baking sheets. I'm following her lead. I feel clumsy and uncomfortable, but I'm doing it.

"It happened by accident, actually. I was having a really bad weekend and decided to bake everything under the sun. Cheesecakes, cookies, cupcakes, you name it."

"I bet the guys loved that."

Lulu smirks and grabs a fork for me and one for her. "We're going to squish the dough balls, just like this." She shows me how to flatten the dough with the tines of the fork and then continues with her story. "Rome wasn't happy that I was upset, but they all loved the outcome, yes. When Julian saw the peanut butter cookies, he claimed the whole container for himself and drew a gun on Mateo when he tried to grab one."

I can't help but laugh at that because I can totally see it happening in my head.

"That's both hilarious and alarming."

"What is?" Julian asks as he walks in the room. He

lifts an eyebrow when he sees the peanut butter cookies ready for the oven. "My favorite."

I smile at him. He's only been gone for a few hours, and damn it, I missed him. "So I heard. Lulu was just telling me about the lengths you'll go to protect your cookies."

Julian smirks. "I've killed men for far less than trying to steal dessert. Hi, Lu."

"Hey," she says with a smile. "I don't think Natasha will be trying to burn the house down anymore."

"I know you hired a chef," I tell my husband, "but she can't work every single day. I can limp through her days off."

"Whatever you say," my husband replies before kissing me on the forehead. "I'll be in my office."

He shoves his hands in his pockets and walks away, and I can't tear my gaze away from his truly spectacular ass.

"He has to do a *lot* of squats to look like that in those pants," I murmur, and Lulu bites her lip.

"They all work out a ton. Okay, these go in the oven for about fifteen minutes."

I've loved spending the day with Lulu. She doesn't talk to me like I'm an idiot just because I don't know how to cook. She's an excellent teacher, and by the time she leaves, I have three dozen cookies, three full meals saved in the fridge, and even more self-confidence than I had when she arrived this morning.

With a plate of delicious peanut-buttery goodness in hand, I wander back to Julian's office. The door is open, so I stride in, and then stop when I see that he's on the phone.

My husband gives his head a little shake and gestures for me to come closer, not caring if I overhear his conversation.

"It's happening on Tuesday," he says as I set the plate on the desk. Rather than sit across from him, I sit in Julian's lap when he scoots back, giving me room. His hand lands on my hip, and I rest my face in the crook of his neck, breathing in his comforting scent of cedarwood and leather, and nothing feels better than the warmth of his body holding mine.

Okay, I lied.

The orgasms this man has given me over the past week are *incredible*. He knows my body better than I do, and hasn't been shy about taking me wherever he wants me. Kitchen, piano, outside on the patio under the stars . . . nothing is off limits.

And I'm lapping it up like a kitten with cream.

"Tuesday at midnight," he confirms, and kisses the top of my head. "Forty million. You heard me. I'll have six men there. Yes, just six. Draco is heading this, and he's the best I have, next to Jack. He's got it handled."

He hangs up and sets the phone down before wrapping his arms around me and hugging me to him.

"Did you have fun today?" he asks.

"Yeah, I think Lulu is actually my friend." I blink up at him. "I really like her."

"Why does it surprise you that she'd be your friend, Angel?"

"Because I don't have friends. Well, except for you. I

was never allowed to get close to people. So, this is new. And I like it."

I might have said too much. I don't want my husband to pity me.

"You were a prisoner, not part of a family," he says, shaking his head, and then he sees the bandage on my finger and scowls. "What's this?"

"I shredded my finger instead of cheese." His eyes jump to mine, and I offer him a little shrug. "Now I know not to do that."

"I don't like you being hurt," he says before he kisses my finger, right over the bandage.

That comment makes me giggle, and he narrows his eyes at me.

"You torture men for a living, and my little cut makes you uncomfortable?"

He tips his head to the side, considering my comment, and then he simply nods. "Yes."

I laugh and kiss his cheek. "I brought you cookies. I helped bake them, and I'm pretty sure they won't kill you."

"Only *pretty* sure?"

I press my lips together, enjoying this lighthearted side of my husband. "I'm ninety-nine percent sure."

"I try not to put myself in danger at home, but I'll risk it for you." He reaches out to grab a cookie and takes a bite, and his eyebrows climb in surprise. "Delicious. And all mine. We're not sharing these with anyone."

With a smile, I brush my fingers into the hair at his nape. "They're all for you, greedy man."

"Mm." The groan is full of satisfaction as he returns

the uneaten portion to the plate and then moves it to a side table, clearing the top of the desk. Standing with me in his arms, he sets me on the desk. "You know what's even more delicious"—he presses his lips to my neck—"and also all mine?"

"What?" My eyes close as I tip my head back, giving him more access. I *love* it when he bites my neck. I have all kinds of marks on me from the past week, and I love every single one.

"My wife." He grazes his nose along my jawline as his hand cups my pussy through the leggings I'm wearing. "And this pussy."

Suddenly, the crotch of my leggings is ripped, and cool air hits my already heated core just as his finger brushes through my slit.

"Fuck, baby." Julian sits in his chair, scoots forward, and with his hands on my ass, he pulls my pussy to his face and licks me, from entrance to clit. "Better than cookies."

"Oh God." I'm resting back on one elbow and plunge my hand in his hair, holding on as he works me over. "You're so good with your mouth."

He hums, his fingers dig into the globes of my ass, and I know they'll leave bruises.

I can't wait to see them later.

"I'm going to come." Is that *my* voice? All breathy and needy and full of lust. "Fuck, Julian, I'm going to . . . *fuck*."

He sucks on my clit, circling his tongue around it, and I come apart, unable to stop the intense orgasm that washes through me, leaving me panting and whimpering.

Julian stands, unbuckles his belt, and opens his slacks, unleashing his cock, and then he pushes inside me, filling me so completely, I fall over another edge, squeezing around him.

"Jesus, you're going to be the death of me," he growls against my ear before slamming his mouth to mine. I can taste myself on his lips, and I *love* it. I lap at him, licking every drop from his mouth. His cock expands inside me even more as he cants his hips back and forth, chasing his own release. "So. Fucking. Mine."

He pushes his thumb against my clit, and that's it for me. I fly over into oblivion with him, screaming his name as my body lights on fire for him.

"I'm going to make cookies every day," I say as he peppers kisses over my neck, "if this is my reward."

"Angel, I'll eat this perfect cunt whenever you want, cookies or not. I'm always hungry for you."

Twenty-One

JULIAN

"I'LL MEET you back at my building in a few hours, after you're finished shopping with the girls," I tell my wife as we ride into the city from the mansion.

"We've been talking about this shopping trip for the past three days straight in the group text," Natasha says with a smile, tapping on the screen of her phone as she types out a message. "Apparently, there's a new line at Dior that Lulu's dying to see. Until you, I've never worn luxury brands. But I have to admit, they're nice. The materials feel . . . well, luxurious."

I smile and reach over to tuck her silky blond hair behind her ear. She's wearing a blue dress that falls past her knees, the color of her eyes, with brown sandals and a brown Dior saddlebag that matches. She's fucking beautiful.

Of course, she's just as stunning when she's in sweats, with her hair in a wild bun at the top of her head and no makeup.

I'll take this woman any way I can get her.

"Your card finally came." I pass her Black Card to her. "There's no limit, Angel. Buy whatever you want."

"That's dangerous," she whispers, and tucks it into her purse. "I won't go crazy."

"I just told you to buy whatever you want."

"But it's *your* money. I'll get a job, and then—"

I unfasten her seat belt and slide her over to me, then buckle her into the middle strap and tip her face up so I can kiss the fuck out of her.

"What was that for?" Her voice is breathy, the way it gets when she's turned on, and it makes me want to fuck her, right here in the car. And I don't give a fuck that we're not alone.

"You don't need to get a job, unless you want one. I have more money than we could ever possibly need, Natasha. Have fun today. Go buy out Dior, or Chanel, or wherever the three of you end up. I don't care in the least about what you spend, I just want you to you enjoy yourself."

"You're a good man, Julian Stavros."

The driver coughs, covering a laugh, and I don't bother to hide my own chuckle as I brush my thumb over the apple of her cheek.

"Only for you, Angel." I love that she thinks of me as good. I'm not, not even a little bit, but I'll always treat her well. "Each of you will have a detail with you today, but just call me if there are any issues."

"There won't be," she says with confidence. Once we've dropped her off with the others—and I make sure that all six men of their detail are acceptable, and make it clear that I'll skin them alive if any of these women get so much as a hangnail—I head to my building.

Jack, waiting for me outside the cell, passes me the chair that I requested before unlocking the door and opening it for me.

I stride in, carrying the metal chair, and resist cringing at the smell in this room.

My son is still sitting in the corner. His clothes are filthy, and he's listless and has lost even more weight.

Please let him hear me today. I might enjoy torturing men who deserve it, but this makes me sick to my stomach.

I turn the chair backward in front of him and straddle it, resting my forearms on the back as I watch him sleep.

He didn't even stir when I walked in.

"Elliott." My voice is hard but not too loud. His eyes flutter open, and he looks up at me, then swallows hard. "Are you ready to talk?"

"Yeah." He coughs as though his throat is dry, which it likely is. "Yes."

"Good. You have two choices, and I want you to listen to me very carefully."

His eyes don't leave mine.

"The first is, you can stay in a cell like this one for the rest of your natural life. You'll be fed and watered, but that's it."

His eyes well with tears, and I clench my jaw shut. *Take the second choice, son.*

"The second choice is, I let you out of here, and you start from scratch. No money. No car, nothing. You'll work as a janitor at one of my buildings, and when I feel that you've earned it, you can come back to the organization as a soldier. You won't set foot in another casino to gamble ever again. You'll also get a handle on your drinking."

Elliott swallows hard.

"Neither option is easy. You'll have to decide which *hard* you want to take on."

"I can't live in here for the rest of my life." His voice is raspy, but full of conviction. "Where will I live?"

"You'll have a small apartment. You won't come to the penthouse or the mansion until you've been invited, if ever. I don't want you anywhere near my wife."

His eyes flare and then he frowns. "Wife? You got married?"

Ah, that's right. He doesn't know.

"I married Natasha."

I stay still, watching him to see how he reacts to this news. He blows out a breath and then hangs his head.

"She deserved better than me."

Those words both surprise me and give me hope that my son is actually capable of changing into a man I can respect.

"Yeah, she fucking did. You're going to toe the goddamn line, Elliott. You're twenty-five, not a child. I raised you to be a better man than this. If you fuck up *once*, you won't see the light of day again. And if you *ever* so much as lay your pinky finger on my wife, I'll put a bullet in your skull myself."

He presses his lips together, his lower lip quivers, and then he swallows it all down and nods his head.

"Yes, sir. I'll take that option, please."

"That's maybe the smartest thing you've ever done. Prove yourself to me, and you'll earn a place in my organization, but nothing will be handed to you because of your last name, and you'll never inherit my empire. Do you understand?"

He nods once more, and I call out for Jack. He immediately opens the door of the cell, and three of my men follow him inside.

"Take Elliott to our infirmary and call Dr. Asgood. He'll need medical attention. Make sure the apartment is ready for him when he's been released."

"Yes, boss," Jack says with a nod. "Come on, kid. Let's get you fixed up."

The guys help my son off the floor, and before they can lead him away, I step forward and cup his face in my hand.

"You're going to be okay," I tell him.

"Thanks for not killing me," he replies. "I guess you're not as soft as I thought."

"No, I'm not *soft*. And you won't make that mistake again."

He shakes his head, and then he's led away, and I make my way up to the penthouse.

It's time to get ready for the next part of my day.

"Hi." Natasha's smile is cheerful, with just a little sleepiness added. Which is appropriate, since she spent about a hundred and sixty thousand dollars over the course of three hours this afternoon.

My accountant called me, concerned that the card had been stolen.

I told him to approve every single charge.

She's just stepped out of the SUV and moves right into my arms, presses her head to my chest, and hugs me close.

"Did you have fun, Angel?"

"More than I should have," she says with a laugh. "Those two girls are *enablers*. Don't ever ask them if you should get something because the answer is immediately *yes, and you should get it in every color*. I have a bag on order at Chanel because I loved the style but not the color, so it's coming from a store in New York. Should be here in a couple of days."

"Excellent. I'm glad you had a good time." I brush her hair behind her ear and lean in to kiss her perfect bee-stung lips. "Now, I need you to come upstairs so I can get your opinion on something."

With my woman tucked into my side, I lead Natasha to the elevator. When we're alone inside, I press her against the wall, push my hands in her hair, and kiss the fuck out of her.

She whimpers and clings to me, giving as good as she gets, and when the doors open again, we're both panting, and I'm wishing I still had a bed in the penthouse.

"Come on, before I boost you up and fuck you in my elevator."

"*Your* elevator?" she asks, walking next to me.

"I own the building." I kiss the back of her hand, and then she looks around, and her blue eyes widen in surprise.

"Julian."

"This is what I need your advice on."

"It's empty. It's just walls and concrete."

Nodding, I pull her deeper into the penthouse. "There were too many bad memories for you in here, so it all had to go. You'll be meeting with someone named MaryBeth to go over designs. You'll make this into whatever pleases you, since you didn't get the opportunity at the mansion, although we can change anything that you don't like there too. I want you to be comfortable wherever we are, and there will be times that we'll be staying here."

"I don't know anything about decorating a penthouse. This place is massive."

"It's actually not that big. Only about five thousand square feet."

"That sounds pretty big, if you ask me. Wait, how many square feet is the mansion?"

I can't keep my lips, or my hands, off this woman. I kiss the top of her head and drag my hand down her back.

"About twenty thousand."

"For *two people*, Julian? That's nuts."

"It won't always just be the two of us."

Her gaze whips up to mine and I shrug.

"You want more kids?" she asks, so surprised that it makes me smile.

"I'm not that old, Angel. Men in their forties have kids all the time."

"It's not that." She shakes her head and strolls away from me. I don't like that she's out of reach, but I can see that her mind is whirling, so I give her the space she needs to process. "I know you're not too old for children, I'm just surprised because you have Elliott, and I didn't think you'd want to start all over again. I had prepared myself to not have any kids."

I shove my hands in my pockets so I don't reach out for her.

"I didn't think I would ever remarry or have more children," I reply honestly and watch as her cheeks darken.

I fucking love it when she blushes.

"And I'm not in a rush to start right away, but I also didn't have you before. So, when and if you're ready to start a conversation about it, I'm here. Are you on birth control?"

She bites her lip and her cheeks darken. "No."

I can't help but laugh. "Baby, we've been fucking like rabbits, and I don't plan to stop or put anything between us when I'm inside you. So if you don't want babies, you'd better make yourself an appointment with a doctor."

Her lips roll in, and then she lets out a little laugh. "I'm so stupid. I didn't even think of it. But it's never been something I've had to consider before."

I love that she hasn't been with anyone but me.

I especially love that my son was never inside her. Because then I *would* have to kill him.

"Call yourself stupid again, and I'll put you over my knee and make your ass glow."

Her eyes widen, and she shifts on her feet. *She likes that idea.*

"You didn't have to tear all of this out just for me," she says quietly, spreading her arms wide, and I nod.

"Yeah, I did. I don't want to see Elliott hitting you every time I walk into the fucking living room, Angel. We'll change it all and make new memories."

She licks her lips, looking around. "The view is so amazing up here."

Ideas are starting to form in that smart-as-fuck mind of hers. And I can't wait to see what she comes up with.

"The view is why I bought the building," I tell her and watch as she walks around what used to be the kitchen.

"Can we have a piano there, by the windows?"

"You can have literally anything in the world that you want. How many times do I have to tell you that before you believe me? There's no limit to what I'll give you, Angel."

"Why?" She blinks quickly, surprised at her own question. "I mean, thank you."

"The *why* is easy. You're my wife. Are you hungry?"

Her stomach growls before she can answer, and I nod.

"Me too. I'm taking you out tonight."

"To the Rapture building?" She pauses, watching me, and I shake my head.

"No. To a restaurant. How do you feel about Mexican food?"

"I'm having a love affair with chips and queso. I'm sorry, I can't give them up for you," she says, keeping a straight face. "But we'll accept a third into our relationship."

"How generous." I reach out, offering her my hand, and without hesitation, she slides her palm against mine. "Let's go get some queso, then."

"And margaritas?"

"You bet."

"And carne asada?"

"I'll get you everything on the menu."

JULIAN

"WHAT IN THE ACTUAL *FUCK* HAPPENED?" I demand as I walk into my warehouse, Mateo, Carson, and Rome right behind me.

Jack's already here. He was closer when the call came in.

I left my wife, asleep in our bed, so I could get here too fucking late.

"They took it all, boss," Jack says. He's pale and shaken, and my number two is *never* pale and shaken.

"There's no way," Mateo says, shaking his head, but I move to where three of my men are standing at attention, clearly shaken up.

The other three, including Draco, are fucking dead.

"Report." I sound calm. I *always* sound fucking calm. When in reality, I'm ready to blow the whole world apart. The guys shuffle and look at each other, and I yell, "REPORT!"

"We were ambushed," Tony says, shaking his head.

"The product arrived, on schedule. We accounted for everything. It was routine, nothing out of the ordinary."

"We had just finished inventory," Shawn adds. "Moved everything to the containers you specified, and then suddenly, smoke bombs rolled in through the big doors and filled the room fast."

I can still smell it in the air.

"About a dozen men, all in black and armed to the nines, ran inside," Tony continues. "Shot Draco first, then the other two. They were out the door, with the shipment, in less than five minutes."

Motherfucker.

"What did they look like?" I ask them.

"They were in gas masks," Shawn says. "Black clothes, like special ops or some kind of professionals. These guys weren't foot soldiers, boss."

I glance over at Carson, and he's already making calls. He has contacts with exactly the kind of professionals Shawn is describing.

"I need to get to my office so I can watch security cam footage." I pace away and drag my hand down my face before I kneel next to Draco.

This man served under my father. He'd been with our organization for decades and dedicated his life to us. He had no wife or children and always said that the job was his life. He didn't have room for anything else.

He was a good friend and someone I respected.

The motherfucker behind this is going to pay dearly.

"Clean this up," I say to Jack. "Pay the other two's families."

"I'll handle it," Jack says with a nod, and I walk over to where my brothers stand talking.

"No one knew about this," I tell them and feel exhaustion settle in.

"It's just like LA," Rome replies. "*Someone* knew, Julian."

Shaking my head, I run it down for them. "Obviously the men in this room, along with the supplier. That's it."

"Then you have a mole," Mateo says grimly.

"Fuck no, I don't." The mere thought of it makes me want to come out of my skin. "My men have been with me for years."

"How careful are you about what you say in front of your pretty little wife?" Carson asks.

"That's out of the question."

"Why?" Rome counters. "Because she's beautiful and young? Listen, I've been in your position. My brothers insinuating that my wife was a plant. But you don't know her well, and although her father is a grade A piece of shit, he's still her father. Is she funneling intel back to him?"

"Absolutely not." I laugh at the absurdity of the idea. "She's not a plant for her father. She hates his guts."

"Or maybe her father planted a bug on her." Mateo shrugs. "You have equipment that can scan electronics to see if they have tracking or listening devices."

"Of course I do."

"So use it," Carson says. "Go through her things and make sure it's not her."

"It's *not* my wife," I grit out, so fucking frustrated

that I want to stab them all in the neck. "For fuck's sake. We don't even know that there *is* an informant."

"There has to be," Jack says as he joins us. "This was locked down, Julian. Only this team knew about it. Forty million in gems are gone, three of our men are dead. There's either a mole, or it's an inside job."

"Thanks for the recap," I snap at him. "I'm going home, and I'll degrade my wife by going through her things, just to prove to all of you that she's not at fault for this."

"Excellent," Mateo says with a nod. "Then we can go hunting for the real mole. It's a logical place to start, brother. Shit didn't start to go down until you married her. I'm connecting the dots here."

"Fuck all of you," I growl as I stalk off to my Porsche and climb inside.

I'm fucking *livid*.

It's a complete waste of time to go through Natasha's things, but I'll do it to appease the others so we can move forward and make whoever's responsible for this pay. It's *not* my sweet wife. She can't stand her father. She's afraid of him.

By the time I get home, dawn is breaking, and I'm surprised to find Natasha already up and in the kitchen. She's holding a mug of coffee and smiles at me when I walk inside.

Immediately, my body calms down.

There's no way that the woman who soothes me in every way, who lights me on fire, and makes me feel emotions that I never have before is double-crossing me.

It's not fucking possible.

"Good morning," she says as I walk to her. "I couldn't sleep without you."

"Have you been up since I left?" I ask as I pull her to me and bury my lips in her hair, breathing her in.

"I woke up about an hour ago and didn't go back to sleep," she says before placing a kiss over my heart. "God, you smell good. Is everything okay?"

She takes another deep breath, and it makes me smile.

"I need to ask you some questions."

With a frown, Natasha turns that gorgeous face up to me, and I tuck her messy blond strands behind her ear.

"You can ask me anything."

Good girl.

"Some shit went down early this morning that's pretty fucking bad, Angel. I need to know if you know anything about that."

Her eyebrows climb in surprise, and I can see it written all over her face that she has no idea what I'm talking about.

"I—no. I don't."

I nod and then let out a breath. "I need to look through your electronics."

She pulls out of my arms and backs away from me, scowling. "What exactly are you accusing me of, Julian?"

"I'm not accusing you of anything. I'm trying to rule it out. I don't think that you've done anything at all, but you're the newest member in my circle. I think I have a mole, Natasha."

Realization dawns in her eyes and she nods slowly. "And you think I'm the mole. For my father."

"No, I'm proving that you're *not* the one doing this so I can move on to hunting who is."

Without a word, she turns and walks out of the kitchen, to where her new laptop—the one I bought for her after she informed us that hers was taken away—is sitting in the living room. She opens it, types in her password, and passes it to me.

"Here. I'll go get my phone."

"Natasha—"

"I'll be right back. If you need to watch me to make sure I don't delete anything, I understand."

Without a word, I follow her, and she unplugs her phone, which was sitting next to her side of the bed, and passes it to me.

"Do you need my Kindle too?"

"No."

She presses her lips together and crosses her arms over her chest, and I want to pull her against me and kiss her until we're both calmed the hell down. Reassure her that this is just a formality.

"Do what you have to do," she says, nodding to the electronics in my hands.

"Follow me." Grimly, I walk down to my office, and Natasha walks next to me. First, I quickly scan her incoming and outgoing emails and texts, but there's not much here, and nothing that catches my eye as suspicious.

Next, I open a drawer in my desk and pull out the device that scans for tracking and listening bugs.

Powering it on, I run it over both the laptop and the phone, but the red light stays lit. If there was anything here, it would change to green. I have it programmed not to make any noise, in case I have to search in front of an audience that I don't want to be privy to the results of a scan.

Standing, I approach Natasha.

"Run it over me," she says, putting her arms out wide. "I don't have anything to hide from you."

Grimly, I do just that. If her father implanted something subdermal, this would pick up on it. I start at the back of her body and scan over her skin, and when I circle to the front, I work my way up from her feet.

Nothing.

Until I get up to her chest and move the device over the pendant hanging around her neck.

Green.

I do it again, just to be sure, and keep my face impassive as I run it over her head and then set the device aside on the desk.

"See?" she says. "Nothing."

Either she doesn't know, or she's a *very* good liar.

Shoving my hands in my pockets, I will my heart to calm down and keep my face neutral. She's watching me closely.

Are you double-crossing me, Angel?

"Thank you," I tell her softly. "And I'm sorry—"

"You don't need to be sorry," she replies and pushes her hands into mine, linking our fingers as she boosts up on her toes, offering her plump lips to me for a kiss.

I oblige her, but my mind is whirling.

"Now you can focus on finding the person trying to

hurt you," she says and pats me on the chest. "Is that what you'll be doing today?"

"It seems so." She's never asked me about my plans before.

Is this who I am now? Questioning every word my wife says? Every question? Every smile?

Someone is listening to us through that pendant. She doesn't wear it every single day, and she doesn't wear it at night, but most days she has it on her.

She says it's because it's sentimental to her, but now I'm not so sure that's true.

"I'll be at warehouse six today," I tell her, even though she has no idea what that means. "I have a smaller shipment coming in at around nine, and I want to be there for it personally."

There's no shipment. I'm testing out this pendant of hers.

"Please be careful." She leans her forehead to my chest. "I'm going to meet with Scarlett and Lulu for breakfast. I guess it's at a diner in Carson's building. The one with the casino?"

"You'll like it there," I tell her and brush my hand down her hair. Christ, I've been falling in love with this woman, and all the while, has she been fucking spying on me? "You'll take your detail."

"Of course." She smiles again, and then her face falls as she watches me. "You're not okay, Julian."

No, Angel, I'm not in the same vicinity as okay.

"I'll be fine."

"If you want me to skip breakfast with them, I can, and—"

"No, you should go. Enjoy yourself. I'm glad that the three of you are becoming close."

But if you do something to hurt them, I'll make your life a living hell.

Christ, I'm all fucked up. I need to set this plan of mine into place to test my theory.

And pray that I'm wrong because if I'm not, my wife is my goddamn mole. And I don't think my heart can take that.

Twenty-Three

NATASHA

"SOMETHING BAD HAPPENED LAST NIGHT, you guys," I say to my friends after we order our breakfasts. Julian was right, I do like it here. The diner is old-fashioned, like something from the 1950s, with rock and roll memorabilia all over the place. It's bright and fun, and even the waitstaff is wearing old-timey uniforms. The three of us are sipping coffees and leaning forward so I can speak lower. "Like, bad."

"Our guys left in the middle of the night," Lulu says, and Scarlett nods. "They must have gone to help Julian."

"Julian didn't say what it was, but he scanned my electronics and stuff to make sure that I wasn't responsible for anything."

"What?" Scarlett scowls over at me. "Why the fuck would he think that?"

"That's ridiculous," Lulu adds.

"I think he's being paranoid and just wants to make sure. I mean, I guess someone could have planted something in my stuff without me knowing. He said that I'm the newest member of the circle, so he had to eliminate me first. But he checked, and there was nothing to find, like I knew there wouldn't be. I didn't like it, though. I don't like feeling like he doesn't trust me."

"He trusts you," Lulu says with a frown. "Julian's crazy about you. Whatever it was that went down, it must have just really rattled him."

Nodding, I feel my phone vibrate in my pocket, so I pull it out and find a text from my father.

He hasn't reached out to me since I got married.

Not a phone call, not one message.

So, what does he want now?

I open it and read his text.

> Papa: You will come to lunch
> tomorrow. Noon at Tolstoy's Lounge.
> Do not be late.

Yep, that's my father. He's not asking, he's *demanding*. And because I want to keep the peace, I'll go. Conveniently, Tolstoy's is in the same shopping center as the store where I bought the Chanel bag, and I can pick it up at the same time.

I quickly reply.

> Me: I'll see you then.

"We should hit the spa at Rapture sometime soon," Lulu says, catching my attention, and I shake my head.

"No offense, but I don't want to spend any time at Rapture."

"It's not attached to the club," Scarlett says. "It's way

different and *so relaxing*. You won't even know that you're in the same building, just like when we're at Lulu's penthouse."

I take a deep breath, watching my friends with apprehension. I do *not* want to be in that building.

"You can trust us," Lulu adds.

"Oh, I trust you both. Implicitly. You guys have become my best friends, and I know that you'd never hurt me. I kind of hate that I'm afraid of a building. It's so ridiculous."

"You're entitled to your feelings," Scarlett reminds me. "But the building, even the *club*, can't hurt you. Maybe if you go with us, you'll see that there's nothing to worry about. I promise you, it's *perfectly* safe. Lulu and I both work *and* live there."

"You're right." I nibble my lip and then decide to trust my new friends. "Okay, I'm down for the spa."

"Holy shit, let's go *today*." Lulu does a little dance in her seat. "I'm not letting you change your mind."

I grin as she pulls her phone out and starts making calls. "Looks like I'm not changing my mind."

Twenty-Four

JULIAN

"SO, you suspect that because you told Natasha that you had a delivery coming to this warehouse this morning, that whoever's been stealing your shit will show up." Rome is sitting next to me in my Porsche. We're alone. No security. I've hidden the car in the trees from a vantage point where we can see anyone coming or going from the warehouse, but they can't see us.

"Her necklace lit up," I tell him again, and feel nausea roll through me once more, the way it has from the minute I saw that motherfucking green light. "Jesus, Rome. *Fuck.*"

"Let's see if your hunch is right. Don't lose your shit until you know for sure."

I sigh, hoping with everything in me that I'm wrong. *It can't be her.*

It can't be my angel.

Fuck, I love her. I'm crazy about her. If she's been playing me this whole time, I won't just lose my shit. I'll go crazy. I don't know what my life looks like without her in it anymore. After such a short time of being married to her, she's *everything*.

"Maybe the device I was using had a low battery," I mutter, grasping for *any* other explanation.

Rome doesn't say anything.

He knows that's not the case. I don't ever let anything I own have a low fucking battery.

"I sound like an idiot."

"No, you sound like a man who wants to believe the best of his wife. You're not an idiot for that. You're an idiot for a whole host of other reasons." Rome sighs and drags his hand down his face. "Five minutes."

I nod silently. I haven't been this nervous in . . . *ever*. I've never been nervous a day in my life. There's no place for it in my line of work. I'm sure about every step I take, every decision I make, and I never question myself. If you falter, you die.

But for the first time in my life, my hands want to shake.

Jesus Christ, I never expected to be brought to my knees by a curvy bombshell of a woman with perfect lips and a sassy mouth. She's finally starting to open up and tell me what she needs and wants. She's just coming out of a shell that I know was built out of a lifetime of abuse and pain.

At least, that's what she's told me.

She touches me without a second thought, and *never* flinches when I touch her, and it feels like I finally soothed a broken animal.

I've completely fallen for Natasha in every way. Her body that I know better than my own, her smart-as-fuck mind, the way she laughs, and even how horrible she is in the kitchen. And don't even get me started on how her music is like medicine for me.

I could listen to her play for weeks on end and never tire of it.

But for all I know, her father treated her like a motherfucking princess and her experience with Elliott was the first time she's ever been mistreated. Maybe her father beat the hell out of her as a decoy, to make me *believe* she'd been hurt.

I don't have any proof to the contrary, and that's what's sending me out of my goddamn mind.

"Shit," Rome mutters, and my gaze comes up to see the armored SUV roll up in front of the warehouse. "Fucking *shit*."

"We don't have any backup," I mutter. "But we can attack and kill these fuckers."

"I'm with you."

Rome and I both grab extra firepower out of the front of the car, and then we're silently on the move, coming around the warehouse from behind.

I hear them bust down the door, and I can hear voices. I motion for Rome to stop, and we listen.

"He said nine," someone growls. "I heard it plain as day. He must have been fucking her for all I know, his voice was so clear."

They're all going to die.

And then I have to deal with my *wife*.

"Well there's nothing here," another says, and I nod at Rome.

We move through the door to behind them, still silent. There are four of them.

Two are dead from blades slicing their necks before the other two realize what's happened.

"Shit!"

They don't have time to say anything else before we have them on the ground, restrained and gagged, and then I call Jack.

"I need transport," I tell him. "I have two for the cell."

IT'S BEEN MORE THAN TWENTY-FOUR HOURS. Actually, it's well past noon now, so we've been working these assholes over for a long time, taking shifts.

I haven't been home. What little sleep I got was in one of the extra apartments upstairs in my building. I can't stomach looking at her right now, let alone being in the same room with her, and as good as I am at keeping a straight face, I'm afraid that I'll let my rage take over and I'll put a bullet in her head.

I'm so fucking pissed off.

She knows that I'm working, and that's all she needs to know. I have men keeping an eye on her. She spent yesterday at the spa and then stayed in last night.

And I fucking hate myself for missing her.

Because all the evidence points to Natasha being the one feeding information to her father to fuck with my business. Putting my men, my *family*, in danger. Men are dead because of her. *And she is going to pay for that.*

"Wake up," Mateo barks at the first of the two men that we have hanging in the basement of my building. He slaps him across the face, making him moan.

These two have had a shit twenty-four hours.

Their faces are both swollen, barely able to see through eyelids the size of golf balls. We relieved Number One of his left foot, then cauterized it so he didn't bleed out.

Number Two no longer has fingernails or molars, and just an hour ago, we decided he could live without his hips being in their respective joints.

That had to fucking hurt like a bitch.

And yet, they still don't want to talk. So, it's time to get more creative.

"Don't know," Number One mutters, and I get closer.

"What did you say?"

"Don't know anything."

I nod slowly and pace away from him. Fuck, I'm tired. Bone-, soul-deep tired.

"Except, you've been listening to me with my wife." I turn and see him wince. "Have you listened in while I fucked her? While she screamed my name?"

"No."

"Yeah, I don't fucking believe you. I'm going to take your cock for that, but first I want to know who you fucking work for."

Say Sergei Ivanov.

"Contract."

"You know who you're reporting to," Mateo says. "You know exactly what's going on. You can try to wait us out, but we won't kill you for a long fucking time, asshole, and every last minute of your life is going to be in agony. So you might as well just tell us."

"I wonder if they think we're stupid?" I turn to Mateo, as if we're just hanging out with a couple of beers, shooting the shit. "You know? Like, we haven't been doing this for the majority of our lives. We have practice at this."

"A lot of practice," Mateo agrees with a nod. "Did you know that death by a thousand cuts is really a thing? You can keep a man alive for *years* that way. Sounds pretty shitty to me, but I might be up for the challenge."

"I don't have anything else going on right now." That's a lie. But these assholes don't know that. "Maybe we should split them up, then go at them. I bet they're not so brave if they're alone."

"True." Mateo tilts his head, watching the two men hang and listen to us. "Or?"

"Or."

I pull my knife from the sheath on my belt and slash it across Number Two's throat and watch as the life drains out of him.

Number One whimpers.

"There, now it's just the three of us." Number Two continues to bleed out, the drip, drip, drip of the thick liquid loud in this empty concrete cell. "And I'm going to torture you until you tell me everything you fucking know. You're not getting out of here alive. That's a given. But how long you suffer is completely up to you."

"And he's pissed," Mateo adds. "So the torture will be . . . extra shitty."

"Extra shitty," I agree. "Did you know that I can remove every inch of your skin from your body while you're conscious? I mean, you'll eventually die of hypothermia, but that could take a while."

He whimpers again. *Pussy.*

"Who do you fucking work for?"

"Ivanov."

Without another word, I slit his throat and walk away, pulling my phone out of my pocket as I go.

I missed three messages from my wife.

> Wife: I missed you last night. I hope you're safe.

> Wife: I'm going to the shop where I bought that bag I told you about. It finally came in!

> Wife: Please just let me know that you're okay.

"Fuck."

Mateo and I have just reached the parking garage when Jack strides over to me, his face more grim than normal.

"You need to see something, boss."

"Show me."

He passes me an iPad, and I narrow my eyes and press play on the video.

Natasha walks into a restaurant and greets *her father*. He kisses her cheek, and she smiles at him.

She fucking smiles at him.

With my heart thudding in my chest, I watch as they talk for a minute, and then Sergei's face turns angry. He reaches out and swipes the necklace, snapping it off her throat, and then tosses it on the table.

Because he knows exactly what it is.

"Where is she now?" I ask as I pass the iPad back to Jack.

"On her way to the mansion."

I nod once and stride to my car.

I have to go take care of my perfect, sweet little traitorous wife.

Twenty-Five

NATASHA

I SHOULD HAVE TOLD Julian that I'm meeting with my father for lunch. I should have called him and let him talk me off the edge of this meltdown that I'm about to have. Not to mention, I don't like keeping secrets from my husband. It feels wrong.

It feels like a lie.

But Julian didn't come home last night, and he said he was busy with work, so I didn't want to interrupt him. Distractions could mean the difference between life and death, and I need him to be safe.

God, I've fallen in love with him. I hated being in our bed by myself last night. I'm too used to sleeping while wrapped up in his arms. Our home is too cold and quiet without him. I did break down and send him some meaningless messages, but he never replied, so I stopped.

Now I'm wishing I had at least texted him one more time about my father because I could really use his deep, soothing voice in my ear right now, assuring me that everything will be okay and that my father can't hurt me.

But I can handle this on my own. We'll be in a public place. And I'm so much stronger since I've been with my husband.

He makes me feel like I can do anything. I need to thank him for that later.

I have two men with me, like I always do. They're sitting up front, and we're all silent as we drive into the city. My detail never says much to me. I don't know if that's because Julian has told them to keep a distance from me or if they simply don't like me. But if these two are going to be with me for years, I'd like to get to know them.

"So, you're Benji," I say, gesturing to the driver. "And you're . . . ?"

"Gary," the other one replies.

"Thanks for taking this assignment."

"We don't volunteer for things," Benji reminds me. "We're told. The boss wants us with you, so we're with you."

"Do you not like this assignment?"

Benji shrugs. "It's fine."

"I just wondered because you guys don't say much."

"We're not here to be your friends," Gary says. "We're here to make sure no one can take you or kill you."

"Maybe we could do both?"

They smirk at that, and it makes me relax a bit.

"We don't have to be best friends, but we don't have to be so formal."

When we reach the shopping center, I go to the store first to pick up the bag I had on order, and then I leave my shopping bag with Gary and make my way to the restaurant to meet my father. I feel better knowing that these big, scary guys are just a few feet behind me.

They won't let Papa hurt me.

When I walk inside, I turn to both of them and offer them a shaky smile.

"I shouldn't be too long."

"We'll be right here, watching," Benji says with a nod. "Take your time. Signal if you need us."

I draw in a deep, nervous breath and walk into the dining room, spotting my father at his favorite table, and to my surprise, he stands as I get closer. Even Viktor stands, but he doesn't smile or say anything.

He's always leering at me, though. Always has a smarmy sneer on his face.

My father, however, *smiles* at me and reaches out to hug me, plants a kiss on my cheek.

"It's good to see you, malyshka."

"Um, hi, Papa." I offer him a smile, but everything in me is on high alert. This is *not* how my father usually treats me. Not even close. I don't remember the last time he kissed my cheek. He certainly never smiles at me.

"Sit, sit." He points to the chair across from him and takes his seat once more, and I fold my hands in my lap, waiting for him to start the conversation. "I haven't seen you in weeks. How is everything going with your new husband?"

His face is calm and pleasant. *Who is this man?*

"It's been going well," I reply carefully. "He treats me well, and I don't have any complaints."

"Good." He nods at me and then gestures for the

server to leave us alone rather than order lunch. "Does Julian discuss business around you, *malyshka*?"

He wants information.

I should have known.

"No, he doesn't do much work from home." I keep my eyes on his and don't so much as flinch. I may not like keeping things from my husband, but I'll lie to this motherfucker all day long. "Is that why you brought me here?"

"How much time do you spend with the other three men?"

"None."

All pleasantness leaves his face, and he drops his voice. "You listen to me, you worthless little brat, I put you in that luxurious life with that man, and you're going to do your job and tell me everything you know."

His eyes fall to my necklace, and he glares.

"I thought you loved your grandmother."

Um, what?

"You know I did."

"Yet, you don't wear her necklace all the time."

Confused, I sit back in my seat and scowl. "How would you even know that?"

He shakes his head in disgust and then, to my horror, reaches across and rips the chain from around my neck and tosses it on the table.

I grab for it and hold it tightly in my fist.

"Why did you do that?"

"You don't deserve anything from her," he snarls, his lip curled in disgust. "She'd be disgusted by you. You whore yourself to him—"

"He's my *husband*," I hiss back at him, and he lifts his arm, like he's going to strike me, and I flinch back, my heart pounding, feeling so damn small again.

"You may not live under my roof, but you won't talk back to me, Natasha. Do you think your husband gives a shit if I hurt you? I'm your father, I can do whatever I want to you. I can't believe he stepped up to marry you. You're so fucking worthless, so *stupid*. He deserves far better than you. He must have pitied you, after the way even his son discarded you. How does it feel to be married to a man who never wanted you in the first place?"

"That's not true." It's a whisper, because that's all I can force out of my throat. I'm shaking, and I just want to hide.

I want to disappear.

No one can make me feel as small as my father does.

I need Julian to hug me and tell me that Papa's wrong. He married me because he wanted to. He's grown to care about me.

I know he cares about me.

"Those four men, the Kings of Vegas"—he smirks—"they're excellent liars. Manipulators. I've been told that Julian is the worst of them, and it seems that rumor is true, given how devastated you look. You know this world, malyshka. It should come as no surprise to you that he married you for the deal and nothing more. When we're finished, he'll cast you off. That should be any day now."

Shaking my head, I feel tears push their way to the surface. He's wrong. Julian wouldn't cast me aside. He told me that he'll give me anything I want. That I'm safe with him.

Was it all an act?

I've never been treated as well as my husband treats me, but maybe that's because it's not real.

"He wouldn't do that."

"Oh, he would. Do you think his late wife's death was an accident?" Papa laughs as if the thought is ridiculous. "You'll be lucky if he just kicks you out rather than killing you when he's done."

"You're my *father*."

"And you're my pawn," he says, his voice hard. "Now, you go back there, and you listen to everything that goes on in that house. You ask questions. You get information. And then you feed it to me. If I'm satisfied with your work, I won't let Julian kill you."

"No."

His eyes narrow menacingly. "What the fuck did you just say?"

"No, I won't spy on my husband for you. He may be a bad man, and he might throw me out when he's done with me, but I won't betray him."

"So, you'll betray *me*?"

"I've already done what you asked. I married him. That's all I'll do for you."

Papa leans forward, pure hate staring back at me now. "You'd better hope and pray that the piece of shit you're married to never tosses your ass out because you won't be welcome at my house. I'll kill you before I'll let you through the door. I don't care what he does with you. He can share you with his men or slit your throat, it means nothing to me. If you don't get out of my sight in ten seconds, I'll break both of your knees."

With a soft sob, I stand on shaking legs and rush out of the restaurant. My guards share a look. Gary is on the phone, but the ringing in my ears is so loud, I can't hear what he's saying, and then they follow me out to the car.

I need to get home.

I need my husband.

God, it feels like just before my wedding all over again. Worthless. Helpless. So fucking terrifying.

What if everything he said is true?

My husband *is* the head of a Mafia family. I should know better than to trust anyone in this world.

But he's been so sweet and tender with me.

You're letting that horrible man get in your head. That's not Julian. That's not your husband. Think of all of the times he's spoiled you, held you, smiled at you. He shares his family with you. He's not going to discard you.

I almost believe myself when we pull up to the house. When I step out of the SUV, I frown at the two black garbage bags sitting on the steps.

That's unusual.

Twenty-Six

JULIAN

"THEY'RE HERE," Jack says at the doorway of my office, where I've been standing and staring out the window. I arrived ten minutes ahead of her because I texted Benji and told him to take the long way home.

I wanted to be waiting for her.

With a nod, I leave the room and stride out in time to meet Natasha in the kitchen, where she sets her shopping bag on the counter.

It seems that's *one* thing she didn't lie about.

"Hi," she says softly. She won't meet my eyes as she rubs her hand over the back of her neck. She looks pale and shaken, and two days ago, I would have pulled her to me and demanded to know what's wrong so I could disembowel whoever made her feel this way.

Right now, I'm telling myself that I don't fucking care.

It's a lie, but I'm telling myself anyway.

"You no longer live here." I have to force the words out. I didn't mean to start with that. I'd planned to interrogate her, to ask her *why*, to intimidate and do what I do when it comes to my enemies.

But at the end of the day, the answers don't matter. *She* was what mattered the most, and she betrayed me. She put my family in danger. Because of this woman, some good men are dead. So I don't give a shit about her answers. She went against me, and that means she has no place by my side.

I need her out of my sight.

At first, she doesn't react to my statement at all, as if she's lost in her own mind, and then what I said finally registers, and her head slowly comes up. She frowns at me, as if she's sure she misheard me.

"What?"

"You. No longer. Live here. The belongings you came with the day I married you—the worst day of my life, as it turns out—are in the bags out front, which are being loaded into the car as we speak." I have to shove my hands in my pockets, balling them into fists, so I don't reach for her. Christ, my chest aches. I can't believe she's been lying to me, *deceiving me*, all along, while I was falling in love with her. Becoming addicted to everything about her.

"I don't understand." I'll hear that voice in my dreams for the rest of my life.

"I don't give a fuck what you do or don't understand. I don't live with traitors."

She shakes her head, and I glare at her.

"You met with your father."

Her jaw drops and then she swallows hard. *Yeah, Angel, I fucking know.*

"You were working, and—"

"Get the fuck out of my house." I put all the rage and disgust I have running through my veins into my voice and eyes as I stare down at her. She cowers back, as if she's afraid I'll hit her. It makes my stomach roll, but she *should* be afraid of me right now. "If I ever see you again, I'll fucking kill you without hesitation."

The gasp is small but unmistakable, and she stumbles back, catches her heel on the corner of a table, and falls backward, crying out when she lands on her hand.

Instinctively, I start to move toward her to help her up but then bite the inside of my cheek and stay rooted where I am.

I need her gone before I do something fucking stupid.

"Get up and get your ass out of my house, Natasha."

She cradles her hand against her chest as she pushes up to her feet, watching me with terrified eyes. Her lips wobble. She's shaking.

She's an excellent fucking actress. Don't forget that.

"Wh-where am I going?"

I tilt my head to the side and glare at her. "I don't give a fuck."

"I'm sorry," she whispers, and then she stumbles away, out of view. After the door closes behind her, I walk back to my office and slam the door shut before I scream and shove my hands in my hair.

Fuck.

"Jack!" I yell, storming out of the office again, and find my number two walking down the hall toward me. "Have some of my personal things packed up. I'm not staying here."

"Are you going to the penthouse, boss?"

The penthouse is gutted, and I'll never live there now anyway.

"No, the apartment below it," I reply. His eyebrow lifts, but he doesn't say anything as I stride away. "And I want anyone who's ever fucking crossed me in the cell by the end of the day. I need to make someone bleed."

Twenty-Seven

NATASHA

HIS EYES ARE what destroyed me. The hate in them, the way he stared at me as if I disgust him. I was still so upset after meeting with my father, and then Julian was there, so cold and hard, the way he used to be when I first met him. The man standing before me wasn't my husband.

He was the ruthless made man that my father warned me about, and with Papa's words still ringing through my mind, I stood there and watched everything he told me come true.

My Julian discarded me, and the whole time, I did what I'd been raised to do.

Stay small.

Stay quiet.

Do as you're told.

He called me a traitor, but that can't be right. I told my father no.

"I told him no," I murmur, holding onto my aching

wrist. It's starting to hurt worse, with its own pounding heartbeat, and I cradle it to my chest.

"Shut up," Benji barks, glaring at me in the rearview mirror.

My hand comes up to touch my necklace, and then I remember that it's gone. I dropped it when I fell at the house, and I have no idea where it skidded off to. There was no time to look for it.

When the vehicle stops, I look up to find that we're at the gates of my father's estate.

You'd better hope and pray that the piece of shit you're married to never tosses your ass out because you won't be welcome at my house. I'll kill you before I'll let you through the door.

I can't go in there. I *can't* be here.

"Please don't leave me here."

"Boss's orders," Gary says with a shrug, and the two of them climb out of the car, open my door, and roughly yank me out, then do the same with the trash bags. They toss them next to me and leave me at the gate as they drive away, kicking up dirt in their wake.

I don't hold the tears back as I look around helplessly. What am I supposed to do? I can't go to my father's house. Julian has done the one thing he swore he'd never do. He cast me out.

I'm sure that means that I'm not allowed to contact Lulu or Scarlett, either, since they're his family.

I don't have anyone.

Pulling my phone out of my purse—thank fuck I still had it looped over my shoulder—I order an Uber. It takes me a long time to figure it out because I can only use one hand and I have to get my payment information set up.

Shit, payment information.

I don't have any money.

My heart is hammering as I punch in the numbers on the credit card that Julian gave me. I don't have a choice but to use it to pay for this ride.

I have to get out of here before one of my father's men alerts him to my being here and he makes good on his promise.

"CAN YOU PLEASE WAIT WITH MY THINGS?" I ASK the rideshare driver as he pulls into the parking lot of the pawn shop. "I don't have a way to carry the bags, and my wrist is injured."

The guy sighs and looks back at me, as if he's bored. "I can't. I have to go pick up another ride. I can't afford to sit here and wait for you all day."

"I'll add a hundred dollar tip," I offer, but he shakes his head no. "Will you help me—"

"Get the fuck out of my car," he growls, making me flinch. I manage to drag the bags out of the vehicle one at a time, and then do the same, pulling them into the pawn shop where I can watch them.

"I can tell you that I don't want anything you've got in those bags," the woman behind the counter says.

"I'm not selling them, I just don't have anywhere else

to put them right now." I stride to her and gingerly pull the engagement ring off the finger of my injured hand, the movement making it hurt even worse. "I'd like to sell this."

Her eyes widen as she stares at the diamond. "Lover's spat?"

"Something like that. Can you tell me what you'll give me for it?"

"Hmm." She takes it from me and examines it, weighs it. I know it's worth well into the six figures, maybe even seven, but I'm hoping to get at least fifty thousand for it. I'd be able to get a place to stay, and it would give me time to figure out what I'm going to do.

How did my life go so wrong so fast?

"I'll give you two grand for it."

I blink at her, sure I've heard her wrong. "You have to be kidding."

"That's all I can do."

"But it's worth—"

"Doesn't matter what it's worth. Only matters what I'm willing to pay for it. And I'm willing to pay two grand."

"Twenty-five hundred. *Please.*"

She sighs, and then nods. "Fine. Twenty-five hundred."

She opens her till and counts out the cash and passes it to me, then walks away.

I don't sign anything. *That can't be right.*

"Wait. What if I want it back?"

"You didn't pawn it, sweetie. You *sold* it. I'll sell it back to you for ten grand."

Oh my God.

I shake my head and put the money in my bag, then return to the garbage sacks. I can't carry these. Maybe the next driver will help me.

Finally, I manage to drag them outside and look up some hotels. There are a few rooms available for fifty dollars a night.

I don't even want to know what kind of hotel room is fifty dollars a night.

But I don't really have a choice either. I don't have enough money to stay in a nicer place for any amount of time. I'll go broke too fast.

So, I reserve the room and then order a car. I'll have to put one more charge on Julian's card, and then I'll cut it up.

THREE HOURS LATER, I'M SITTING IN THE middle of a saggy queen-size bed in the seediest place I've ever seen, finally letting emotion wash over me. I checked into this motel—thankfully this rideshare driver was nicer and helped with my bags—and then walked across the street to a pharmacy, where I bought a brace for my wrist, along with some basic toiletries and snacks. Bottles of water. Pain medication.

I took some medicine and then got in the shower. The water only trickles out, and it smells dubious. Like mildew and metal and I don't even know. I'm not even convinced that this place is all that clean.

The dust bunnies are something to behold.

But I have the door barricaded, and now I can finally stop moving.

All the anguish and fear and pain washes over me in waves. It feels like I'm standing in the ocean and a riptide of emotion is pulling me under, threatening to drown me.

I don't care about the money or the mansion or the fancy things.

I want *my husband*. The man who looks at me with so much affection and humor and lust. The man who fucks me like I'm everything he's ever needed in his life. I want my best friend, my partner.

My love. God, I love him so much, even though he kicked me out so heartlessly. How could the universe be so cruel, to *finally* allow me to experience so much kindness and happiness, only to have it ripped away?

I roll onto my side and bury my face in my hands, crying so hard I can barely breathe.

"He should have just killed me."

JULIAN

COVERED IN BLOOD, I make my way upstairs to the apartment I've been living in, and walk straight through to my bedroom and then into the shower.

I don't even give a fuck that I'm still dressed when I turn the water on as scalding as I can stand it and let it soak me through.

It's been a week of fucking hell.

Every minute without her is torment that I wouldn't wish on anyone, even Ivanov. And I'm going to kill that fucker.

My brothers have all called me out on my shit, with Mateo even taking me into a boxing ring to kick the hell out of me.

I welcomed it, and I let him beat me until I almost passed out.

And still, despite the bruises and what's likely a broken rib, I don't feel a fucking thing.

The only thing that brings an ounce of relief is when I'm in the cell, terrorizing one of my enemies.

I mean, I knew I was a shit human. Might as well play the part.

Finally, I strip out of the wet clothes and wash the blood out of my hair, off my face. Arteries really spray like a motherfucker. Then I dry off, throw the clothes away, and dress in a T-shirt and sweats.

When I walk out to the kitchen to pour myself some whiskey, I pull the gun from the small of my back and aim it at Rome, who's sitting at my island, already drinking a glass of his own.

He doesn't even bat an eyelash.

"It's just me," he says, sounding completely at ease and not at all intimidated. "Also, your reaction time is slow as fuck. I could have killed you about a dozen times before you noticed I was here."

Not answering him, I pour my own glass and swallow it down in one gulp before pouring another and then lean my hips against the countertop behind me and stare at him.

"What do you want?"

"First of all, why are you living here? This place is tiny, has nothing on the walls, no view. You like looking at the next building over?"

It doesn't matter. I'm hardly here.

"What do you want, Rome?"

He blows out a breath and sips his whiskey.

"You've missed two family dinners in a row, and you're hurting my wife's feelings."

Wife.

"I love Lulu, you know that, but family dinner isn't high on my priority list these days."

"No, disemboweling and dismembering men seems to be all the rage for you." His ice-blue eyes hold mine as he takes another drink of the whiskey. "At the risk of sounding too soft, I'm worried about you."

Shaking my head, I push off the counter, but he doesn't leave it alone.

"If you're this upset, it's because you're second-guessing yourself."

"No, I'm not."

Yes, I fucking am.

"We saw the evidence, Julian."

"I'm not talking about this with you. It doesn't matter. It's over. She's gone."

"It does fucking matter." He stands and follows me into the living room. "Because now you're being reckless."

"No, I'm not. I'm taking care of business. I've let things slide for too long, was too lenient. It's time the people in this city remember who the fuck we are."

He nods slowly. "Or, you're—"

"Stop." My voice is hard as fucking granite.

"You're grieving," he says quietly. "I get it. If it was Eloise . . . I can't even think it."

"It's not Eloise," I remind him. "And it's my own fault for buying her innocent doe-eyed act, thinking that she was sweet and perfect and not as ruthless as her piece-of-shit father."

"Natasha isn't ruthless," Rome says, shaking his head.

"Are you telling me that you think I was wrong?" I stare at him, incredulous. "You were *fucking there*, like you said. You saw it all. I sent you that video of her with her father. She was fucking spying on me. On *us*."

I throw my glass against the wall, not feeling any better when it shatters, and then push my hands into my hair.

"I know what we saw," he says quietly and then takes a deep breath. "I hope we're right, Julian."

"We *are*. Because if we're not, that means I kicked my innocent fucking wife out on her ass and left her at her father's doorstep."

He winces and then nods. "What are we going to do about Ivanov?"

"His days are numbered, but I don't just want him. I want his entire organization, and to do that, we need to plan. I've been a little busy."

"We'll all help you," he reminds me. "Now, really, you need to move the fuck out of this apartment. It's depressing as fuck. No wonder you want to kill everyone."

I glance around, taking in the bile-colored, empty walls and plain hardwood. It's bare bones. No decorations, just the simplest furniture. And like he said, there's no view.

I took the worst apartment in my building. We never use this unit.

But this is what I deserve after I got my men killed and tore my own heart out of my chest.

This is what I deserve for forgetting who the fuck I am.

I'm not the kind of man who lives happily ever after.

I'm the head of the Greek Mafia. That's my job. My whole reason for being.

"Whatever you're thinking to yourself right now is bullshit," Rome says, and I just flip him the bird, making him laugh.

"Are you done?"

"Will you make Eloise happy and come to dinner next week?"

"It's been *one* week, Rome."

"Yeah, but two Sundays." He shrugs. "When my wife worries, I'm sent out to make sure the people she loves are okay. And you're not okay."

"I will be."

Another lie.

"Yeah, you will be. Come to dinner next week. In the meantime, come to the club. Get laid. If nothing else, let Mariah give you a blow job."

"Get the fuck out," I growl, and Rome shakes his head, a smile spreading over his face as he glances down at my hand, the one still wearing a wedding band.

Yeah, I need to take that off, but every time I do, I put it right back on again.

"It was just a suggestion."

When I'm alone, I sit on the couch and lean my head back with a sigh.

I could go to the club. Rome was right, Mariah was always my partner of choice. She gives one hell of a fucking blow job, and she doesn't look anything like Natasha.

But the mere thought of another woman anywhere near me makes me sick to my stomach.

I'd rather kill people.
I'm a sick fuck.
And I miss my wife.

Twenty-Nine

NATASHA

"SHIT, THAT HURTS," I mutter, trying to wrap tissue around my hand. I started a job, cleaning rooms in the motel I'm currently living in, actually. Does it suck? So, so much.

But I get to live here rent-free in exchange for the work, along with a small salary, and it's the best thing I could come up with right away. My phone died on day two, so it's not like I can send out résumés.

I don't even *have* a résumé.

Of course, my left hand or wrist . . . *something* . . . is still horribly injured, and I can hardly use it. It's probably broken, but I can't afford to go to the hospital.

It'll heal with time.

I hope, someday, I'll be able the play the piano again, but just the thought of it makes me cry, so I blink fast and focus on trying to cover up this wound.

"What happened," Sue, my boss, asks.

Shit.

"I slipped and cut my hand," I reply. "I just need to cover it up, and then I can get back to work."

"Listen, Natasha, I like you. I think you're a nice girl who's going through a shitty time in your life, but I have to let you go."

I feel all of the blood drain out of my face.

"I've only had this job for a week," I protest. It's been two weeks since Julian kicked me out, and every single day has been a nightmare. Getting this job was the only thing keeping my emotions under control. "Please don't fire me."

"You move at a glacial pace," she says, shaking her head with sympathy. "I know it's because your wrist is hurt, but you're just too slow, sweetie. And now you've hurt your other hand. As much as I like having you around, I need someone who can actually do the work at a decent rate of speed."

I press my lips together, willing myself not to cry.

"Please," I whisper. "I need this job so badly."

"I'll tell you what. I'm giving you the next two weeks off. You won't get paid your salary, but you can still keep your room benefit. I want you to rest and heal, so in two weeks, you can come back good as new and kick ass."

A tear falls down my cheek, and I stare at Sue, shocked by her offer.

"You'd do that for me?"

Aside from Julian and his family, no one's ever been this kind to me. I don't know what to do with it. I don't know if I can trust it.

"What's the catch?" I ask her.

"Get better," she says. "Eat something. In the two

weeks I've known you, you've lost ten pounds. Take care of yourself for a while, get your feet under you, and the job will be waiting for you."

"I'm so grateful," I reply, overcome with emotion. "Thank you."

"You're welcome. Now, go clean that cut on your palm and rest."

With a nod, I walk back to my room. It's not good that I won't have a salary for two weeks, but at least I can still stay here for free. I borrowed some extra cleaning supplies from my cart when I started the job and did a deep clean of my room. My wrist sang with pain afterward, but I felt better knowing that it was cleaner.

I walk into the bathroom and examine the cut over the sink. It's deep. It should probably have stitches, but if I'm not willing to go to the hospital for a likely broken wrist, I'm not going for a cut either.

I've just started cleaning it up when nausea rolls through me, and I fall to my knees in front of the toilet, throwing up what little food I had in my system. Then I wrap a towel around my hand and climb onto the bed, lying on my side. I stare at my dead phone on the bedside table. I could go over to the pharmacy and probably buy a charger for it, but I don't have anyone to talk to.

I should eat, but I'm not hungry.

I'm just sad.

Everything hurts—not just my hands, but my heart, my stomach, my *soul*.

I'm exhausted from crying every night. After working all day, I come back in here and cry for hours until I fall into a fitful sleep.

Then I get up the next morning and do it all again.

Eating isn't on my mind, and it's really not in my budget either.

SOMETHING'S WRONG.

I'm so sweaty. Out of breath. Exhausted.

So fucking tired.

And I throw up a lot, even though I haven't had anything to eat in days. I've always been the type to toss my cookies when I'm anxious, scared, nervous. And I've been all of those things pretty much from the minute I met my father for lunch so many weeks ago now. It doesn't surprise me that I can't keep food down, but the other symptoms are worrisome.

My cut hand is killing me, so I walk into the bathroom and remove the towel that I've been using to keep it covered.

That doesn't look good.

There's puss and redness. A red streak runs up my forearm. Is it infected? Is that why I'm so hot? It's been a week since I cut myself. It should be healing.

It shouldn't look like hamburger.

Ugh, just the thought of hamburger has me dry-heaving over the toilet again, and then I fall onto my side on the cool tile and fall asleep.

I'M SO COLD. SHIVERING. TEETH CHATTERING.

Hands hurt.

With a whimper, I pick myself up off the floor of the bathroom, dizzy when I get on my feet. How did I get here?

I go to turn the AC off, but it's not on. Why is it so cold in here?

Maybe I have a fever and need medicine.

I check the bottle on the table and see that I'm out. I'll have to walk across the street to the pharmacy to buy more, and just the thought of doing that is exhausting. I want to lie down and sleep. Get under the covers to warm up. But if I have a fever, I'll need both ibuprofen and acetaminophen for the pain and to get the fever down. I think I still have some money in my purse.

Twenty-five hundred dollars doesn't go far in this town.

Making sure I have my key card for the room, I push outside and sigh in relief as the hot midday sun hits my face. The warmth feels so good, I can't help but tip my face up to the sun.

I'm sweaty as I make my way across the street and into the store. I shiver when I walk inside because it's so cold in here. As quickly as I can, I find the medicine I need and grab a couple of bottles of water before making my way to the counter.

"Natasha?"

I frown into my purse, trying to find my cash. I should have enough for this. *Please let me have enough.*

"That's twenty-six ninety-five."

"Okay." I pull all the bills I have out of my purse and lay them on the counter, feeling embarrassed when the cashier has to unwad them to count them. I just don't have the energy, and my hands are *killing me.*

"Natasha."

I blink and turn at the sound of my name, and then feel the blood leave my face as terror takes up residence in my stomach.

"No." I shake my head, trying to keep the nausea at bay, and back away. "I didn't do anything."

"Hey." Elliott looks concerned, and he doesn't make a move toward me, he just holds his hand up like he's trying to approach an injured kitten. "Natasha, you don't look good."

"You don't have enough money," the cashier says.

Immediately, Elliott takes his wallet out and taps his card, paying for my medicine.

"You don't have to pay for the junkies," she says to Elliott.

"She's not a motherfucking junkie. She's sick. She's buying *medicine* for fuck's sake."

Elliott shakes his head and offers me the plastic bag full of my things. He tries to hand me my cash as well, but I can't bring myself to get close enough to him as terror continues to race through my body.

Will he hurt me? Will he tell Julian where to find me?

"Okay, I'll put your money in here." He drops the cash into the bag and then passes it to me.

I snatch it out of his hands and back away. God, I'm so dizzy. And so cold.

"Did you hurt your wrist?" He asks, gesturing to the brace on my left hand.

"Doesn't matter," I whisper. "Please don't tell your dad you saw me. Please just forget this, okay?"

"Natasha, I can help—"

"No!" Panicked, I keep backing away, shaking my head and trembling. "No. I'll scream. I'll call the police."

"Christ." Elliott's frowning at me, and I leave as fast as I can, looking back to make sure he's not following me.

I don't see him.

I'm afraid I'm going to fall down from weakness and dizziness, but I force my eyes to stay open as I maneuver back across the street and let myself into my room. I have to hurry to the bathroom because I have to throw up again.

I want Julian.

I don't care that he kicked me out. I want him. I want him to hold me and kiss me and tell me that it'll be okay.

Nothing is going to be okay.

I can't do this by myself. I'm hurt, I'm scared. I'm so fucking sad. Life without him isn't worth living at all.

I manage to take a couple of pills, not even seeing which ones I'm taking, and then I crawl back into bed, so exhausted from the trip across the street and seeing Elliott.

He looked genuinely concerned, but I can't have him going back to Julian to tell him where I am. He said he'd kill me if he ever saw me again.

I believe him.

He will kill me. I just wish I knew what I did that made him hate me so much. It can't just be because I had lunch with my father.

That's ridiculous.

"Don't hate me," I mutter, sounding delirious to my own ears. "I wanna go home. I just want to go home."

I turn my hot face into the pillow, enjoying how cool it feels on my skin, and cry myself to sleep again.

It's the only way I ever sleep at all.

JULIAN

IT'S BEEN weeks since I stayed here at the mansion, and I need to check in on things before I have a realtor come out here to list it.

I can't live here. She's embedded in every inch of this house. Her music, her laughter. Jesus, I can still smell her.

And it makes me ache.

I should storm over to her father's house, demand he hand her over to me, kill the fucker, and bring her back here. Paddle her ass for betraying me and then fuck her into submission.

That actually sounds really good.

If no one had been hurt because of her little stunt, I might be able to find a way to work through it, but damn it, my men died.

Because of her.

Frustrated with myself, I push my hands through my hair and then notice the sun sparkle off something on the floor. When I get close, I see that it's her necklace, and I scoop it up and roll it around in my palm.

The one with the listening device in it.

She must have dropped it when she fell. The chain is broken from her father ripping it off her neck.

I could hack into it and hear her voice.

I fucking miss her sweet voice. I feel like a complete idiot for not hating her guts and wanting her to suffer.

I want to feel those things.

But I don't.

Without overthinking or beating myself up about it, I walk back to my office and turn on all my equipment, then pull out the device that will scramble the one in the pendant and get to work hacking into the software attached to it.

I want to hear her.

Maybe if I actually hear the words that she was selling me out to her father come out of her fuckable little mouth, I can find the hate I so desperately need right now.

It takes me a while, but soon, I have the audio files pulled up on my computer, and I cue it up to that last day, around lunchtime when she met with her father behind my back.

"Does Julian discuss business around you, malyshka?"

I narrow my eyes at the sound of his voice and lean in closer to the computer, riveted.

"No, he doesn't do much work from home. Is that why you brought me here?"

"How much time do you spend with the other three men?"

"None."

She lied to him. She spent a lot of time with my

brothers, and I do most of my work from my home office.

She lied to him.

My stomach starts to roll as I keep listening. His words turn more and more abusive, spewing nothing but lies and hate, trying to convince her that she's worthless, that I don't care about her, and making it clear that he hates her.

"You're my father."

"And you're my pawn," he says, his voice hard. "Now, you go back there, and you listen to everything that goes on in that house. You ask questions. You get information. And then you feed it to me. If I'm satisfied with your work, I won't let Julian kill you."

"No."

I sit back in shock at the hardness in Natasha's voice.

She told him no.

Fuck me, she told him no.

"No, I won't spy on my husband for you. He may be a bad man, and he might throw me out when he's done with me, but I won't betray him."

"So, you'll betray me?"

"I've already done what you asked. I married him. That's all I'll do for you."

I make myself listen to the last of it. He makes it clear that she's not welcome at his home ever again, and *I fucking sent her there.*

Spiraling, I stand and pace my office, my hands pushing through my hair and over my mouth, wrapping my mind around the fact that *she didn't betray me.*

She was upset that day because her abusive-as-fuck

father had taken verbal punches at her at lunch, not because she was keeping something from me.

She was fucking upset.

And then I kicked her out.

Jesus, did he kill her when she was dumped off at his house?

Is my wife fucking dead?

Shaking my head, I reach for my phone and dial her number, but it goes straight to voicemail. I'm about to suck it up and call Sergei when my phone rings with an incoming call.

Elliott.

With a sigh, I accept. "Hey, now's not a great time, I'll have—"

"Dad, I'm calling about Natasha."

I stop cold. "What's going on?"

"Listen, I don't know what's going on with you two, but I saw her a few hours ago, and she . . . she wasn't right, Dad. She's sick, and she was so fucking scared of me."

My entire fucking world tilts off its axis.

"Where was she?" I demand, already walking through the house toward my car.

"At a pharmacy, getting some medicine." He gives me the area, and I scowl.

"What the fuck is she doing on that side of town? Wait, what are *you* doing over there?"

"I needed a prescription, and the doctor's office sent it to the wrong place. Had to hunt it down. Anyway, I don't know what Natasha is doing over there, but she didn't have enough money for her meds, so I paid for them and tried to give her the cash back that she'd spilled onto the counter, but she wouldn't let me near her. Dad, she looks *really bad*. Skinny and fragile."

What the fuck have I done?

"Did you see where she went?"

"Yeah, she walked across the street to a motel. She must be staying there? I can show you."

"Send me your location, and I'll meet you there. You said this was hours ago?"

Elliott clears his throat. "I'm sorry, but you warned me to stay away from her, and I didn't want to piss you off. But—"

"You did the right thing. Fuck. I'll be there as soon as I can."

I hang up and call my finance guy.

"Hello, Mr. Stavros."

"When is the last time my wife used her credit card?"

I can hear tapping on keys in the background and then he says, "Roughly three weeks ago."

"And what did she spend it on?"

"There were three charges that day. She spent six grand at Chanel, and then thirty dollars each on two Uber rides."

My wife took a fucking *rideshare*, by herself.

"And nothing since?"

"No, sir."

I hang up and dial Benji's number. He's the one who was supposed to take Natasha home.

"Boss."

"I gave you instructions to take my wife to her father's home."

"Yes, sir, we did."

"Did you take her to the front door?"

There's a pause. "No, we left her at the gate. Pulled her out of the car and dumped her bags with her, then left."

I end the call and fist my hands around the wheel, driving entirely too fast into the city. Jesus fucking Christ, what have I done?

Elliott waves me down as I pull into the parking lot, and when I slam out of the car and race toward him, he points to the door marked *Eight*.

"She's in there," he says. "At least, she was earlier this afternoon."

I nod and gesture for him to follow me. The lock on the flimsy doorknob is nothing at all to jimmy open, and when I push inside the room, revulsion rolls through me.

"Fuck," Elliott whispers behind me.

The room isn't just old. It's musty and dirty. Dark. Her bags lie just inside, mostly untouched, some white clothes spilled out the top of one of them.

And my girl is on the bed, on her side, curled up in a ball.

"Call Dr. Asgood," I bark at Elliott, all calm gone

from my voice, "and tell her to meet us at the infirmary with a full staff."

"On it," he says as I approach Natasha, not wanting to scare her. "Baby, I need you to wake up."

She's thrashing her head side to side, and she's so fucking sweaty. She's soaked through her clothes and the bedding. Her phone is beside the bed, but it's dead, and I slip it into my pocket.

"Natasha," I say a little louder as I press my hand to her head. "Christ, you're burning up, baby."

"Asgood will meet us there and will be on standby," Elliott says. "What do we do?"

"Grab her things and put them in your car. I'm going to carry her out to mine."

My son nods and immediately follows my orders, and I push my arms under my wife. She's wearing a brace on one wrist, and a dirty towel is wrapped around her other hand. Her hair is full of sweat, and when I pull her against me, she's clearly lost weight.

Too much weight. She's not eating. Is it because she didn't think she could afford it? Fuck, I should be tortured for years for what I've put her through.

"Baby, I'm so fucking sorry."

She whimpers and buries her face in my chest for a moment, but then she opens her eyes and shrinks back when she sees me, tries to get out of my arms.

"No. Nonono. I didn't do anything."

"I know. I know, Angel. I'm not going to hurt you. I promise, I won't hurt you."

"Can't fight you," she says, shaking her head. "It hurts."

"Baby, I'm so sorry. We're going to fix you up. I'm going to fix this."

I carry her out of that godforsaken room and out to my car just as Elliott shuts his trunk.

"Hey! Where the fuck do you think you're taking her!" The tiniest woman I've ever seen comes running out of a neighboring room, scowling at us.

"I'm taking her home," I reply coolly. "She's my wife."

She stops short, and her jaw drops in surprise. She eyes my car, and then scowls up at me. "You drive that, and your wife was living *here*? Asshole."

She shakes her head and starts to walk away, but then turns back.

"I guess she won't be coming to work next week?"

My entire body goes very still.

"And what work would that be?"

"She was working for me. Cleaning rooms in exchange for her rent." She shrugs, and my stomach flips again at the thought of my gorgeous wife cleaning rooms in this filth, just to keep a roof over her head. "Be nice to her, yeah? She's a good one."

"Fuck," Elliott says, which is exactly what I was thinking.

Natasha's teeth chatter as I lower her into the car. I don't want to let go of her, but I have to get her back to my building so Dr. Asgood can examine her.

"I'll follow you over," Elliott says, and all I can do is nod as I sprint to the other side of the car and get behind the wheel.

Natasha whimpers again, clearly in pain and uncomfortable from the fever, and it makes my already-broken heart ache.

"Did I die?" she whispers, and I whip my gaze over to find her watching me through glassy eyes. "Or is this a dream? You smell so good."

"Neither."

"Are you going to hurt me?"

"No." Christ, I'll keep reminding her over and over again. "No, Angel, I won't hurt you. I'm going to get you some help."

"Can't afford a hospital," she whispers, and then she's asleep once more.

If I could, I'd string myself up and slowly, *very* fucking painfully, skin myself alive.

I make a quick call to Rome and give him the watered down version of the past hour, and after he swears in my ear, he promises to tell the others, and then hangs up on me.

Yeah, I'm pissed at me too.

As soon as I pull into the underground garage, my car is surrounded by my men, including Jack, who has a gurney waiting for us.

"How—"

"Elliott called me."

I glance over at my son and give him a nod. His eyes are filled with worry as he nods back, and then we work as a team to get Natasha on the rolling bed and up to the medical care that's waiting for her.

My brothers and I hired Dr. Asgood years ago. She's exclusively on our payroll and is on call for us twenty-four seven. She's an amazing doctor, and she's discreet, which makes her perfect for our organization.

"Over here," the doctor says as we walk inside, gesturing for us to roll Natasha to the corner where four other medical staff are waiting. "What do we know?"

"Not much," I reply grimly. "We found her like this. I have no idea what her injuries are, or just how sick she is."

"A puzzle," Dr. Asgood murmurs as she takes Natasha's temperature. The others work on taking her blood pressure, putting in an IV, and all the other things they need to do. "Her fever is too high. 104.8. There's definitely an infection or a virus of some kind."

"Found the infection," someone calls out. They've just unwrapped the towel from her hand, and my stomach climbs into my throat as I stare down at a wound so red and angry, it looks agonizing. "This cut should have had stitches. It's not fresh."

"I'm going to run some blood tests, so we get the big picture," Dr. Asgood says as she keeps poking at and examining my wife. "But this wrist is broken. I need an X-ray to determine exactly where, but it shouldn't be this swollen. This brace has been on here for a while."

She fell backward at the house when I was kicking her out and was cradling her hand to her chest afterward.

"Three weeks," I say roughly. "If it's what I think it is, it would be three weeks."

"If that's the case, this woman has been in a lot of pain."

She shakes her head, and they continue to work on

her. Carson and Mateo stride into the room, both looking serious as fuck as they stare at my wife.

"Take me down and kill me," I say to them. "I deserve it."

"I'll kill just about anyone," Carson says, "but not you. This isn't your fault."

"It's absolutely my fault."

Thirty-One

NATASHA

COOL HANDS ARE on my face. It feels really good. I don't hurt as bad as I did before, but I feel like I have to throw up again, and I flail about to get out of bed and run for the bathroom.

"Easy. You can throw up in here."

Someone guides my head to the side of the bed, and I throw up until I'm heaving, and then there's a cool cloth wiping over the back of my neck and face, and it helps with the nausea.

I don't even open my eyes. I can't. So tired.

I think I smell Julian. *Is my husband here?* I want to snuggle into that comforting scent. I want to ask for him, but I can't.

I lie back down and return to sleep.

"I'm so sorry, Angel." Is that Julian's voice? It must be, but how did he get in my room? How did he find me?

I whimper because I'm starting to feel nauseous again, and my hands hurt.

"Shh, it's going to be okay."

"Dreaming."

"No, baby, you're not dreaming. We're getting you better. Please forgive me. I'm so sorry."

Lips brush over my forehead. It feels so nice.

I want to open my eyes and look at him, but I'm so tired. Maybe I really am dreaming. If he were really here, he'd be mad at me.

"I want to go home."

"I'll take you home as soon as you're better."

"You'll hurt me."

"No, Angel." His voice cracks, and I want to see his face so badly. "Never. I'll never hurt you again."

He smells so good. It's calming. I feel like I've had that thought before, but I just keep falling asleep.

Thirty-Two

JULIAN

"IT'S normal for her to be in and out of consciousness," Dr. Asgood says. She's standing with me beside my wife, filling me in on test results. "She has a horrible staph infection, and it's gone septic. Meaning, it's through her whole body. So, we're running a broad spectrum of antibiotics in her IV along with continuous fluids. Her blood pressure is lower than I'd like. I want to see a big improvement in the next four hours. If that doesn't happen, we'll take her to the hospital."

I nod, all the words floating through my head.

"If she'd gone even one more day without being found, she might not have survived, Julian."

I pull my hand down my face and swallow hard. "Fuck."

"You should go home, and—"

"I'm not leaving."

She nods and pats me on the shoulder. "I figured as much. I'll be back in an hour to check her vitals."

When she's gone, I sink into the chair at Natasha's side. She's not in a coma, but she's sleeping almost constantly. We've been here for about four hours, and she's hardly surfaced. When she does, she babbles and doesn't make much sense. She keeps thinking that I'll hurt her.

And who the fuck can blame her?

"Hey, sweetheart." I kiss her temple and reach for the bowl of cool water and the washcloth, get it wet, and then gently smooth the cloth over her face, cleaning her up a bit. I wish I could sit in a bath with her, but she's too sick.

Sponge baths it is.

"Sorry," she whispers, and my eyes fly to hers. She's not looking at me.

"You don't have anything to be sorry for. *I'm* the one who failed you. Failed us. And we can talk about all of that later. For now, you just rest and get better."

"Missed you," she whispers. "Don't leave me."

"I'm not going anywhere." She's not pulling away or saying no anymore, and that's a huge relief, but she might still be delirious. When she's better, she might tell me to go fuck myself.

And she probably should.

Because I don't deserve her.

I'll also never let her go.

Three days later, we're at the mansion, and my wife is in our bed, where she belongs. She's still sleeping well over twenty-two hours a day, but she's still fighting the last of the infection.

I haven't been able to ask her about anything that's happened over the past few weeks yet. She honestly hasn't stayed awake long enough for much of a conversation.

But I've spent a lot of time holding her. Kissing her head, her cheeks. Her hands are healing, but the wrist is going to take a while before it's as good as new again.

"You need to sleep."

When I glance down, I see my wife looking up at me. She doesn't look afraid, but she also isn't looking at me with love.

Not like *before*.

"You're so tired, Julian. I'm fine. Lie down."

I shake my head, but she reaches for my hand with her injured one and holds onto my pointer finger.

"Get in this bed, Julian."

Fuck, I love it when she gets bossy.

Finally, I strip down to my boxer briefs and slide between the sheets with her, but I'm afraid to pull her into my arms.

"I don't know what to do," I admit with a whisper. "I don't know what you want."

"I'm going to yell at you when I'm better," she replies, making me smile, but she doesn't smile back. "But right now, I need my husband. Just be my husband, and we'll figure the rest out later."

Gently, I gather my wife into my arms and cradle her

close, pressing my lips to her hair. I was able to put her in a bath this morning and wash her hair, getting her the rest of the way clean, and I think it helped her feel better.

"I have so much to say to you," I whisper in her ear. "Are you awake enough to talk?"

"Yeah."

"I need you to know how fucking sorry I am for everything that's happened."

She sighs and nuzzles her sweet nose against my chest. I should feel relieved that she's with me, but I'm still on edge.

There's so much to resolve between us. So much to talk over.

"Jesus, I feel horrible."

"You should." She shrugs when I blink down at her. "But that's for another day. When I'm better, you can just take me back to the m-motel."

Her voice quivers, and I roll her onto her back so I can push the hair from her face and kiss her forehead.

"Hey, no. No, baby."

"You don't want me." Her voice is so damn small, just the way it was in the beginning, and it fucking *hurts*.

"I want you more than anything in the world, and I'm never letting you go again. You will be wherever I am, always."

"You said that before."

My eyes close at the truth of that. I did make promises to her that I blew apart.

"I'll show you," I whisper. "Go to sleep, baby. We'll talk more later."

"Julian?"

"Hmm."

"My father said that you'll eventually get tired of me and get rid of me—"

"Don't you ever listen to another fucking thing that man says, Natasha Stavros."

She smiles up at me, and then her smile falls and more tears fill her pretty eyes.

"What is it?"

"My ring is gone."

With a frown, I look down at her hand and realize for the first time that the diamond is missing from her finger.

"What happened?"

She presses her lips together. "I don't want to tell you. You'll get mad."

"It's okay. You can tell me anything."

"I had to sell it. I didn't have any money."

"If you sold it, you should have been in a much better place than where I found you."

"I only got twenty-five hundred for it."

I stare down at her, and for the first time since I've had her back safe and sound, I feel hot anger pulse through me.

But not at her.

"Who did you sell it to, Angel?"

"I went to a pawn shop. She said it didn't matter what it was worth, it only mattered what she was willing to pay for it. And then she said that I couldn't have it back unless I paid her ten grand."

"When you're better, you're going to tell me which shop that was. And I'll get your ring back. Unless you want something else?"

"I want my ring."

"Then you'll have it."

Thirty-Three

NATASHA

I'VE BEEN STARING at the book in my hands for an hour but haven't actually read a word of it. It's nice out today. Winter in Vegas means that it's not too hot, and I can be outside without having a heatstroke within ten minutes, so I'm sitting by the pool, under the shade of an umbrella, breathing in the fresh air and the scent of the flowers nearby.

How Julian's gardener keeps this all in bloom and looking spectacular in the middle of a freaking desert, I have no idea.

But I love it.

It's been a week since Julian found me. It's both a relief to be home and terrible because I don't trust him.

I can't.

He promised me so much before. Treated me like I mattered to him, like he cared about me, and then he discarded me like I was trash. Like it was the easiest thing in the world to cast me aside.

Just like my father would have.

And I just can't let go of how he looked at me that day, as he watched me fall and hurt myself and then kicked me out.

I'm not stupid. I'm not going to insist that he take me back to that horrible motel. Julian has made it clear every single day that I'm staying and that he'll never let that happen again.

However, just like my father warned me, the men in this world are manipulators. Liars. I don't know what Julian's game is right now, but I don't trust that he magically wants me with him again. I don't even know what happened to have him kick me out in the first place.

My husband is always home. To my knowledge, he hasn't left the mansion once since he brought me here days ago, and he's never far away. He must be babysitting me. Keeping watch, in case I do something to betray him again.

I glance through the glass doors into the house and see Julian pacing the kitchen, his phone to his ear.

I wonder what happened to my phone.

Until this moment, I haven't even thought about my cell. It had been dead for so long that I was out of the habit of reaching for it, and today's the first day that I'm starting to feel well enough to spend most of my time out of bed.

I really don't want to lie around anymore.

That must mean that I'm getting better.

With my eyes still on my husband, I settle back against the lounge chair. *He's so handsome.* He's in his standard black slacks and button-down, sleeves rolled up, top two buttons undone. I'm quite sure all his clothes are custom because they mold around his perfect body like a second skin.

He's been so tender with me over the past week. I know he was worried, and I can sense that he means it when he says he's sorry and that he'll never hurt me again.

I want to believe him.

At least, I think *he* believes what he says. But a month ago, I would have sworn on my life that Julian Stavros would *never* put me in danger, would *never* cast me aside.

But he did.

I know I'm safe here, for now. And I'll go back to being the dutiful wife, doing what I was raised to do.

But I need to guard my heart. Because I don't think I could survive another heartbreak like the one I just went through.

Julian slides the glass door open and steps out to join me, smiling down at me.

"I'm so glad you're feeling better."

"Me too. I don't want to be in bed anymore."

"That's a good sign." He sits on the chair next to mine, facing me. "Angel, what was the store called where you sold your ring?"

I frown over at him.

"I'm going to get it back for you."

I glance down and run my fingertip over the skin where my diamond usually sits.

I miss it.

Even if this marriage is in name only, it's *mine*.

"I'd need my phone to remember the exact name of

the business," I reply softly. "I know that it's not too far away from where I was staying."

Julian pulls my phone out of his pocket and passes it to me. "It's charged. I didn't turn it on because I didn't want to invade your privacy."

I lift an eyebrow, and he blows out a breath.

"You're going to learn to trust me again."

I don't reply as I press the button on the side of the device and wait for it to come to life.

To my surprise, hundreds of texts come in, all from Lulu and Scarlett, and it makes tears come to my eyes.

"What's wrong?" Julian asks, jumping to his feet and standing over me.

"They cared."

I look up at him and see that he's staring down at my phone.

"Angel. Of course, they care. They're your friends."

"No." I shake my head sadly. "They're *your* friends. Your family. I was just borrowing them."

He doesn't say anything as I maneuver to my search history and then show him the name of the pawn shop where I sold my ring.

"This is it."

"Would you please text me that location?"

"Sure." Quickly, I tap the screen and send it to him. "Do you want me to have dinner ready for you when you get home?"

"No." He sits next to my hip on the lounger and reaches out to brush his fingertips down my cheek.

I flinch.

His eyes narrow, and his jaw tightens.

"I will *never* hurt you."

Pressing my lips together, I nod. "Okay."

"I don't want you to have dinner ready for me today or any other day. We've been through this before. Chef will be here at five to get dinner started for us."

I nod and look away from him, staring at the blue water in the pool. If my hand wasn't in a cast, I would go for a swim.

"Would you please take the piano away?"

He's quiet for a moment and then takes my chin in his fingers and makes me look him in the eyes.

"Why would I do that?"

"Because it hurts to look at it." A tear falls down my cheek, and I hate myself for showing vulnerability in front of him. I want to be strong. I don't want him to pity me. "I don't think I'll be able—"

"Don't finish that sentence." He leans in and presses his lips to mine, so unbearably softly that it makes more tears fall.

It hurt when I didn't have him, and it's just as horrible being this close to him and holding myself back.

"You'll play again when your hands have healed, baby. But if you want me to have it moved until you're ready, I can."

"We had good times at that piano." It's whispered. I didn't mean to voice it out loud.

"And we will again."

I shake my head slowly and pull my chin away from his fingers.

"I know you're angry," he says. There's no malice in his voice. He sounds perfectly calm, but when I glance over, I see torment in his gorgeous dark eyes. "You *should be*. All I can do is prove to you, every day, how much you mean to me and that I'll never let you get hurt like that again. I *will* prove it to you, Natasha. Just promise you won't leave me."

"I don't have anywhere to go." My lower lip trembles, and I try to firm it. "I learned that the hard way."

"Fuck, baby. I need to hold you. Tell me I can hold you."

That's the other thing: Since I've been back here, he only wraps his strong arms around me when I give consent.

I brush away my tears with the back of my cut hand and then give him a nod, and he gently wraps his arms around my shoulders, tugging me against him.

He's so warm. So fucking strong.

And he smells so damn good.

"You break my heart every fucking day," he whispers into my hair.

"Same," I whisper back.

Suddenly, the glass door opens again, and when I look over, I see Lulu and Scarlett rushing over to us.

"Oh my God," Lulu says, wiping tears from her cheeks. "He can't keep me away from you for another minute. Oh, honey, we missed the fuck out of you."

"You go," Scarlett says, pointing to Julian. "Go do Mafia shit. This is girl time."

Julian glances at me and lifts his eyebrow.

"Go do Mafia shit," I repeat with a soft smile. "These two can take over the babysitting duties."

"I haven't been—"

"Girl time," Scarlett says again, leaving no room for argument.

Julian sighs and presses his lips to my forehead, then brushes his lips by my ear, and little tingles explode over my skin.

I'm still attracted as fuck to my husband.

"I won't be gone long. Call me if you need me."

And then he walks away, leaving me with Lulu and Scarlett.

Thirty-Four

JULIAN

I DIDN'T WANT to leave her, and it isn't because I'm babysitting her like she says. It's because whenever I'm more than eight feet away from her, I physically ache. I start to have panic attacks, wondering if the infection is coming back, if she's feeling better, does she still hate me.

Natasha may be at home with me, but there's a wall a mile high between us. I'm grateful that she wants to sleep in our bed, but she only cuddles me if I ask her to. She *never* initiates physical touch, and now she's flinching again when I reach for her.

We've gone all the way back to the beginning, and I want to *rage*. I want to get on my knees and beg her to forgive me, for things to go back to the way they were before I fucked everything up.

I know she needs time. She's still healing and coming to terms with everything. She's still angry, and damn it, I get that.

But when she asked me if she should have dinner

waiting for me, she might as well have opened my chest and plucked my heart from my body.

I need my wife back.

Jack pulls into the parking lot of the piece-of-shit pawn shop where *my wife* sold her million-dollar ring, and when he cuts the engine, we sit in silence for a moment.

"We offing someone in there?" he asks.

"Maybe." I glance over at him. "Depends on how this goes."

I push out of the vehicle and walk to the door, and when I stride inside, I see a woman behind the counter staring at her phone. She's middle aged, has sallow skin, dull and lifeless, after a long life of poor nutrition and smoking. And when she looks up at me, her eyes narrow with curiosity and maybe a little fear.

When she stands, her eyes travel down my body, and with what I'm sure she thinks is a flirty smile, she leans on the counter, showing off tits that I'm absolutely *not* interested in.

"Hey, fellas. How can I help you?"

"My wife came in here a few weeks ago and sold you a ring."

The smile turns into a sneer.

"Don't remember. I buy a lot of rings."

"You'd remember this one. It's an eight-carat oval solitaire, and you raped my wife with the price you paid for it."

This bitch sets her jaw and digs her heels in.

This is going to be fun.

"She agreed to the terms."

"I don't agree to your fucking terms."

"You're not the one who sold it, are you?"

"I assume you still have it because it would be difficult for you to find a buyer for a million-dollar ring when you don't know where to sell it. I'm going make this offer only once. I'll reimburse you the twenty-five hundred you paid for it, and you're going to give it back to me."

She snorts and shakes her head. "Or what?"

I lean just a little closer to her, like I'm going to tell her a secret. "Or I'll go find Stephen at his little community college in Van Nuys and disembowel him slowly. You pissed off the wrong man, Britney Ann Lewis, of 688 Huntington Drive, Social Security number . . ."

I rattle off the number, along with every other piece of personal information I could find on this cunt, and watch as what little color she has leeches from her wrinkled face.

"I won't kill you. I'll destroy you. I'll make every fucking day of your miserable life a terror and agony that you can't even comprehend, and I'll make sure you live to be a hundred fucking years old. You fucked with a Mafia queen, you idiot. A woman walks in here with a ring like that, and you just dick with her?"

"I didn't know who she was!" Her voice is shrill now as panic starts to set in.

"Well, now you do. And you know who I am. But the most important piece here is, I know who *you* are. Now, where is my wife's ring?"

She licks her lips, and her faded brown eyes flick over

to Jack, but my man is stoic as fuck, and he looks scary with his beefy arms crossed over his chest. She won't find comfort there.

"It's in the safe," she finally says.

"Lead the way."

"Oh, I can just go get it."

I smirk at her. "I don't need you slipping out the back door."

Britney turns and leads me to the cheapest fucking safe I've ever seen. It's not even locked.

How she hasn't been robbed blind, I'll never know.

The woman pulls out a sandwich bag full of diamond rings, and plucks Natasha's out and holds it up, just out of my reach.

I should break her fucking fingers.

"I want fifty grand for it." She raises her chin defiantly. "If you paid a million, you can afford it."

"You're under the impression that we're negotiating." I take a step closer, and she swallows thickly, takes a step back. "That's not what's happening here."

My hand snatches the ring from hers faster than she can react, and I slide it into my pocket, then walk away.

"Hey! You owe me money, asshole."

Jack lifts an eyebrow as I come out of the back. He heard every word, of course.

"She thinks I'm an asshole," I tell him.

"Well, there are days . . ."

I smirk and then turn back and scowl at Britney as I pull the cash out of my pocket and drop it on the smudged glass of her countertop.

Without another word, I walk out to the car, and Jack and I climb in.

"Home?" he asks.

"No, we need to see Malis. I need a new setting for my wife's ring. That bitch touched it."

Jack nods and heads toward my jeweler's office.

Thirty-Five

NATASHA

"THIS POOL AREA IS *NICE*," Scarlett says with a sigh, leaning back on her shaded lounge chair. Lulu's on the other side of me.

I'm sandwiched between them.

"I haven't been able to read your texts," I tell them quietly. "I just got my phone back today."

"He took your *phone* away?" Lulu demands, staring at me incredulously.

"No, I had it with me, but I didn't have a charger, so it died early on. I never bothered to find a way to plug it in."

I shrug a shoulder, and the girls continue to watch me.

"You could have called us," Scarlett says.

"No, I couldn't." I shake my head and take a deep breath. "You're Julian's family, not mine. And he made it clear that I wasn't welcome when he kicked me out."

"Jesus," Lulu mutters. "He *really* fucked up. We haven't seen him since before it all went down. He kind of became a hermit. Rome said that he didn't live here, he moved into a shitty apartment in his building."

"Luke said that Julian went a little mad," Scarlett adds. "He was beside himself. So angry and frustrated."

"Sad," Lulu adds. "Rome said he was grieving and hurt. He felt betrayed by you, Natasha."

"That's what he told me. That he doesn't live with traitors. But I swear to you, I didn't *do anything*. I wouldn't do that."

Lulu shakes her head with sympathy. When the girls first got here, I was convinced that they came because Julian had to run errands, but he still wanted me to be watched, so he brought in my friends to keep an eye on me.

But the more we've talked, the more I realize that they really missed me.

And I missed them too.

I just don't know how much I can trust them.

"I hate how your light has been snuffed out," Lulu says softly, and tears fill her eyes. She sniffs as she watches me, and then a tear glides down her cheek. "You look so . . . sad. Something must have happened to make him act the way he did, Natasha. Because I can fucking guarantee you that the man loves you."

I bark out a laugh, the first one since before I got sick. "No, he definitely doesn't love me. He just didn't want me to die. There's a difference."

"He touches you and looks at you like he loves you," Scarlett says. "Also, if you still don't know why he kicked you out in the first place, you need to ask him."

"A dutiful wife doesn't ask questions," I reply, my

voice sounding hollow to my own ears. "She keeps quiet and does as she's told."

"Oh, fuck that sideways," Lulu said, shaking her head. "Absolutely fucking not. That's not how it works in this family."

"I'm not a part of this family." God, those words hurt.

Suddenly, both women are on my lounge chair, and I'm hugged between them.

"Don't ever say that," Scarlett says, with tears of her own. "You're absolutely part of this family. Julian fucked up so bad, but don't punish all of us for it. Lu and I didn't have anything to do with it."

All I've ever wanted in my life was to be included, to feel loved and be part of a close family. My parents are assholes and treated me like shit.

But this, these women, is where I was finally starting to feel like I fit in.

"It wasn't your fault," I finally say and pat them gingerly on the back. "And it wasn't my fault. But you need to understand that he made me feel like I didn't deserve the friendships, or the life I was starting to carve out here. He just shut it all down and discarded me like I could be replaced with the snap of his fingers."

"We tried to find you," Lu says and sweeps my hair back from my face, then wipes her thumb over my cheek, brushing away tears I didn't realize were falling. "Scar and I learned some hacking tricks, and we tried to find your phone, but it was dead or turned off, and we couldn't locate you."

"We sent hundreds of messages," Scarlett adds.

"Tried to call. It was so damn frustrating. We would have helped you."

Now that the tears have started, for the first time since I woke up with the fever finally gone, I can't make them stop. I finally break and tell them everything because I *need* them.

"I don't know what to do," I say at last. "This was an arranged marriage. It's not real. I knew that from the beginning, but I let myself fall in love with all of you. I let myself *fit in* for the first time in my life, and I was finally finding my voice. I was so happy. I had everything I ever wanted, and I'm not talking about money."

"Trust me, I totally understand," Lu says with an encouraging nod.

"Same," Scarlett agrees.

"And then I had that fucking lunch with my father, and he made me question everything. He broke me down, verbally beat me back into that quiet, mousy woman who does what she's told. Who stays quiet."

"Oh, sweetie," Lulu says, brushing her fingers through my hair softly.

"And when I got back here that day, I just wanted *my husband*. Because my dad had told me that Julian would eventually toss me away when he was finished with me, and all kinds of shit that I would have sworn were lies just said to hurt me. I wanted to tell Julian about it and have him hug me and reassure me."

I swallow hard and take a breath because I'm crying and talking at the same time, and it's not easy.

"But his face." The last word is said on a shaky whisper. "He was so cold. So fucking angry. The Mafia king was back, and my husband was long gone. He told me I no longer lived here, warned me he'd kill me if he ever saw me again. When I fell, I broke my wrist, but he didn't pause long enough for me to speak or cry, or anything. And then I was taken away."

I'm a blubbering, snotty mess. I can't even get the rest of the story out. I can't tell them about the sleazy motel, or hurting my hand. Those delirious days of being so sick, I didn't know reality from dreams.

And finally, when the tears have slowed down, Scarlett wipes my face with her shirt and kisses my cheek.

"We're right here," she says softly. "No matter what."

"Always," Lu agrees. "Elliott found you?"

"Yeah. Fuck, I was scared. And so sick. I didn't think he followed me back to where I was staying, but he must have. I don't really remember much after that."

"Thank fuck they found you." Lu and Scarlett hug me, and we sit like this for a long time, snuggled up together, watching the breeze blow through the flowers and the birds flit around.

"How are your hands healing up?" Scarlett asks.

"The cut is doing much better. It should be pretty much normal in another week or so. But the wrist is going to take some time. Thankfully, I didn't need surgery."

"Are you able to use them at all?" Lu asks.

"Just well enough to get by. And let me tell you, it's annoying. Julian had to feed me for days. Finally, I can hold my own utensils."

"I'm going to say this one more time, and then I'll leave it be," Lu says. "You need to talk to your husband about what happened. If you still don't know why he did what he did, *ask* him. He owes you answers."

I nod, agreeing with her.

"I have to find my voice again."

"It's still there," Scarlett reminds me. "You just need to use it."

An hour later, after we've talked about other things, and actually napped for a bit, we're in the kitchen snacking on fruit when Julian walks into the room, followed by Rome and Luke, who each make a beeline for their girls.

It's adorable, really. How those big, scary guys dote on their women.

Julian's eyes are pinned to mine as he stalks toward me, but he doesn't touch me. His hands bunch into fists, and I decide to take pity on him and open my arms for a hug.

Without hesitation, he presses his lips to my forehead and hugs me against him.

"How was your afternoon, Angel?"

"Fun, actually." I glance at the girls, and we share a smile. Then, I look at their men. "Hi, guys."

"It's good to see you," Luke says, and Scarlett beams up at him.

"You look much better since the last time I saw you," Rome says with a wink. "Welcome back, Natasha."

"Um, thanks." I offer him a smile, and then to my horror, I yawn. "I'm so sorry, it's not the company."

"Yes it is, they're boring as fuck," Julian says with a smug grin. "My girl is tired, guys."

"That's our cue," Rome says as he kisses Lu's neck. "Let's go home, Firefly."

The girls hug me once more, and then the four of them head out, and I'm left with my husband.

I want the affection back. I want to pretend the past month didn't happen.

"Do you want to nap?" Julian asks softly.

"No, I'm going to try to stay up until a normal bedtime."

"It's okay to rest."

I press my lips together and lean back in my chair so I can look up at him. "We need to talk."

His brow furrows, and then he nods and stands back, not touching me as I push off the stool and stride into the living room, where I lower myself onto the couch and fold my legs under me. Julian sits on a chair across from me.

He's so far away.

Use your voice, Natasha.

"I like it when you sit next to me."

With a surprised lift of his eyebrow, he crosses to me and sits just a foot away, facing me. I adjust myself so I'm facing him as well, my crossed legs resting against his shin. If he wanted to, he could lean in and press his lips to mine.

Julian rests his arm on the back of the couch, and his fingers ghost over the ball of my shoulder.

"Let's talk, Angel."

With a nod, I lick my lips and dive right into the deep end.

"What happened?"

He frowns down at me, so I elaborate.

"That day when—" I have to swallow and press my lips together. "What did I do that you thought was a betrayal? I know I met my father for lunch. He texted me the day before, when I was with the girls, and demanded that I meet him. I didn't see you at all because you'd been working, and I was trying to be strong and handle it on my own. You shouldn't have to fight all of my battles for me."

"Christ," he mutters and rubs his hand through his hair.

Should I stop talking?

Feeling brave, I keep going.

"I wanted to talk to you before I got there because I was scared, and I could have used some encouragement, but you hadn't replied to my texts, and I didn't want to distract you and put you in danger."

His jaw firms, but his fingers are still gentle on my skin.

"It was not a good lunch."

"I know," he says at last, and I blink in surprise.

"You do?"

"Yes. I heard every fucking word."

My stomach drops. "Wait, you heard what he said, and you still—"

"No, I didn't hear it until the day I found you." His face is ashen as he starts to lay it all out for me. How he suspected there was a traitor in his organization, like he'd told me. How my necklace lit up when he scanned it.

My necklace.

And everything else that happened until the day Elliott found me in that pharmacy.

When he's finished with his story, I'm crying again. Because all of this was a fucking *misunderstanding*?

"Where's my necklace now?"

"In my office. I scrambled the feed to your father, and I can have it fixed for you, if you want."

"I don't want it. I want you to throw it away. Julian, you didn't even ask me to explain myself. You just assumed—"

"You're right. I did. Natasha, the evidence was pretty fucking damning. It all pointed to you putting my entire family and organization at risk. Men that I respected and who put their lives on the line for me were killed because of information that only you could have been privy to. I don't tolerate betrayal from *anyone*. And I was hurt, okay? It fucked with my head that the woman I was falling for could have double-crossed me because I don't let my guard down like that. I don't let *anyone* in. My circle is real fucking small, so when I thought that the most important part of that circle had betrayed me, I—"

"You freaked out," I finish for him.

His shoulders sag.

"Yeah, I fucking freaked out. And I hurt you, and *fuck*, baby, that's something I have to live with for the rest of my life. I'm ashamed, and the guilt has me by the throat. I'm a Mafia boss. I'm a ruthless piece of shit, and I'm not a good person. Except when it comes to *you*. And what I put you through fucking kills me. I will never get over how you looked lying in that fucking room, so damn sick and small and practically *dying*."

"I wished for death often," I admit with a small voice. "Because it would have been better than living without you."

Finally, Julian gently tugs me into his lap, careful of my hands, and lies back so we're snuggled up together on the couch, and this is *exactly* what I need.

"Please don't ever say that again." His voice is rough with emotion. "I'm so fucking sorry for everything that happened, and I will do whatever you need me to do to show you that I will protect you and never let anything like that happen again."

I sigh, letting myself sink into him and soak up his warmth, his amazing scent. His arms feel so damn good around me.

"What do you need me to do, baby?"

"I think it'll just take time. I trusted you so completely. You weren't the only one falling, Julian. I finally had a *home*. A family. And in the blink of an eye, it was just yanked out from under me."

He cups my face and brushes his nose over mine.

"You *have* a home and a family, and I'll give you anything you want to show you how much I—"

He closes his eyes and clears his throat, and I don't even breathe, waiting for him to finish that sentence.

"I love you," he finally says.

I simply stare at him, unable to speak.

"I wouldn't have reacted the way I did if I wasn't in love with you. If I didn't feel like I'd given you my heart, and you'd set it on fire in front of me. It wasn't simply that I felt betrayed, I was *destroyed*, and I didn't know how to handle it because I've never felt the way I feel about you. You're my life, Natasha."

I want to say the words back. I want to so, so badly. Because I *do* love him, and now I understand what happened.

I don't agree with it. I definitely don't like it.

But I understand.

"I need you to know that if anything even *close* were to happen again, I won't come back to you. I wouldn't be able to do it again."

He's peppering kisses all over my face. "I'll kill myself before I ever hurt you again, Angel."

"I promise you, I will *never* betray you or your organization. I'm loyal to you. You never have to question that. If something is amiss, just ask me, Julian. I'm not a liar."

"I can't promise that I'll tell you whatever I can when it comes to my business. You won't want to know everything, and I can't put you at risk legally. But I will be open with you. You'll have the same access that my brothers have, and that's a big step for me. Even Jack doesn't have that, baby."

"Thank you." I nuzzle my face into his neck and take the first deep breath in a month.

JULIAN

"WHAT," I bark into the phone when I see Sergei's name on the screen.

"I want you to talk to Carson about allowing me into his casino," Sergei says, making me scrub my hand over the back of my neck. "We're family now. There's a poker game I want in on."

"I don't run Carson's business," I reply, my voice hard as fuck. "Is that really why you're calling me?"

"I gave you *my daughter*. The least you can do—"

I don't let him finish. I hang up on the stupid son of a bitch. I already knew that he's been trying to get in on card games at King of Spades. Carson told me a couple of days ago, just to keep me in the loop.

The old man has some audacity to think that I'd help him with literally *anything*.

He can go fuck himself.

I can hear my wife playing the piano from my office. The cast is off her left wrist now, but it doesn't feel good enough to use it yet. I can tell that she's playing with just one hand.

She's been so frustrated and brokenhearted that she can't enjoy the piano over the past month, and it's just one more thing that I feel so fucking guilty about.

I miss my wife.

I have her here with me, and we talk and cuddle, but I haven't fucked her since she's been back. I wanted her to heal, not just physically but also emotionally. I needed her to feel all the emotions before I brought sex back into things.

And that's not like me at all. I don't even know who I am anymore.

Apparently, this is who I am when I'm in love. I had no idea.

With all the plans for the next few days set into motion, I stand from my desk and push my hands in my pockets as I walk out to where Natasha is. When she notices me, she stops playing immediately, and her face flushes.

"You don't have to stop on my account."

She nibbles that plump lower lip and stares down at the keys. "I wish I didn't suck at this. I know I need to practice, but my hand doesn't want to work the way it should."

"We can find a physical therapist," I tell her. "Dr. Asgood recommended that when we saw her last week."

"I was hoping I could work on it myself, but I need help." She looks up at me and shrugs a shoulder. "Let's find someone."

"I'll make some calls."

Natasha nods and slides over on the bench, inviting me to sit next to her. I'll never deny this woman anything. She leans her head on my shoulder, making me grin as I kiss the top of her head.

"Will you play for me?" she asks quietly.

This has been our thing this past month. We sit here, sometimes late into the night, and I play for her. Everything from classical Bach to Taylor Swift. My girl loves a wide range of music.

"What do you want to hear, Angel?"

"Something fast and happy."

I grin and start playing "All That Jazz" from *Chicago*, and Natasha starts to sing with the music, surprising me.

"You can play *and* sing? Add in gorgeous and smart as fuck. Jesus, what can't you do, baby?"

"Cook," she says between lines, making us both laugh.

Christ, it feels good to laugh with her.

When the last notes fade, my wife smiles up at me, and I can't resist tipping her chin up so I can kiss her, sweetly at first, but it heats up quick, and I sink into the taste of her. She makes that whimpering noise in the back of her throat, and I glide my fingers into her hair, enjoying the fuck out of her.

"Thanks for playing for me," she says when I pull back. "You're so good. I never would have pegged you for a concert pianist."

I snort and tuck her hair behind her ear.

"Far from it. I learned when I was a kid and never

stopped playing. It's the thing that always soothed me. I don't drink a lot, I don't smoke. I play the piano. And now, I have you."

"I soothe you?"

"Yeah, baby. You do." I kiss her again and then stand so I can move to the side and face her. "I have to go to LA this afternoon, and I'm taking you with me."

She blinks in surprise and then firms her chin.

"I don't need to be babysat, Julian. I keep telling you that. You can go, and I'll be fine here alone. I won't do anything to hurt you."

I take a deep breath and rub my hand over my mouth.

"Angel, will you please join me in California? I want you with me because I enjoy being with you and going without you for three days sounds like fucking torture. Please come with me."

She presses her lips together for a heartbeat. "Was that so hard?"

"Is that a yes?"

She stands and bushes her hair over her shoulder. "I'd love to come. What do I need to pack?"

I plan to keep you naked as much as possible, so just bring yourself.

Instead of that, I tell her to pack for a couple of nights, and then she starts to walk to our room, but stops and looks back at me.

"Do I have luggage, or will I be using trash bags?"

"Never gonna let me live any of that down, are you?"

"Are you kidding? Absolutely not."

There's that sassy fucking mouth that I love.

NATASHA FOLDS AND UNFOLDS HER HANDS where they rest in her lap for the tenth time in as many minutes, so I reach over and cover them with my own.

"Why are you nervous?"

"What? Oh, I'm not."

"We're not even at the airfield yet. What's going on in that perfect brain of yours?"

She stares out the window for a moment and then glances at me, and the fear in her eyes slays me. "I've never flown before."

Jesus.

That's right, she told me that she'd never left the state. Her piece-of-shit father, with all of his wealth, never took her on a goddamn vacation.

"It's a short flight," I assure her. "Less than an hour. And we'll take my jet."

"*Your* jet?"

"Yes."

"Oh God, that's *worse*."

Not expecting that response, I frown. "Why?"

"Because, what if I do something stupid and hurt your plane?"

She's so fucking adorable.

"You can't hurt it, Natasha."

"Oh, I'm pretty sure I can." She shifts in her seat, looking terrified, and I bring one of her hands to my lips, peppering kisses on her knuckles.

"Listen to me, it's going to be great. And I have to amend what I said. It's not *my* jet, it's just habit to phrase it that way."

"Then whose is it?"

"It's *ours*."

She swallows hard. "That doesn't help."

I grin and squeeze her hands, and before long the SUV pulls up in front of the private plane that's ready for boarding.

"Wait for me."

Natasha nods, and I step out of the car, scanning the area for any potential danger, then circle to her side and help her out.

My crew grabs our luggage—Hermès for my wife, not fucking trash bags—and loads it aboard while I guide her up the stairs and into our plane.

I love this jet. I spent a fucking fortune on it, customizing it. It's comfortable, with the softest leather seats, plenty of space to spread out, and it's fancy as fuck.

I hope she likes it because I plan to take her all over the world in it.

Once we're on board, Natasha stands in the aisle, taking it all in, her blue eyes wide.

"Have a seat, baby. Anywhere you want."

"Where do *you* want to sit?" she asks as she reaches for my hand, and I love that she wants to be close to me.

"Next to you. So, you pick, and I'll be happy."

She's still nibbling that lip as she moves to a seat in

the middle of the plane and sits, and I take the seat across from her, facing her, then reach down for her foot, remove her shoe, and start to rub the arch.

"Oh, that's nice."

"I'm going to get you to relax, sweetheart. I want you to enjoy this trip."

She sighs and looks around, and the flight attendant approaches, not even sparing my wife a glance as she smiles at me.

"What can I get you, sir?"

"What would you like, Angel?"

Natasha just shakes her head.

"Two ginger ales, please," I reply, not even glancing up.

Did I fuck the flight attendant once on a trip to South Africa? Yes. Obviously, there will be no repeat performance.

She saunters away and Natasha watches her, those sapphire eyes narrowing.

"What's wrong?"

"If she eye fucks you *one more time*, I'll pull your gun—"

"Jessica," I bark out, and the attendant returns seconds later. Natasha's still glaring at her. "You're fired. Get off my wife's plane. Now."

"What? Sir—"

"I won't tell you twice."

Her jaw drops, and then, with burning red cheeks, she spins on her heel and exits the aircraft as I make a call.

"I need a new flight attendant in the next twenty minutes."

I hang up and smile over at my wife.

"I like it when you're territorial, Angel."

"Did you fuck her?" *My girl is pissed.*

"Yes. Before I married you."

"And yet, you're married now, and she still worked for you."

I hold her gaze with mine, not wavering. So fucking proud of her for standing up for herself.

"An oversight on my part, obviously. My apologies."

"Do you have other women—"

"No. There's no one else under my employ that I've fucked."

She lifts her chin, and I want to fucking *applaud*.

"Good. That's a new rule of mine. If you've touched a woman, she no longer has access to you."

"I'm more than happy to live by that rule, sweetheart."

Within fifteen minutes, another woman boards the plane and comes right over to us. She's in her thirties, dressed in her black uniform, her hair pulled back in a tidy bun, and smiles kindly but not inappropriately.

"Hello," she says, addressing Natasha first. "Mrs. Stavros, Mr. Stavros. I'm Chloe. I'm happy to be part of your crew today. Can I get you a refreshment before we take off?"

"I'd like a ginger ale," Natasha says with a genuine smile. "Thank you, Chloe."

"The same for me."

"Of course, I'll be right back with those."

She walks away and Natasha nods.

"That's more like it."

"How are your nerves now?"

"Better." The engines start, and she lets out a little squeak. "Maybe not."

"Those are the engines. Nothing that's happening is out of the ordinary. Soon, we'll taxi to the runway and take off. We'll be flying at about thirty thousand feet, and the flight lasts less than an hour."

"Okay."

Chloe sets our glasses in front of us, then walks away, and Natasha gazes around the plane.

"It's fancy," she says. "And really pretty. I'm afraid that I'm going to spill something and ruin the leather."

"You won't. And if you do, who the fuck cares? It can all be replaced."

"It's expensive."

"I can afford a hundred of these jets, Natasha. You can't do any harm. Besides, I want you to remember something. Are you listening?"

"You're three feet away, of course I'm listening."

"I fucking love your sassy mouth," I growl at her, making her smile smugly. I love that the light has come back to her eyes over the past few weeks. "You're the boss here. Yes, they all answer to me, but you're my wife. You're a Mafia queen, Natasha. If you don't like something, or someone, you say so, and it changes immediately."

"I just snap my fingers and—"

"And whatever you want to happen, happens. Jessica's gone. You want steak and lobster for the ride over? Done. You want the color of the leather changed to bright fucking orange? It might not happen today, but I'll arrange it. This is your empire too."

She blinks at me, obviously stunned, and then nods slowly. "Thank you."

"Remember that when you start to get nervous because you're in new territory. You don't need to be afraid or worried that you'll say or do the wrong thing, because you're at the top of the food chain, Natasha. Don't forget that."

She presses her lips together and then nods again. "Thanks for the reminder. I'll work on it. Now, what are we doing in LA?"

"I have work. While I take care of that, you're welcome to enjoy the spa at our resort, or go shopping, or sit by the pool. You can do whatever you want."

"A facial and a mani-pedi sound really good," she admits.

"Done. I'll be back every evening with you, and we'll decide what we want to do from there."

"So I get to relax, and you have to work. That's pretty on brand for us."

I chuckle and sip my drink. "Are you getting bored?"

"Not bored, but maybe antsy. I still *really* want to teach music." She sips her ginger ale as the airplane moves, headed for the runway.

"Hello, Mr. and Mrs. Stavros. Thanks for joining us this afternoon. We've been cleared for takeoff, so we'll be in the air here shortly. Flight time is approximately fifty-seven minutes from wheels up to wheels down. There's no weather to speak of, so it should be a smooth flight. We'll see you on the ground."

"You were right about all of the things," Natasha says with a smile.

"I go to LA often. I have a port near there where I receive most of my product. Now, back to you teaching music. I think that once your wrist is rehabbed, you'll be good to go there. We talked before about me buying you a building for it. Where would you like it to be?"

She frowns, thinking it over. "Do you have an office in the same building as the penthouse?"

Surprised, my brow furrows. "I do, yes."

"Can I have space in that building, so I'm close to you? And then, once the penthouse is finished, I'll be close to home too."

She wants to be near me.

Fuck, nothing's ever sounded better.

"You can have all the space you need, absolutely. When we get back to Vegas, we'll check it out, and you can choose the area. We'll get started on it right away."

"I can advertise with local schools, letting them know that I'm available. I've been doing research on curriculums for different ages and abilities. I'm *so* excited."

"We'll get everything you need."

The plane revs down the runway and then lifts into the air, and Natasha's eyes widen as she watches me.

"Oh God."

"You're fine. You're completely safe. Look." I point out the window at the city below. "The Sphere looks like the moon right now."

"It's so beautiful from up here," she says quietly. "I love our city."

"I know you do. But I'm excited to show you the ocean."

Within a few minutes, the *Fasten Seat Belt* light goes off, and I unbuckle myself, then her, and lift her into my arms before sitting on a sofa with her in my lap.

"What are you doing?"

"Getting more comfortable. I want you in my arms, baby."

Thirty-Seven

NATASHA

I ADMIT, I don't have any experience at all with travel or hotels—aside from the one I don't want to think about—but I'm pretty sure that most people don't get to stay in this kind of luxury.

I mean, I *knew* my husband was rich, but he's also bougie as hell. This Mafia boss, who I know is scary and ruthless and comes home in blood once in a while, loves the finer things.

And I kind of think it's adorable.

"This resort is insane," I whisper-shout to him as we walk across the marble floor to a counter marked *Concierge*. We're surrounded by about eight of his men, all of them huge and tattooed and mean looking, and I admit, it makes me feel safer.

"The accommodations are acceptable," he says as he pulls my hand up to his lips, and I shake my head at him. He smiles down at me, but when we reach the man at the counter, his face goes stony, and he's all business.

Shit, he's hot.

I know he's been giving me time to heal and settle back in, but if this man doesn't *really* touch me soon, I might spontaneously combust.

"Hello, Mr. Stavros, I'm Lawrence, and will be your point of contact while you're with us."

We're given keys to our room, and Julian turns to his men.

"You two are out front. You two stay here in the lobby by the elevators. You two will be upstairs by the elevators on our floor, and the rest of you will be on patrol."

"Boss." They nod their heads and disperse to their positions, and with my hand in his, Julian leads me to the elevators. When we get on, two of the men join us, and two stay just outside, as ordered.

"Are we safe here?" I whisper up to him, feeling the two men behind us. "You have a lot of guys with us."

"The most valuable asset in my life is with me," he says simply. "And you'll be protected at all costs."

The elevator doors open, and we all step out, but the guards stay back as we walk to our room.

"There's no one else on this floor," he informs me as he unlocks the door and gestures for me to go in ahead of him.

This isn't a hotel room. This is a luxury condo.

The color scheme is white and beige with black accents, and it's open and breezy. The living room spills to a dining area, and a huge set of double doors lead to the bedroom, in the same colors, with a bathroom that I could get lost in. You could have a party for eight in that shower.

We could have so much fun in that shower.

But the best part? It's the outdoor space. Both the living area and the bedroom have doors that open to the biggest balcony I've ever seen, with plush furniture, a fireplace, and a view that takes my breath away. We're *right on* the ocean, and the sun is hanging just above the water, making the churning water sparkle so incredibly, it brings tears to my eyes.

"This is the most beautiful thing I've ever seen," I say, my hands on the railing.

"I couldn't agree more."

I glance up and find him watching me, his jaw tense, his hands in his pockets, and *God, I love him.*

He reaches out to tuck my hair behind my ear, and I don't flinch. I haven't flinched since that day by the pool.

Because I know, deep down, that he loves me. That he won't ever hurt me again. The past month has been magical, full of late nights at the piano, sitting by the pool, and walks through the garden. He's *not* babysitting me, he's spending time with me because we almost lost each other, and now we don't want to be apart.

"What are you thinking, Angel?"

"I think I could live here," I reply, making him smile. "It's seriously amazing. Let's buy the resort and come here whenever we want."

"Done. Now—"

"Wait, I'm kidding."

"Do you want this place or not, Natasha? Just say the word."

I feel my jaw go slack, and then I start to laugh because he's *absurd.*

"You would not buy this entire resort just because I love it after being here for three minutes."

"I think you grossly underestimate exactly how much I love you and will give you anything you want," he replies, and kisses my forehead. "But you think about it. Now, shall we have dinner up here, or do you want to go down to the restaurant?"

"Oh, can we eat out here on the patio and enjoy the view?"

"Of course." He pulls me to him and lifts my chin, gently kisses my lips, making me want to purr. "What else do you want, baby?"

"You," I whisper, my eyes dropping to his lips. "I just want *you*."

His dark eyes sober as he picks me up and carries me inside, leaving the doors open so the salty ocean breeze floats through. He sets me down beside the bed and frames my face in his big, warm hands.

"Are you sure? I'm fine with waiting. I don't want to rush you."

Nibbling on my lip, I frown up at my husband, worried that I've overstepped and he's just not . . . attracted to me anymore. "Do *you* not want to?"

Julian shocks the hell out of me when a laugh bursts out of him, and then he's tugging my clothes off, casting them aside.

"Keeping my hands to myself is torture, wife. Do I *want you*? No. I fucking *crave* you. I need you. Every glorious, perfect inch of you."

His words are intoxicating, and my hands are all over him. We're a tangle of pure lust as we strip each other naked, and then he guides me onto the bed, where he covers me, bracing himself above me on strong, muscled arms covered in those tattoos, and it makes me burn for him. He's kissing me with lips so soft and sure and *ravenous*, my legs scissor, trying to ease the ache between them.

"You're so beautiful, I physically ache," he growls against my ear before his lips ghost down my jawline to my neck. "You're everything I've ever wanted in my life. More than power, more than money. You're the beginning and the end, Natasha."

Before I can reply and tell him how much I love him, he covers my mouth and kisses me while his hands do delicious things to my skin. His fingers tug on my nipples, so hard it makes me gasp, and then they soothe the sensitive skin before making the trip down my belly and over my smooth pubis to my aching core.

His fingers slide through my slit, and he groans, clearly happy with what he finds.

"So. Fucking. Wet for me." His lips tickle mine as he speaks, and I cling to him, my nails digging into his shoulders, needing more of him. I need *all of him*. "Tell me what you need, Angel."

"You."

He smiles, so damn smug and happy that I can't be irritated with him, and then licks over the seam of my lips, and I invite him in eagerly as I arch my back and then push my fingers into his thick hair, holding on.

"What do you need me to do for you?"

I whimper as he kisses his way to my collarbones. "Make me come. Please, make me come, Julian."

"You're going to come all night long, sweetheart. For this first time, do you want me to do it with my fingers?" He pushes two thick fingers inside me, making me gasp. "Or my mouth?" He circles his tongue over my nipple. "Or my cock?"

"Yes."

With a chuckle, Julian kisses his way down and pulls my clit into his mouth, and that's all I need to burst into a million pieces, screaming out his name.

And even when I come down from that high, he doesn't stop. He's planting wet kisses along my inner thighs, and then he covers my pussy with his mouth again and watches me as he laps at me, pushes his tongue inside and then up to my clit again.

"So fucking delicious," he says. "God, I love the way you taste. I've been *starving* for you."

I'm so impatient for him. I haven't felt him in what feels like forever, and I don't want to wait anymore.

"Julian . . . *please*."

"Please what, baby?"

"I need you inside me."

His eyes are on fire as he groans into my pussy, and then he kisses up my body and settles between my thighs, rocking his huge, talented cock through my slit before he pushes inside me, and we both moan with how fucking *incredible* it feels.

"It's like coming home," he whispers against my lips, and then he flips us, so I'm on top, and I smile down into his perfect face. His hands glide down my back to my ass, and I kiss him, relishing in the taste of myself on his lips, before I push up and start to ride him.

"Fuck, you're the prettiest thing," he growls, his hands planted on my hips, guiding me up and down his shaft. "You take me so damn well, Angel."

I thought I would be uncomfortable, since we haven't done this in so long, but he's right. It's like coming home, and nothing feels better than this.

"Julian."

"I'm right here, baby." He leans up so he can tug my nipple between his lips, then presses the sweetest kiss to my sternum. "I'm right fucking here. Always."

"Oh God." I have to lean down and rest my forehead on his as I ride him, chasing another orgasm. "I'm gonna . . . *fuck*."

"Come for me. Make a mess of my cock, you perfect girl."

I couldn't hold back if I wanted to. My muscles quiver, and I grind down, coming so damn hard, I collapse on top of him. Julian nibbles his way down my shoulder, and then he flips us again, but this time, I'm on my stomach, and he's trapped my legs between his thick thighs, spreads me open and pushes inside, and *holy mother Mary*, I've never been so full.

"Julian!"

"I can't hold back." His voice is thick and rough. "Jesus, this pussy is what I'll pray to for the rest of my life."

His fingers will leave bruises on my ass, and I can't wait to see them later. He's pounding hard, relentlessly, and then he lets out a loud groan as he comes, grinding into my pussy and coming inside me, and it sends me over once again.

He kisses up my spine, over my shoulders, and then brushes my hair aside so he can pepper kisses on my cheek.

"Holy shit, Julian."

"Are you okay, my love?"

"Never better." I giggle and feel him smile against my shoulder blade. "Now I'm *really* hungry."

"Let's feed you, and then we'll do this again. All night long. Now that I've had you, I'll never get enough of you."

Thirty-Eight

JULIAN

FINALLY, work is going smoothly. The shipments that have come in over the past two days have gone off without a hitch. No sign of Sergei's men, no interruptions. The product is now off to its new owners in Vancouver, Canada, and I'm richer than I was when we landed.

Today is my last full day here, and I'll be spending it with my wife, spoiling her like crazy after this last meeting.

"Hello, Sir." Antonio nods with respect. He's carrying two briefcases, and he's flanked by two guards, both armed to the gills.

They should be. He's carrying roughly a hundred million dollars in precious gemstones.

I'm sitting at my desk in the office of my building, casually tapping my closed switchblade on the wood, waiting for Antonio to unpack the gems and spread them out on the black velvet laid out before me.

Jack is standing behind me, and I have six of my soldiers with us. No one will fuck with these stones.

Antonio puts on his gloves, and then starts spreading out the gems. My heart speeds up, the way it always does when I see stones like this. This is what I nerd out over. I can talk about carat weight and clarity and color ad nauseam.

But Antonio doesn't know that. He and his boss think I'm just another buyer, another go-between who buys the stones and then resells them.

That's mostly true.

I will sell these for a tidy profit.

But I also know what the fuck I'm looking at.

Calmly, I pull the loupe out of my drawer and pick up the first stone, taking my time with it. I weigh it. And when I'm satisfied, I set it aside and pick up the next.

Pink diamond from the Argyle mine in Western Australia. One of the rarest diamonds in the world. Roughly four carats.

"Are you going to examine all of them," Antonio asks, and I lift my eyes to him, raising an eyebrow.

He shifts on his feet and clears his throat as I pin him in a stare, not saying anything for a long moment.

"Do you have somewhere else to be?" I finally ask.

"No, of course not. Carry on."

My eyes flit from his face to his guards before I return to the task at hand.

Blue diamonds. White diamonds. Everything I discussed with Antonio's boss is here.

But there's one stone we need to have a conversation about.

I fist the one in question in my hand and then nod for Jack to take the others away. He quickly rolls them in the velvet and stows them in a locked hand-carry safe.

"This one." I open my hand and keep my eyes on Antonio, who licks his lips and has a light sheen of sweat on his brow. "Let's talk about it."

"What would you like to discuss?" he asks, trying to look innocent.

He's a bad fucking liar.

"Tell me about it."

His brows pull together for just a heartbeat. "Well, it's a blue Cullinan diamond, eight carats—"

"What's it worth," I cut in.

"Approximately eight million dollars."

I stare at him, unblinking, until he clears his throat and tugs at the collar of his shirt.

"This is worth about, oh . . ." I look down at it and tilt my head side by side, as if I'm pondering it. "Jack shit. It's fucking *fake*."

Antonio starts to shake his head, but I stand, and his eyes widen with fear.

Good.

He should be afraid.

"It's not fake," he says.

"Here's my loupe," I say, passing it over to him. "Have a look for yourself."

Carefully, he takes it from me and examines the stone, and by the time he looks back up at me, his face has gone white.

"I don't know how this happened."

Nodding, I sigh and put my hand out. Jack passes me a hammer, and I swing it at my side.

"The thing is, Antonio, I think you're skimming. I think you planted this fake, and you have the real stone, which you're going to sell yourself. That *really* pisses me off."

I glance at his guards.

"He's been paid in full for the real gemstones. You can leave."

Without thinking twice or arguing, the two men leave the room, and Antonio starts to shake.

"I swear, I don't know what happened. I would *never—*"

"Sure you would." I lean on the desk, as if we're just having a nice civilized conversation and Antonio isn't about to lose the function of his right hand. "It's eight million. A nice little take for someone like you, Antonio. I bet you only make about a million a year, so if you swipe one of these every six months or so, that puts you in a nice spot. Makes it so you don't have to do this forever. You can retire on a beach somewhere and disappear."

I shake my head, as if I'm disappointed in him.

"The thing is, I'm damn fucking smart. I've already learned everything there is to know about you. I know what your taxes look like, the balances in your bank accounts. Those match."

His shoulders loosen.

"However, they *don't* match the twenty million you have stashed in the Caymans. I also know that you have a sister in Orlando, who likes to go to Disney every Saturday. Your niece is in Paris, studying abroad."

He's sweating profusely now, and it brings me immense satisfaction.

"You see, I don't appreciate it when someone tries to double-cross me. What do I do when that happens, Jack?"

"You destroy them, boss."

"I've heard," Antonio mutters, and I tilt my head to the side.

"What have you heard?"

He shakes his head, like he didn't mean to say that out loud. So I get closer and stand over him. I have at least six inches on him.

"What. Have you. Heard?"

"You almost killed your wife," he whispers.

"Idiot," Jack mutters as anger moves through my veins.

"Is that what you heard, Antonio?"

He nods and licks his lips, and I turn to Jack.

"Different tool."

He takes the hammer and replaces it with my cleaver, and when I turn back, Antonio takes a step back, but I shake my head.

I strike fast, grab his hand, pin it to the desk, and then remove it with one hard chop of the cleaver.

Antonio starts to scream as one of my soldiers fires up a butane torch to cauterize the wound.

I can't have him bleeding out in my office.

"Now, you listen to me, you piece of shit. You're lucky I didn't kill you for simply *thinking* about my wife.

You stole from me, and not only will you pay for it, but you'll send a message back to your boss. If this happens again, I take your head without warning, am I clear?"

Tears roll down his face as he nods.

"Good. Have a nice day."

I turn my back on him, and my men escort him out. Jack sighs.

"Did you have to take the whole hand? This is going to be a bitch to clean up."

"You haven't cleaned up blood in a decade," I remind him. "We have people for that. And yes, I did. He mentioned my wife."

Jack shakes his head but knows better than to say anything else.

"That concludes my business," I tell him. "I'll be out with Natasha today. You can take the jet back if you want. I'm keeping eight men here with us."

"When will you be back in Vegas?"

"Tomorrow afternoon."

"I'll go back, then. Call me if you need me."

"Same goes."

Thirty-Nine

NATASHA

"I DON'T THINK there's much left in Beverly Hills for anyone else to buy," I say as we walk into our suite, and I drop my handbag on the entry table. It's our last night here, and I wanted to be back in time to see the sunset.

Watching the sun sink into the water, the sky shifting from blue to orange and purple, is the most magical thing I've ever witnessed. I know that we'll be back here —as guests; I don't need to own this resort—but I don't know when that might be, and I want to enjoy it.

"But did you get everything you wanted?" Julian asks as he follows me inside. All my purchases today will be on the flight to go with us tomorrow. They were taken straight to the plane rather than back here to the hotel.

"I got things I didn't *know* I wanted," I reply with a grin, and let him tug me into his arms, offering my lips up for a kiss.

This trip is exactly what we needed. I've never felt closer to Julian than I do now, and it's absolute bliss.

I'm also a little worried that it might all get ripped out from under me, but I'm choosing to trust him.

To trust *us*.

"Come on," he says, taking my hand and leading me out to the balcony.

My hand comes up to cover my mouth as I stare in wonder.

There's a full table set in the middle, with white plates covered with silver domes. Candles flicker, flowers cover every surface in red, pink, and white. It smells fucking amazing.

Music even plays from hidden speakers.

"Well, who knew you could be this romantic?"

"Literally no one," he says with a little laugh and wraps his arms around me, pulling my back against his front. "You said you wanted to eat here tonight, so . . . dinner is served."

He pulls my chair out for me, and when the dome is removed, my mouth waters at the sight of steak and potatoes with roasted vegetables. I'm starving.

Buying out Rodeo Drive will do that to a girl.

"You spoiled me today."

Julian lifts an eyebrow. "I simply took you shopping."

"Yeah and bought everything I looked at. You don't have to do that."

"I don't have to do anything at all, Angel. It was fun. I haven't shopped with you before."

"It *was* fun," I agree. "Thanks for going with me. It would have been boring without you."

"You'd have your detail with you," he reminds me, and I tilt my head to the side and stare at him like, *really?*

He chuckles. "How are you getting along with them, anyway?"

I refused to have Benji and Gary as my personal guards after the way they left me in front of my father's house that day. Julian didn't argue with me and assigned Danny and Jeremy as my guards. They're both strong and big and they never smile.

"I actually like them," I reply honestly, finishing my steak. "They're respectful, and they don't say much, but that's okay. They're giant and scary looking, and I feel safe when I can't be with you."

Julian nods. "Good. That's the goal. They're two of my best men, both trained in hand to hand, excellent marksmen, and they're smart."

"If they're two of your best, maybe you need them elsewhere," I say after pushing my empty plate aside. "Doing something more important."

Julian stares at me for a full heartbeat, his brows pulled together, and then he stands and offers me his hand.

"Let's go get comfortable."

We sit on the sofa that looks out to the water, and the sky is bright orange right now, reflecting in the ocean.

I love it here.

"Angel, I don't want Danny and Jeremy assigned to anyone but *you*. Because you're the most important assignment I could give them. They understand that if they fuck up and anything happens to you, I'll have their heads."

My jaw goes slack at that, and then I scowl up at him. "Julian—"

"Don't argue with me, Natasha. It's the way it is. They protect you, with their life if need be, or they die at my hand. I might also remind you that although it's the most important job, it's also one they enjoy because you don't fight them, don't try to evade them, and you're kind to them."

"I've had guards all my life." I shrug a shoulder. "I'm used to it. There's no reason to be a jerk to guys who are doing their job."

He brushes my hair behind my ear, and then reaches into his pocket and pulls out . . . *my ring.*

Except, it's not my ring. The setting is similar, and I'm pretty sure that's my diamond, but there are more stones, and it's set slightly differently.

I frown up at my husband as he turns it so I can see all of it.

"I altered this a bit," he says casually. "This is still your stone, the eight-carat diamond. But I added pink diamonds on the sides, and it's in a new setting."

"Why the new setting?" I ask as he slides it on my finger, and I turn it, admiring the way the light makes it sparkle.

"Because that bitch at the pawn shop touched it. And I wanted you to have something fresh."

To be honest, I hate that she touched it too.

"It's beautiful," I murmur, staring down at it, and then I lean up to kiss him. "Thank you."

He moves in for another kiss, but I hold up a finger

and hurry inside to where my oversize handbag is and pull out the box I've been carrying around since Julian left one of the stores to take a call. "I have something for you too."

I pass him the box with the bow, and he goes very still for a moment.

"It's a gift," I say with a nervous smile.

His eyes jump to mine. "You didn't have—"

"I don't *have* to do anything at all," I reply, echoing his own words, and his eyes narrow. "Just open it. If you hate it—"

"I won't," he says as he tugs the bow free and then opens the box, and his lips tip up in a small smile.

"I know you don't wear cuff links often, but I couldn't resist." They're yellow diamonds surrounded by yellow gold. "When I saw them, I knew you had to have them."

"Thank you." He tips my chin up and kisses me softly. "They're perfect."

I look back down at my ring. "What made you decide to go with pink diamonds?"

"A few reasons," he says, taking my hand and kissing the back of it. "First of all, you look gorgeous in pink. These are Argyle diamonds. The mine in Western Australia closed in 2020, and aside from red and blue diamonds, these are the rarest in the world. Your center stone is what's called fancy white. It's completely colorless and quite rare."

"This ring must be worth the same as a small country."

He smirks at that and then kisses the back of my hand again.

"Maybe."

"How do you know so much about jewelry?" I ask him.

"This is what I do, Natasha. I'm a gem importer. I deal in extremely rare stones."

I feel my cheeks heat. "Well, now I feel stupid."

My husband scowls and cups my cheek. "Why?"

"Because I got you those cuff links because they're *pretty*. I have no idea about the clarity or color, or—"

"You did well," he says, cutting me off. "These are canary diamonds, and without having a scale here to weigh them, I'd say they're about two carats each."

I blink at him in surprise. "They're exactly two each."

He nods and pulls a jeweler's loupe out of his pocket.

"You just carry that around with you?"

Julian laughs as he scoops me into his lap and picks up the cuff links. "I had work this morning, remember? I want you to look at them through this."

I do as he instructs, and he goes into great detail about all the things that make these diamonds an excellent choice, but I'm too busy getting turned on by the deep timbre of his voice and the feel of his arms around me, his lips near my ear.

God, I want him.

"So, you see, you made an excellent decision with these. I'll wear them often, Angel."

"I'm glad you like them."

He sets them aside and then cups my face and

captures my lips with his, kissing me in that firm, demanding way that he does, and I sink into him.

But before the kiss can go deeper, I hear a . . . *noise.*

I pull back and frown, listening.

"I hear something."

His lips twitch, but he doesn't stop me as I wiggle out of his lap and move to the railing, listening closer, and then I realize what I'm hearing.

"Yes, please, just like that . . ."

I stretch so I can look down, and *holy shit.*

"Julian," I hiss, and he's already laughing. "Get over here. You have to see this."

He stands and walks to me, but he doesn't look over the side of the railing. He brushes my hair away from my neck and leans in to press kisses there, making my skin tingle with awareness.

Was there really a time when I couldn't bear the thought of him touching me? Because now I can't live without his hands on me.

"There's a couple below us," I say softly.

"Mm-hmm." He nibbles down my shoulder, pulling my dress out of his way. "What are they doing, baby?"

"Fucking."

"Describe it to me."

Oh. Well, that sends a little thrill through me, and I look down again to see a woman bent over, grabbing onto the railing.

"She's bent over, and he's going to town on her. Oh! He just spanked her."

Julian chuckles next to my ear as he lets my dress puddle around my feet, and his fingers dive down the front of my panties. He groans when he finds me already wet.

"You like watching them, don't you, my dirty little angel?"

I tip my head back against his chest, unable to talk as he sinks those fingers inside me.

"Keep looking down," he says into my ear, moving those fingers in and out of me, brushing against my walls, over my G-spot perfectly. I follow the order, just in time to see the man turn her around and lay her out on one of the chairs on their balcony.

"They moved." I swallow hard when his thumb flicks my clit. How am I supposed to talk when he's doing these delicious things to me? "Now she's on her back on a chair and he's, oh God, he's . . . his face is . . ."

"What? Where's his face?"

"Between her legs." My own knees threaten to give out when his fingertips brush over my G-spot. "Oh my God, Julian."

"Are they naked?" he asks. "Where are her hands?"

I have to swallow thickly before I answer. "They're naked. And her hands are in his hair, and she's tugging on him, pulling him closer to her."

"You do that too," he murmurs directly into my ear, making me gasp at the gravel in his sexy voice. "You love to pull my face into your greedy little cunt while I feast on you, don't you?"

"Yes." God, I'll never survive his mouth. "He just spun her around again, so he's fucking her from behind."

"Mm, good idea." He rips my panties off my body, and then he's guiding the tip of his cock—when did he unfasten his pants? I didn't even hear it—through my sopping-wet slit, making sloppy noises, teasing me.

"Julian, please."

"What, Natasha? Be my good little slut and use your words."

"Fuck me."

I don't have to tell him twice. He slams into me, making me cry out and then slap my hand over my mouth to keep the sounds at bay, but my husband pulls my hand away, twists my arm back and holds it over my low back.

"Don't you *dare* keep quiet. I want you to scream my name when you come. I want every fucking soul in this resort to know who you belong to. No one gets to see you but me, but I'll be fucking damned if I won't let them all hear you while I wreck this gorgeous pussy."

Jesus Christ, the things his mouth does to me.

He yanks me back against him with every hard thrust. This isn't sweet, tender lovemaking.

This is primal, hard fucking, and I love it so much.

I've started to shake, my pussy grips onto him, and he growls before biting my shoulder blade.

"Fucking come, Natasha."

"Julian!" I cry out, not holding back at all as the orgasm washes through me. "Fuck yes, it's so good."

"Your pussy was made for me." He pushes in three more times, and then he's rocking against me, coming so hard that it spills out around him, coating my inner thighs.

I glance down, and the couple that was fucking are gone. I don't see anyone.

But I'm quite sure that someone heard us, and I don't hate the idea of that. In fact, I kind of love it.

At just the thought of it, my pussy spasms around him once more, and he chuckles as he kisses up my neck.

"Come on, my little voyeur, let's go do that again in the shower."

Forty

JULIAN

"I HATE THIS BUILDING," Natasha whispers next to me. We're in the elevator, headed up to the penthouse for family dinner.

I fold her into my arms and press my lips to the top of her head.

"This building will never hurt you. There's nothing here that can harm you, Angel. You're with me."

"I know." She clears her throat and steps away when the doors open. "It just gives me the creeps."

"Someday, I'll talk you into a tour of every inch of that club. I'll show you why it's safe and why you'd love it."

I press my lips to her ear.

"I know intimately how much you like to watch, Angel. We can explore all of your fantasies down there." I kiss her temple and then stride to the door with her hand in mine. "But for tonight, we're in the penthouse."

Her eyes are bright, and her lips are parted as she stares up at me.

She doesn't hate the idea of a private tour.

I move that up on my to-do list.

Not bothering to knock, I rest my palm on the security plate and then push inside. Jack won't be joining us. He and Spider are currently working on a project together.

In fact, he should be checking in with me soon.

We find everyone else in the kitchen, hovering around the island, taking bites of what looks like bruschetta.

"Hey!" Scarlett wraps her arm around Natasha's shoulders and gives her a squeeze. "You look *fab*. LA was fun?"

"It was great," Natasha confirms and smiles up at me. "How are you guys? What did I miss while I was gone?"

"Well, one of the guests got a little handsy the other night, and when Luke saw the dude with his hand on my ass, he took him downstairs and cut it off."

Natasha chokes on the sip of wine I just handed her and then stares at Luke, who's smiling smugly.

"Good job," I say to him, and he nods at me.

"You cut off *his hand*?" Natasha demands.

"There's a strict no-touching-Scarlett policy," Luke says with a shrug.

"Like, at the club in general, or is that a *Luke* rule?" Natasha asks.

"Both." He pops an olive in his mouth. "Fucker's lucky that his hand's the only thing he lost."

She frowns up at me. "Would you—"

"He'd no longer be breathing, Angel." I kiss her temple, and Lulu sighs as she wipes her hands on a towel.

"You two are adorable," she says with a smile.

I've never been referred to as *adorable* a day in my life.

Rome checks his phone, and then looks up at us.

"Guys, I need you to join me downstairs." He kisses his wife's temple. "We'll be back before dinner's ready, Firefly."

Natasha goes very still before her face turns up to me. She's suddenly fucking pale. "You're going to the club?"

I hate the uncertainty in her voice.

I smile down at her and then lean in to rest my lips near her ear. "No, baby. I'll never set foot in there without you again. You don't need to worry about that."

When I pull back to see her face, she doesn't look convinced.

"If you're not going to the club, where are you going?"

The room has grown silent, but I only have eyes for my Angel.

"Do you really want to know what this is, Natasha? I won't lie to you, but—"

"No," she interrupts and presses her lips together. "I don't think I want to know. But it's *not the club*."

"It's business," Rome replies before I can.

"Enjoy your friends, sweetheart." I kiss her forehead and then join the others, headed to the elevator.

"Your woman breaks the heart I don't even have," Mateo says, shaking his head.

"She's doing much better, but the club is a trigger," I reply, and Rome growls deep in his throat.

"I fucking hate that," he says.

"I'm going to come up with a way to change her perspective," I tell him. "She won't be afraid of it forever."

"How's Elliott doing?" Mateo asks.

"He hasn't been in my casino," Carson says.

"He's doing well." Frankly, I'm surprised by the improvement my son has made. I'm proud of him. "If he keeps his shit together for a few more months, I'll bring him in as a foot soldier. What's going on in the cell, Rome?"

"Do we get to kill someone?" Carson asks, speaking for the first time. I can tell that he's in one of his moods. If he's not joking and flirting with our girls, that means his dark side is itching to come out. And that's always bad news for someone and their will to live.

"Potentially," Rome says as we file out of the elevator and walk to the door at the end of the hall. Rome's men step out of the way, and we file inside the cell.

"Mendoza," Mateo says in surprise. "Looks like we *do* get to kill someone, brother."

Carson smiles.

It's not a happy smile.

It's a *I'm going to pull his lungs out of his throat* smile.

Correction: It's a happy smile for Carson.

"You're blowing this out of proportion." Mendoza looks clean and relaxed, as if he were watching Netflix in the comfort of his own living room. There's no blood. He's lounging in a metal chair, one leg crossed over the other, checking his manicure.

I glance at Rome and lift my eyebrow.

Rome shrugs.

"You were told to stay out of our city," Rome tells the head of the cartel. "And that if you ever did business here again, you wouldn't leave alive."

"I wasn't doing business," the man says calmly. "I was simply gambling."

"At the Four Leaf," Luke says. "Did you forget that we're allies with the Irish, you smug cunt?"

"No, you're not," Mendoza says, his bravado starting to slip.

"I guess Mendoza says who we are and aren't friends with, boys." Mateo pushes his hands in his pockets and rolls back on his heels. "Maybe we should have him on staff. He could be the secretary, so we're sure to remember who's who. Wait, that won't work. I like to fuck secretaries, and this piece of shit definitely isn't my type."

"Why are you in Vegas," Rome asks as he strides calmly to the tool bench and picks up a throwing star.

Rome has the best fucking accuracy of any of us, no matter the weapon. Sniper rifles, knives, handguns—you name it, and he'll hit the bull's-eye.

"None of your business," Mendoza says.

Rome smirks and throws the star, hitting Mendoza in the upper thigh, right by his dick.

"Good shot," I say with a nod as Mendoza screams.

Ten minutes and eight throwing stars later, Mendoza holds his hand up.

"I'm not doing business, that's the truth. I was just supposed to gather intel. Damien said it would be worth it."

In less than one second, Carson goes from leaning

casually against the wall to hovering over Mendoza with his hands around his neck.

"Say that again."

"He can't breathe," I remind my brother. "Don't kill him yet, we're just getting to the good part."

Carson's face slowly turns to me, and I shake my head.

"Not. Yet."

He loosens his hold and Mendoza takes a breath.

"Who are you spying on?" Mateo asks.

"You," Mendoza replies without a beat. "All of you. That's all I know. I gather whatever information I can and send it to an email address on the dark web, and I get paid."

"I want to know what you've told him," Rome says. "What do you think you know, Mendoza?"

"Mostly that Julian has a pretty new wife."

"Now," I say, and Carson tightens his hands again, squeezing until the man goes purple and the life drains out of his body.

"He might have had more information," Mateo says casually.

"I'll hack into his shit and find out exactly what he has. But I don't buy for a second that he's doing it for Damien. He said that name to get a rise out of Carson."

"Worked," Rome says.

"Did the Irish call to tell you Mendoza had been at the Four Leaf?" I ask.

"Yeah, this morning. My men found Mendoza in a room off the strip and brought him here. His belongings are in the room next door."

"I'll only need his electronics," I reply. "The rest can go with him to the graveyard."

We make our way back upstairs for dinner. When we walk into the penthouse, we can hear the girls laughing in the kitchen.

Christ, I love my wife's laugh.

"They were doing it out in the open," Natasha says, and I pause. We all stop before Natasha can see that we're here.

"You'd enjoy the club," Scarlett assures my girl. "If that did it for you, girl, you're missing out."

I nod and we walk into the kitchen, catching their attention.

"I'm hungry," Mateo says.

"Dinner's ready," Lulu replies with a grin as Rome wraps his arms around her from behind.

"We're going to a show," Natasha tells me. "Just us girls, tomorrow night."

"We'll have guards," Lulu assures me.

"Your detail is invited, but we aren't?" Rome asks.

"Well, the detail isn't technically invited, either, but you won't let us go without them."

"It'll be fun," Natasha says, smiling up at me and pats me on the chest. I capture her hand in mine and press it over my heart. "You'll live without me for one evening."

I love that she's not asking, she's *telling me*. She's come such a long way since we got married. She's so much stronger, so sure of herself.

It's a fucking turn-on.

Of course, everything about this woman drives me out of my mind.

"I'll try, Angel."

Forty-One

NATASHA

"NO."

I'm fastening an earring—pink diamonds, of course, because my husband is over the top—in our bathroom and glance at Julian, who's standing in the doorway, leaning with his arms crossed, watching me with hot, dark eyes.

"No, what?" I frown as I reach for the other earring. My hair is twisted up to keep it off my neck, so I don't get too hot. My makeup looks great, if I do say so myself.

I love a smoky eye.

"You're not wearing that dress."

I glance down at the white slip dress—yes, I went for white voluntarily—and then back at him.

"Why not?"

"That's not a dress, it's something you wear *under* a dress."

"No, it's a dress, all by itself." I smile at him, and when I've secured the second earring, I hold my hands out at my sides and do a little turn.

"It doesn't even cover your perfect ass, Angel."

I glance back in the mirror. "Yes, it does. I mean, I won't bend over, but—"

"If you bent over, I'd have to set fire to the arena. Natasha, *no*."

I sigh and shake my head, frame his face in my hands and lean into him.

"I'm wearing this dress tonight. Because I'm an adult, and you don't get to tell me what I can and can't wear."

"Yes, I do get to do exactly that. You're my wife."

"Fine. I don't want you to wear these shirts anymore. They show off your shoulders, and I don't want other women looking at them."

"Done." He doesn't even hesitate. "It'll be rectified by morning."

I blink up at him, stunned that he'd do that for me. "I was kidding."

"I'm not, Angel."

"*You* bought this in LA."

"I thought you'd wear it for *me*. In the bedroom. Not when you go out with the girls to the Sphere for a goddamn concert."

"Well, that's where it's going tonight." I stomp around my stubborn husband and walk into our closet, where I reach for the gorgeous Dior shirt dress that falls past my knees, so pretty with tigers and blue flowers all over it. I unfasten the row of buttons that fall down the entire front, then I shrug it on and cinch it with a belt, so you can just see the slip underneath, like a peekaboo. The neckline is asymmetrical, so it falls over one shoulder, showing off the spaghetti strap of the dress. "I love a layered look."

I turn and smile at my husband. His eyes have narrowed. His hands are in his pockets.

"Was that always your plan?"

"Yep." I check myself in the mirror as I slide my feet into strappy Dior heels, then grab the crossbody handbag that matches. "If you remember, I've never been one to show a lot of skin, Julian. You never need to worry about that."

He sighs and then he's behind me, holding me.

"I love the way you dress, but I won't ever be okay with other men seeing what's mine. I can't change that."

I turn in his arms and cup his face. "I don't care if anyone else in the world looks twice at me, Julian. *Yours* is the only attention I want."

"I care," he says as he lowers his forehead to mine.

"But you're the only one I love."

He goes very still, and his eyes bounce back and forth between mine.

"Say that again."

"I love you," I say softly, and then he's kissing me like a man starved. I'll have to reapply my lipstick, but I don't care.

"I'd like to be a dick and keep you home with me tonight," he says. "Because I've been waiting to hear those words from you for a long fucking time."

"You'll hear them again," I reply with a smile. "And I *really* want to go to the concert. But I love you, and I'll see you later."

He kisses me again, softer this time, and then once

I've touched up my makeup, I'm in the SUV with my husband and our men.

Danny and Jeremy are up front. They'll go to the concert with me.

Julian's men are following us.

"I'll be with Mateo and Rome, but I'll be available when you're ready to go home," he says and takes my hand in his, linking our fingers. "You're meeting with the penthouse designer tomorrow."

Over the past month, I've mostly worked with her virtually. There wasn't anything to be done on-site, but now things are starting to be installed, and I want to see it myself.

"Yes, at noon. I can't wait to see it all come together. Have you dropped in to have a look?"

"Of course I have." He smirks and then kisses my hand. "You're going to love it."

The SUV pulls up to a VIP entrance at the venue, and as always, Julian gets out first to make sure it's safe.

"Be safe tonight. I love you," I tell him after a kiss to his lips, and then Scarlett and Lulu arrive, and with all six of our guards, we walk inside.

We're shown to a private elevator that takes us up to our premium suite. I shouldn't be surprised by the opulence around us, and yet, *I am*.

"Holy shit, this is *nice*," Scarlett says, and all I can do is nod.

There's a buffet spread out fit for a freaking king. Pasta, sliders, flatbread pizzas. We have an attendant, who immediately takes our drink order, and then I survey the rest of the room.

There are couches, windows where we can sit to watch the concert, but there's also a private balcony with normal seats for us to watch everything unfold.

The stage is *right there*.

"Who arranged for this?" I ask, looking over at my friends.

"I told Rome what we wanted to do, and he said he'd handle the tickets," Lulu says, also looking thunderstruck. "I thought that meant he'd buy eleven seats. We'd be in the middle, our guards on either side, and empty seats at the end. I had no idea he'd buy out a box for the night."

"We need to do this once a month," I decide and hold my glass up to clink with theirs. "Cheers, friends."

AT SOME POINT, I LOST MY SHOES.

I mean, I know where they are. I kicked them off because we'd been dancing around our suite, and the heels were killing me, but now I think I should put them back on. It doesn't seem like a good idea to walk out of here barefoot.

"That was *so fun*," Lulu says with a happy sigh. "And the suite is the way to go. I need to find out who the chef is and ask them for their batter recipe. The chicken fingers were delicious."

"How are you sober enough for this conversation?" Scarlett asks with a snort.

I manage to wiggle my feet into the heels, and we each use the private restroom in our suite before we head out to our guys, who, according to Danny, are waiting for us downstairs.

"Julian didn't text me even once," I say, frowning down at my phone.

So I decide to drunk text him.

> Me: Do you hate me?

The bubbles jump on the screen.

> Julian: Of course not. Why would you ask that?

> Me: Because you didn't text me at all! Are you mad?

I follow the others into the elevator and lean on the wall as it starts to descend, still looking at my phone.

> Julian: You're with your friends, baby. I'm not interrupting. Did you have fun?

I grin and nibble my lip.

> Me: Yes! That suite is INCREDIBLE! We want to do this every month for girl's night. But I miss you. I'm drunk. Ready to get cozy and curl up with you. Naked. With you inside me and your hand wrapped around my neck. I REALLY like that, Julian.

The elevator doors open, and I follow the others as I

wait for a response from my man. Lulu and Scarlett are singing and dancing, and I smile up at them before I turn my attention back to my phone.

> Julian: Jesus, get out here so I can take you home and fuck you, Angel.

I grin and am just sliding my phone in my bag when I hear gunshots. I'm slammed to the ground by Danny, who's covering me with his whole huge body, as people scream and scramble.

Something drips on me, and I realize that it's blood.

"You're bleeding," I yell, but Danny doesn't answer me. He's shooting back at someone and yelling out orders, and it's pandemonium around us.

I try to look for Lulu and Scarlett, but I can't see anything because Danny's blocking my vision.

Then a gun is cocked over us, and I stare up into a barrel.

"Give me the girl, fuck face."

Before Danny can even reply, I watch in horror as the man's head explodes over us, and then Julian's standing there, his face mutinous.

"Baby, are you hurt? Shit, you're bloody."

"Not mine." I shake my head wildly as Danny rolls to the side and Julian pulls me into his arms. "He's hit. Danny's hit. Where's Jer—"

I look to my right and see Jeremy lying on his back with lifeless eyes, a huge hole in the middle of his chest.

"*No.*"

"Let's go," Julian snaps to someone, and then he's carrying me, running, to our SUV. He sets me carefully inside, kisses me hard and fast, and then says, "Stay. I'll be right back."

"Here," Julian says, passing me a glass of whiskey.

We're in a penthouse that I'm not familiar with. Not in the Rapture building—this is closer to the venue.

It's Mateo's home. And it suits him. All dark colors and glass. Spacious. The city lights are an incredible backdrop.

Under any other circumstances, I'd love being here.

"They're Sergei's men," Carson says as he hangs up the phone. "All of the soldiers killed were Russian."

My eyes shoot up to Carson, and he's watching me with a steady gaze.

"Oh, fuck that," I announce and kick off my shoes, then stand to pace. "Absolutely fucking *not*."

"Angel, we got positive ID—"

"That's not what I'm talking about, I'm not in denial," I reply, spinning to face my husband. "I'm so over that piece of shit that sired me. *Kill him*, Julian. I want him gone. I want the entire organization wiped out."

Julian tilts his head, watching me. The room is quiet, and I turn in a circle to take them in. It's our usual crew, sitting all over the spacious room. My girls are sitting with their men. Carson and Mateo are standing. All four of the guys' number twos are nearby as well. And they're watching me like they've never seen me before.

"I've *had it* with that man trying to hurt me and the people I love. My *family*." I shake my head and clench my fists. "He's done. Now, how do we take him out?"

Julian's eyebrows climb in surprise. "I'll take care of it, Angel."

"I want to help."

"You want to kill your father?" Carson asks, and his lips tip up on the side. "I knew I liked you."

"Yes, I want him dead, and I think it's pretty obvious that I need to be the bait that brings him out of his hidey-hole."

"Fuck no," Julian growls. "You will never mention yourself and the word *bait* in the same sentence again, do you understand me?"

"It makes sense," I insist and reach for my husband, taking his hands in mine. "Look, I'm not a good liar. Like, not at *all*—"

"You're not selling yourself well, sweetie," Scarlett says.

"But I can lie to that man all day long. I've done it my whole life. I don't know what he wants from you, why he keeps fucking with you, but I can help end it."

Julian watches me for a moment, his eyes full of emotion. *He doesn't want me to do this.* Then he turns to his brothers, and I follow his gaze.

"I think you should tell her," Rome says with a shrug. "It's her dad."

Julian sighs and drags his hand down my back, as if he's soothing himself as well as me.

"Your father wants to dismantle us from the inside out," he tells me. "He's pissed because we wouldn't bring him into our organization. We don't play well with him. The marriage between our families was supposed to be a peace treaty, but Sergei took it too far, and now he's obviously not upholding the deal."

"After the wedding," Mateo adds, "he came to us and basically demanded we include him in our business dealings, since Julian married you. He's an entitled ass. No offense."

I grin at him. "No offense taken. I already knew that about him."

"I didn't know that Natasha had this badass side," Lulu says to Scarlett, "but it's fucking hot."

"Agreed," Scarlett says, making me chuckle.

"I didn't always feel this . . . *confident*," I reply. "But I'm *pissed*. It's because of *him* that Julian kicked me out of my own house and I had nowhere to go."

Julian swears under his breath.

"My father used to beat the shit out of me. Broke my ribs, stomped my toes. He got off on hurting me, and now he's *still* hurting me because damn it, I *liked* Jeremy. And Danny's hurt. And he could have hurt any one of you. My mom is no better. She used to throw me under the bus with my father all the time to take the focus off of her. I had nannies that showed me more affection. If I died, my own parents wouldn't care. It wouldn't even be a blip for them. They're not my family. *You* are. And now, that asshole is threatening my organization. If I've learned anything since marrying Julian, it's that we don't stand for that. I should know.

So yeah, it seems I do have a badass side when the people I love are threatened. And goddamn it, I'm a fucking queen in this city, and they fucked with the wrong girl."

"I like her too," Spider says to Carson, and I admit, that feels good.

I turn back to Julian, who's staring at me like I hung the moon.

"He made me go to that lunch with him, and he tried to get me to tell him everything I know about you. Let me set up another lunch."

"No."

"Just hear me out."

Julian sighs, clearly on edge, and I keep talking.

"I'll lie and tell him that I'm pissed at you. You did . . . something. I'll make it up. And I'll give him some bogus information and lure him somewhere. I'll make it sound *big*. My father's ego is gigantic. I can feed into that and make it sound like there's something going on that he doesn't want to miss out on."

"Look at you, you little manipulator."

"I would *never* have had the guts to do this before." I shake my head and take a breath. "But if he's not stopped, he'll keep doing this, over and over again. He could hurt you, and I won't have it, Julian."

"He's not going to hurt me, Angel." Julian pulls me into his arms and kisses the top of my head. "You're so fucking brave."

"I'm not brave, I'm pissed."

"Still brave," he whispers.

"It makes sense," Rome says from across the room.

"We'll have eyes on her at all times. We'll make sure she's never in danger."

Julian's grip on me is so tight, as if he's afraid of losing me.

He pulls back and frames my face in his warm hands.

"Are you sure, sweetheart?"

"Absolutely. I'll go in with a wire. You'll hear everything."

"I'll snipe from above," Rome adds. "If he so much as sneezes at her wrong, I'll shoot him between the eyes."

Julian sighs and then reluctantly nods.

"Let's get the plan together."

Forty-Two

NATASHA

IT'S the makeup that's messing with me. Sending me back to that dark place where I'm afraid of everything and everyone, including my own shadow.

A week has passed since the incident after the concert, and on the outside it looks like we're just going about our normal lives. I met with the designer at the penthouse. Julian continues to work. The guys are pretending that they don't know who attacked us that night and have sent out feelers to get intel.

But on the inside, we've been planning.

And every night, Julian has tried to talk me out of this.

"We can come up with a different way, angelos mou." He rests his forehead against mine, holding me so close. *"I don't want you anywhere near him."*

"It's easier this way. And it's my own way of looking him in the eyes so he understands that he didn't win. He didn't beat me."

He's not convinced that he should allow this, but Julian also loves me, and despite wanting to protect me, he respects my need for closure. To do this piece of it myself.

But now I'm standing here in our bathroom, in our *sanctuary*, staring in the mirror, and my stomach rolls.

My right eye is black and purple with yellow around the edges, and I have a bruise on my jawline as well. My wrist is in my brace again.

"Wow, this is pretty good if I do say so myself," Scarlett says as she steps back to take in her handiwork.

She and Lulu came over this morning to help me get ready and for moral support. I had no idea that Scarlett was so great with makeup and costumes, but she's *fantastic*. I don't even look like myself right now.

"I would do a split lip," she says, moving her head back and forth like she's contemplating it, "but I worry about it coming off on a glass, if you drank something."

"Let's keep it simple," I agree. "Okay, now clothes."

We decide on simple jeans and a white T-shirt and sneakers. And then I'm ready to go.

Julian won't be with me, but he and the other men will be nearby. They'll have eyes and ears on me because I'm wearing a wire, and I have the tiniest earpiece in so I can hear Julian's voice.

"Test," he says into my ear, and I grin.

"I can hear you, husband."

"Aww, is he talking to you?" Lulu asks as she walks with us to the front door.

"Yeah. He's nervous."

"Of course I'm nervous. My wife is walking into the fucking lion's den."

I grin and then hug my friends before I climb into the back of the Range Rover and take a deep, shaky breath.

I can't hear what's happening with the rest of the operation. Only Julian, and only when he opens that line of communication. My man is *damn good* with electronics, and he set this whole thing into motion. The eyes and ears, the strategy, everything. Luckily, I was able to tell him where in the restaurant my father prefers to sit, and he could build everything around that.

The ride into town is quiet, and I keep wringing my hands in my lap.

"The makeup is good," Danny says, watching me in the rearview mirror. "The boss won't like it, but it's good."

"It's pretty realistic," I agree with a nod and nibble on my naked bottom lip. I'm not wearing any makeup at all aside from the stuff to make it look like Julian uses me as a punching bag. "How are you feeling, Danny?"

"Never better."

My guard's arm was just grazed, but still, a gunshot wound is a gunshot wound. He refused to take any time off, and he's hardly left my side since that night.

I know that Danny will be with me for a very long time. I trust him implicitly, second only to Julian.

"I don't have any reason to be nervous," I mutter, but I know that's not true. My father is unpredictable on a good day. If I say even one thing that pisses him off, he could pull his gun and shoot me in the face.

I wouldn't put it past him.

"If you don't want to do this, say the word, and it all stops now," Julian says in my ear.

"I'm fine," I reply and do my best to believe it.

This is going to work.

Danny finds a parking space at the shopping center, and then he and my new guard, Elio, walk with me to the restaurant.

"You've got this," Danny says quietly, so only I can hear. "You're not the girl he thinks you are. Just follow the plan. We're all right here. I won't let anything happen to you, Boss Lady."

I nod. I want to smile up at him, but I don't want to break character.

"Thank you," I reply.

"I love you," Julian says into my ear. "If anything feels off, use your hand gesture, and we'll take him out."

"I love you too," I murmur before I look up at Danny. "I'll be out shortly."

He nods, and the two guards stand just inside the restaurant while I'm shown to my father's table. He's nothing if not a man of habit, sitting at the table I knew he would be. He's not alone today. Because of course he's not. He has his second, Viktor, with him, and they're sitting side by side.

Viktor always gave me the creeps. He's got to be close to sixty, and he never takes his eyes off my tits. Even when I was sixteen, he leered at me.

Gross.

Papa's eyebrow climbs when he sees my face. He

doesn't stand to greet me this time, he just waits silently as I slip into the chair across from him.

I'm meek. Timid. My hands shake because I'm nervous, but I know that he'll think it's because I'm afraid of him.

"Daughter," he says tightly. "To what do we owe this lunch?"

I clear my throat and look around, as if I'm making sure no one can overhear our conversation.

"You're doing so great," Julian whispers in my ear.

"I-I needed to see you," I say quietly, not meeting his eyes. "Because you were right, Papa."

My father leans back in his chair, his hands loosening from their fists. He's already starting to drop his guard.

"And what was I right about, Natasha?"

"Everything," it's said on a whisper. "He's not a good man."

I look up at him and see that he's sneering at the bruises on my face.

"He hits me, and I caught him . . . *doing things* with our housekeeper."

Papa snorts and Viktor flat out laughs.

But Julian growls in my ear, and it bolsters my confidence.

"Papa, please can I come home?"

"No, a deal is a deal, Natasha. You're his problem now. His mouth to feed. I told you before that you're not welcome back in my house."

"I should have listened to you." I bite my lower lip and let the tears fall. I can't usually produce tears on command, but right now, I feel for the young girl who endured so much at the hands of this devil. So much pain and fear. How my mother would laugh when he hit me. How they wouldn't care if I fell and hurt myself.

I brush a tear aside just as Julian speaks low in my ear.

"The compound is compromised. Communications are down, and the operation is underway. You've stalled him long enough, Angel."

"Yes, you should have. I know what's best. I *always* fucking know what's best. If you'd just done what you were told, you'd be out of that house by now and back with us."

"That would be a shame."

I square my shoulders and look up at my father, dead in the eye. A muscle in his cheek twitches.

"Do you understand what it is to be beaten every day of your life?"

Papa rolls his eyes, and Viktor shakes his head, as if I'm a young girl who never learns her lessons.

But I've learned more than they'll ever know. They tried to shape me into the proper Mafia wife, but instead, I'm a goddamn Mafia *queen*. I've taken abuse from this man, the one who's supposed to love me, my entire life, and it ends today. *I'm* the one about to take him down, and he's going to listen to every fucking word I have to say. Because I know that Julian and my new family would *never* let these men hurt me.

"Do you, Papa? To be tormented. Taunted. Every day. You didn't let me have friends. You didn't let me do anything except study, play the piano, and wither away in that godforsaken, gaudy, over-the-top eyesore that you call a house."

"I. Will. End. You," Papa says, and I lift my hand, put my pointer finger in the air, and the next thing I know, Viktor falls to the ground with a gunshot wound between the eyes.

"No, you won't."

JULIAN

VIKTOR FALLS out of his chair, and I exhale before I glance over at Rome, who's lying on his stomach, his sniper rifle propped against his shoulder.

"You're lucky you didn't miss."

"I never miss," is his calm reply.

Rome and I are already on the move, down the stairway of the building across from the restaurant, and out the doors, running over to finish this.

"We're with you," Carson says as he and Mateo join us.

"You won't do shit to me," Natasha spits at her father in my ear. "Never again. Because right now, the Kings of Vegas army has infiltrated your compound, and they're leveling it and killing everyone inside, including Mama and her stupid fucking tennis coach."

We burst inside the empty restaurant—Sergei didn't even question why there was no one else here when he arrived—and I'm at my wife's side in seconds.

"No!" He stands, but before he can pull his weapon,

Carson and Rome have him, and they restrain him, but they don't take him away yet.

"Anything else you want to say to dear ol' dad?" Carson asks my wife.

She walks around the table and stands in front of her father. He's glaring down at her, spittle coming out of his mouth. He's breathing hard. Fuck, I'll be lucky if the old fucker doesn't have a heart attack before I can get him in my cell.

"I should have fucking killed you the day you were born," he growls at his daughter.

Natasha tilts her head to the side, watching him.

"Yeah, you should have," she says. "Because I'm the reason you won't live past today. *Me.* Not a man. Not another Mafia don or someone powerful. Your small daughter, who always did as she was told and didn't talk back to you. The one you terrified just for the fun of it."

She rears back and punches him, right across the face. His head knocks to the side, and then he glares down at her again.

"I will haunt you for the rest of your life."

I want to tug her against me, but Natasha steps closer and lifts her chin. "No. You won't. I won't lose one minute of sleep over the pain you're about to feel. You deserve it."

She backs away and reaches blindly for my hand, which I immediately give her.

"I'm done."

Natasha turns her back on her father, and the guys drag him out of here. We have a cell waiting for him.

I can't wait to get started on the son of a bitch.

It almost breaks my heart when Natasha turns her face up to mine.

"Christ, I hate seeing you like this. You need to wash this shit off right now, Angel."

She smiles, and then her perfect face crumples and she starts to cry. I pull her into me and rub my hands up and down her back.

"I'm not sad," she howls into my chest.

"I know, it's the adrenaline wearing off. I fucking hated every minute of that. Never again, do you hear me?"

"No, you can handle all of the Mafia work in this family," she agrees, and lets me lead her out to the car. "I'm officially retired from that. It was my first and only assignment."

"Thank fuck." I kiss her head, her temple, and then tip her chin up so I can ravage her mouth. "You were magnificent in there. I'm so fucking proud of you, baby."

"I'm proud of me too. Are you going to kill him today?"

Fuck no. That asshole is going to live for months in my cell. I'm going to have a lot of fun with him.

"You don't need to worry about it. As far as you're concerned, he died about twenty minutes ago."

She nods and lets out a breath, then leans on me as Danny drives us toward the mansion.

"I'll drop you off at home, and then I have to go back to work."

Natasha scowls up at me. "You don't have to take me all the way home. I'm sure I can go hang out with Lulu.

Or take me to our penthouse. They're delivering bedroom furniture today."

"You don't want to go home?"

"I want to be close to you. So if you're working, just take me somewhere in the city."

I watch her face, to make sure she's telling me the truth, and then I tell Danny to take us to the Rapture building.

"I'd rather you weren't sitting in a construction zone all day, around men I don't know."

Natasha rolls her eyes. "I have Danny and Elio with me."

"I don't care. Text Lulu and see if she's home."

"She is. She and Scarlett have been blowing up my phone, wondering how it went. I just told them I'll be there soon."

"Good."

Suddenly, she unbuckles her belt and climbs into my lap, straddling me on the seat, and buries her face in my neck, holding on tight.

"Angel, you should be in your seat belt."

"I'm safer right here." She kisses my neck so sweetly. "Fuck, I was scared."

"I had you every step of the way."

"I know. You're the only reason I was able to do it." She kisses her way to my lips and then brushes her mouth across mine. "I love you so much."

"I love you too."

"I kind of need you right now." Her blue eyes are on fire as the words are whispered against my lips just as Danny pulls into the parking garage beneath Rapture.

He parks, and I bark at him, "Get the fuck out."

Natasha grins against my lips. "Does that mean that you're going to fuck me in this car?"

"Yeah, Angel, I'm going to wreck your perfect pussy right here in this car."

The windows are tinted, so no one can see inside. I may not care if anyone can hear her, but they won't see her.

I'd have to take their eyes for that.

She shimmies off my lap and works on getting her jeans off, and then she's straddling me once more, her hands on my neck, kissing the fuck out of me.

"You're not in charge here, beautiful girl."

"I know." She presses that hot pussy against my still-covered cock and makes me see stars. "But I need you to fuck me, Julian."

I push two fingers inside her, and she lets her head drop as she moans, her mouth opens, that bottom lip so fucking tempting.

"I'll fuck you, baby. You're already wet. Why are you wet, Natasha?"

"Because I'm free, and I need to feel you inside of me."

Adrenaline is a funny thing. For some people, they need to be reminded that they're alive. And if my wife needs my cock after everything that went down today, then that's exactly what she'll have.

"Take me out," I order her before biting her lower lip hard enough to taste the coppery essence of her blood on my tongue. When her hand wraps around my shaft, I push up into her grip, urging her to touch me harder. "I'm not feeling gentle, Natasha."

She shakes her head manically. "No. I don't need gentle. Fuck me hard. Jesus, please, Julian."

I rip her panties in two and toss them aside, and then slam inside her, making us both groan with how perfect it feels.

"Yes," she whispers as she starts to move. "I love how you fill me up."

"I never stop wanting you," I growl before lifting her shirt, pulling her bra down, and wrapping my lips around her hard nipple. "Christ, you're all I fucking *see*."

Her hips are moving fast, up and down, and I know I won't last like this, with her so desperate for me.

"I need you to come, baby." I press my thumb to her clit, and she shivers. "That's right. I need you to come all over my cock. Give it to me."

She moans, and then her walls contract around me, milking my own release from my body, and I come hard, pushing up until we're a panting, sweaty mess.

"It's a mind fuck to be inside you with your face bruised up, Natasha."

She lets out a surprised laugh and then kisses me hard before wrapping her arms around my neck and holding on tight.

"I'll go up and wash it off. I'll be normal again when you pick me up later."

"I love you."

She smiles down at me, and everything in my world is fucking perfect. "I love you too."

Forty-Four

NATASHA

"I'LL GO UP WITH YOU," Julian insists as he escorts me to the elevator. "I know you don't like this building."

I can feel his come seeping out of me, and I'm reminded that I really do need a bathroom. But also, in the light of day, with everything else that's happened, this building doesn't seem so . . . *scary*.

"It's the middle of the afternoon, so there shouldn't be very many people at Rapture, right?"

Julian's gaze finds mine, and he lifts an eyebrow. "It's not open yet."

"Can you get in anyway?"

He turns to face me now and tips my chin up. "I can get in. Are you saying you want that tour?"

"I'm feeling particularly brave today," I reply with a small smile. "So, if you have the time—"

"I have all the time in the world for you." He pulls his phone out of his pocket as he pushes the button for Rapture, and I assume he calls Rome. "I'm stopping in at

Rapture with Natasha, just for a tour. We won't be long. Thanks."

He hangs up and slips his phone back in his pocket, then threads his fingers through mine and lifts my hand to his lips.

"This is a good idea," he says. "You can see it when there's nothing going on."

He leads me out of the elevator and down a hallway, and we're in the bar area. I remember this from that night that Elliott brought me here.

That was so long ago now.

"Lulu works here," I say softly, taking in the black leather, all the bottles of liquor behind the bar, the low tables with couches surrounding them.

"Yes, part time now," Julian agrees. "Each person is allowed two drinks, max."

"Why?"

He wraps his arm around my shoulders. "So that people don't get too drunk and hurt each other in the playroom."

I nod, taking that in. "I like that rule."

"It's a good one. Are you ready to see the playroom?"

After swallowing hard, I turn a brave face up to my husband. "Sure. Let's do this."

He grins and nibbles on my lips before he guides me to the heavy double doors that lead into the space where people can openly have sex.

Where the lounge is done in dark, rich colors, the playroom is in white with jewel-toned furniture all over the big space. White sheer curtains hang to give it a mystical feel. There are beds, couches, benches. Lots of chains and shackles. Restraints. There's even a cross that I saw someone tied to that one night, getting whipped.

That's a hard pass for me.

I know there are private rooms, too, because I was in one. I'm not ready to go down that hallway right now, so we stay put, here in the middle of the playroom.

"What are you thinking?"

I sigh and shrug one shoulder. "It looks . . . I don't know. Scary. Interesting. Humiliating. Sexy."

"It can be all of those things and more, depending on the person and what they want to get out of the experience."

I turn to him and brace one hand on my hip. "Did you have sex in this room?"

"Yes."

"What did you come here for?"

His face doesn't change. He's somber, and he reaches out to brush my hair over my shoulder, then rubs his thumb over the pulse point in my neck.

"Please remember that I'm twice your age, Natasha, and that you have absolutely nothing to be jealous or uncomfortable about. I came here to fuck. That simple. To get off. I don't have particular kinks that I need to indulge in order to be satisfied. I simply needed to get my dick wet, no matter what hole someone let me do that in."

I wrinkle my nose. "That's . . ."

"The truth," he replies and frames my face in his big hands. "I never claimed to be a good man, Angel. But now my priorities have completely shifted. I want you, and that's it. If you decide that this isn't for you, we never have to step foot in here again. If you want to give it a try, as long as your kinks don't include someone besides me touching you, I'm open to listening to suggestions. You're in control when it comes to this. I don't need it. I have my every fantasy in my bed with me every night. I'm a lucky man."

A slow smile spreads across my face. I'm not jealous over anyone who came before me. There hasn't been anyone else *since* me, and that's all that matters as far as I'm concerned.

And having sex in the open really isn't my thing, but . . .

"Talk to me," he says, and leans down to kiss me softly.

"I kind of like to watch." I press my lips together and grin back at him when he smiles down at me. "I mean, who knew? But I *don't* want anyone to see us because I know that there are already women here who've seen your monster cock, and they don't get that privilege anymore."

"How about this. Whenever you're ready, we'll come back in the evening. We'll just watch others. You can see what goes on when everything is consensual, and then you can decide if you want to play or if you want to go home and let me fuck you until you can't walk for a month."

"I mean, you can *always* do that," I reply with a laugh. "Okay. That sounds good to me."

"I'll always keep you safe, agapi mou." *My love.* I love it when he speaks to me in Greek.

"I know you will." He takes my hand and leads me

back to the elevators, so I can go be with my friends and he can go finish dismantling my father and his empire.

"You're the best thing that ever happened in my life," I tell him softly as I lean my head on his arm. "The best damn thing."

Forty-Five

JULIAN

Three Months Later

MY WIFE IS UPSTAIRS, in our newly finished penthouse, learning how to make pasta from scratch with Lulu. She's safe and happy and so fucking amazing that it still sometimes stuns me that she's *mine*.

She's all mine.

But I had to leave her so I could come down to the cell to finish a project that's been ongoing for three months.

Elliott nods as I near the cell. My boy looks strong and fit. He's added new tattoos to his arms and chest, and he's dressed in dark-gray chinos with a navy button-down. I brought him on as a foot soldier last month, and so far, he's doing me proud.

"How's it going down here?" I ask him.

"He's alive," he replies steadily. I'm surprised that he

volunteered for this duty, but he did it without flinching. "Barely."

"Why are you down here, Elliott?" There's no censure in my voice. I'm truly curious.

"Because you gave me the job."

"I don't mean that. I mean, why did you offer to do it? You spent weeks down here, behind that door. I would think that this is the last place you'd want to be."

He blows out a breath and shoves his hand through his hair.

"I fucked up with Natasha. I'm glad that she's safe and that you two are happy. I really am, this isn't some weird plot to, like, steal her away or anything."

I narrow my eyes, and he keeps talking.

"But I feel bad for the way I treated her. I was drunk most of the time, sometimes I was high or stoned, but that's no excuse. You were right before, when you said that you never taught me to treat women that way. I don't know why I thought it was okay. I guess I feel like I owe her this. I'll babysit her asshole of a father until he's dead, as sort of an unspoken favor to her. And then I'll close the door on it."

I reach out and cup the back of his neck. "I'm proud of you."

His eyes, so much like my own, flare in surprise. "You are."

"Yeah, I am. You're doing well. Keep it up."

Elliott swallows hard and nods. "I will. Are you going to kill him today?"

"Looks like it."

"Good because I want the fuck out of this basement."

I laugh and clap him on the shoulder. "Go. Send someone else in to clean up."

Elliott nods and waits for me to go inside. I don't bother to close the door behind me.

"Hello, Sergei."

The man moans but doesn't form words.

He couldn't if he wanted to. I took his tongue a month ago.

I've kept him alive for ninety long days and nights. It smells like piss and shit and mold in here. Like death. Fuck knows that half the wounds on his naked body are infected, some with gangrene.

The man is rotten, from the inside out.

We keep injecting him with antibiotics, to keep him on this side of death's door, but today, I'm finished.

It seems that death by a thousand cuts really *is* a thing.

"I like to make you bleed, Sergei," I say conversationally. "I've always preferred knives over guns. It's more personal. More direct. And there's all that blood. Does it make me a little, oh, I don't know, *unhinged* that I like to make men bleed so much?"

He can't answer me, but I nod.

"I agree. We don't judge each other for our preferences. I dismantled the last of your empire today, so I thought I'd stop by and tell you all about how it went down. On that first day, when we captured you and killed Viktor, who was a fucking child molester, by the way, we infiltrated your compound. Cut comms, got right in there and killed all of your highest-ranking men first. The soldiers scattered a bit, so it took some time to round them up. We executed the last three of those this morning.”

I grab the box cutter from my table and casually slice his Achilles, severing it completely.

“Your wife? Thanks for asking.” I cut the other one. He doesn’t make a sound. He stopped screaming two months ago. “Don’t worry, we didn’t rape her or anything. She got a clean shot to the head. You should know, though, that she was fucking her tennis coach at the time.”

I wince, as if I’m sympathetic.

“We took care of him too. Call it a favor to you. Sorry your wife was cheating on you, man. That can’t be a good feeling.”

I shake my head and cut the inside of his elbows.

“That was number nine hundred and ninety-eight. I’ve been keeping track.”

His eyes fly to mine and I nod.

“That’s right. Death by a thousand cuts. You’ve heard of it, I’m sure. The thing is, now I only have two left.”

I slice through his lower abdomen, deep enough that some of his intestines spill out and I chuckle.

“Make that *one* left. Do I use it today, or do I let you suffer for another day like this.”

The man whines, and I tsk.

“You and your wife enjoyed making the love of my life hurt,” I say, keeping my voice calm and conversational. “Slap her. Punch her. Kick her. Take away something she enjoyed. But you didn't do that for three measly months. No, you terrorized that perfect woman for *years*."

I set the box cutter down and choose my favorite fillet knife.

"I love her more than anything. And the fact that you *ever* put your disgusting fucking hands on her in any way really pisses me off."

I face him, man to man, and with my eyes locked on his, I swipe my arm out and slit his throat, deep enough that it almost severs his head from his body.

Without waiting to watch the blood run from his veins, I turn and walk away.

I need to get back to my wife.

NATASHA

One Year Later

WE NEVER FUCK AT RAPTURE. *Never.* Even after more than a year, it's not something that I can wrap my head around and do. No matter how safe I feel, I can't relax enough for that, and my amazing husband is all about whatever makes me happy.

Tonight, though, we're at the club, and we're watching a man fuck the shit out of his . . . wife? Girlfriend? Stranger?

I don't know, and it doesn't really matter.

They're in a voyeur room, behind a closed door with a window that Julian and I are standing in front of, watching them.

We're the only ones here.

The man has the woman on her side, her leg raised,

and he's fucking her from behind, rubbing her clit and making her bite the pillow.

I love that position.

I lean into my husband and feel him grin against the top of my head before he kisses me there.

"What's he doing to her now?"

He never likes to watch the people fucking. He wants to watch *me*. He loves it when I describe what they're doing, the way we did at the beach resort last year.

The resort that's now in my name, which was a Christmas gift from my over-the-top, completely unhinged husband.

"She's on her side," I say and gasp when he tweaks my nipple through my dress. "And he's fucking her from behind. Oh, he just gripped onto her throat."

"Is he choking her?"

"I—no. I don't think so. Just holding her."

"Hmm," he growls and slides his own hand up to my neck. "Like this?"

"Shit, you know I love that."

"What else do you love, Angel?"

"Fucking everything you do."

Julian chuckles and plants his lips by my ear. "I'm going to take you home, to the penthouse, and I'm going to fuck you up against the glass, so you can watch your city while I'm inside you."

"Let's go." I grab his hand and march us right out of there and into the elevator, where he pushes me against the wall and kisses the *hell* out of me.

"You're so fucking beautiful," he growls against my

lips. "I can't believe I let you out of the house in this dress."

It's another little slip dress, but this one is red, and I paired it with black heels.

"Hi, I'm a grown-up who can choose her own clothes."

"I'm going to spank your ass and fuck your sassy mouth into submission."

"Now you're flirting with me."

Julian barks out a laugh and cups my cheek as he hugs me to him. "I love your sass, baby. Don't ever change."

Even though our penthouse is only five minutes away, it feels like it takes forever to get home, but once we're inside, Julian picks me up and walks right for the windows.

He's a man of his word. *Bless him.*

With my back pressed against the cool glass, my husband nibbles down my jawline to my neck, and his fingers move under my ass to my slit, covered only by the tiniest black G-string.

"You're fucking killing me," he growls as his fingers slip through my slit. "You're so fucking wet for me, Angel."

"Of course, I am. Have you seen you?"

With a groan, he sets me on my feet and turns me to face the city, pulls my hips back, and then his mouth is on me, lapping at me, making me moan.

"I love this cunt. Christ, you taste like heaven." His hands roam up and down the back of my thighs, down my calves, and back up again. "You feel like velvet."

With his mouth on my pussy, his thumb presses on my tight little muscle above, and I moan against the glass, fogging it up.

"Julian."

"One day," he murmurs, but doesn't press inside. "But not today. Who's pussy is this, Natasha?"

"Yours." *God, I love it when he gets all possessive like this.* "Please, I need you."

He takes one last swipe through my slit with his tongue, and then he stands, and I can hear him unfastening his slacks. Before he's inside me, he brings one hand down on my ass with a loud crack and I moan.

"You teased me all fucking evening," he growls as he pushes inside me. He doesn't pause. He doesn't wait for me to adjust to him. No, my man starts to *fuck me*. So fast and hard that I have to brace myself against the glass, holding on for dear life. "With this perfect body, in that little red dress, smiling at me, batting those eyelashes."

"You like"—I pause, trying to catch my breath—"my eyelashes?"

"Every fucking thing about you is gorgeous," he replies. "And mine. Now, I want you to be a good little wife and come all over this cock."

I've been ready to come for *hours*.

With a loud cry, I fall apart, my hands fist against the glass, and everything goes dark as my body shivers, my pussy contracts around him, and he rocks into me, giving into his own climax.

And then I'm in his arms, and he's carrying me to our bedroom and through to the shower, where he spends so much time pampering me.

Washing me.

Murmuring sweet words of love and affection.

He dries my hair and our skin, and then he carries me to our bed, where we lie down facing each other in the dark.

"We didn't say goodbye to anyone," I say softly.

"Pretty sure they figured it out," he says and drifts his fingertips down my cheek.

"Julian?"

"Yes, Angel."

I bite my lip and then dive right in. "I want a baby."

He blinks down at me in surprise. "Today?"

With a chuckle, I shake my head. "I want to *have* a baby. Soon. I'm not pregnant today, but I want to go off the birth control that I started after . . . well, after."

After I came back home from that horrible motel, sick and broken, I knew that I didn't want to get pregnant for a while. I had to rebuild the trust between us. I wanted to heal and enjoy my husband.

But I'm ready now.

"Throw the pills away, Angel. Let's have a baby."

"Just like that?"

"Haven't you figured it out yet? I'll give you *anything* you want, Natasha. All you have to do is ask."

"Let's start with one baby and go from there."

"Fuck, let's have twelve babies," he counters and pulls me against him. "We have the space."

"One."

He laughs and kisses my forehead. "One baby it is, then."

. . .

If you'd like to read a bonus scene featuring Julian and Natasha, you can download it here:
https://dl.bookfunnel.com/gm9kmmlo65

The Kings of Vegas series continues with *Savage King,* featuring Mateo and Violet! You can preorder it here:
https://bit.ly/45Njsrn

Turn the page for a sneak peek of *Savage King*!

Savage King Preview

MATEO

"How much money?"

Fabian's shifty eyes flit over to Diego, my second in command, but I fist my hand in his collar and force his gaze back to me.

"Don't look at him. He can't save you. I asked you a fucking question. How much money have you stolen from me?"

"I didn't—"

I shove him away and circle the tiny office in the back of one of my gyms. I own twelve gyms throughout Las Vegas. They're just some of my legitimate businesses in the city. They're excellent for cleaning money from my less legitimate holdings.

I'm a man with vast interests.

And this motherfucker thought it would be a good idea to skim money from me.

I turn to Diego and lift an eyebrow.

"Just under a hundred and fifty thousand over two years."

Nodding, feeling the frustration bubbling beneath my skin, I turn back to Fabian and watch as the idiot wets himself.

Why do they always piss themselves?

"Fuck." Exhaling, I look up to the ceiling and shake my head. "The thing is, I pay you well. I'm not unreasonable. However, I'm also not a fucking doormat. If you steal from me, you make me look weak. And if there's anything in this fucked-up world that I can't stomach, it's looking fucking weak."

"No, I—"

I pull the gun from where it's tucked in the small of my back and shoot Fabian right between the eyes. Two seconds later, he falls to the floor.

"Get him to the graveyard," I tell Diego, who sighs but nods grimly. "Is anyone else fucking brave enough to pocket my money?"

"No, boss."

"Good. I'll be out for the rest of the night."

"I wish you'd let me go with you. You know I don't like you being there without backup."

Shaking my head, I ignore my number two and grab my leather jacket on my way through the fitness center. Men spar in the ring, and there are people lifting weights and on cardio machines. It's busy in here, despite the late hour.

It's always busy in here.

I'd often be the one sparring with them, helping, taking some hits, but tonight is the real thing.

I need a night in the cage. I need to pound my fist

into an opponent's face. I want to see their fear. I want to see their desperation.

I need that adrenaline.

The underground fighting in Vegas is another lucrative business that I own. Others have tried to edge me out, and those fuckers are in the graveyard.

This is *my* world. The bets, the fighters, every little piece of this goes through my people. It's not officially attached to my organized crime dealings with my brothers, the other three Kings of Vegas, although if I give them a heads-up, they will gladly attend my fights. I never ask them to invest money in this. I don't need them for that.

It's a well-oiled, profitable machine that I love. It's my passion. It's my baby.

And although no one knows that I'm coming in to fight tonight, I'm crashing anyway. Because I have a lot of pent-up frustration that I need to take out on someone's fucking face. I *could* go to Rapture, the adult club owned by my brother, Rome—which happens to be *his* passion and separate from our usual dealings—and fuck the edge out of me, but this calls for blood.

Violence.

And that's not my kink when I fuck.

I swing into my penthouse to grab my gear and decide to ride the bike the short distance from my building to my fight club. Security sees me pull in, and they're immediately speaking into their comms, alerting everyone inside that I'm here.

That's fine. At least they're doing their jobs.

After parking in my space, I pull off my helmet and

leave it on the handlebars, then look at the nearest armed security and lift my chin.

"Yes, boss."

"Anyone touches this, they die."

"Got it, boss."

I slip inside and make my way to the control room, where twelve screens are hung on the wall, showing live feeds from the entire arena. One screen is dedicated to bets, so we can monitor those as well. There's a match going now, and blood spatters from a particularly rough left jab, and it only fuels my anticipation.

This is going to be fun.

"Who's on the docket tonight?" I ask Pandora, my manager. She's in a tight-as-fuck black leather dress that leaves absolutely nothing to the imagination and might lose its fight with her tits at any second.

"Wasn't expecting you," she mutters, her brows low in a scowl, her bright-red lips pursed.

"Disappointed?" I lift an eyebrow and chuckle when she rolls her eyes.

"Just irritated, that's all." Pandora's not afraid of me. She does too good of a job for me to fire her for insubordination. "I have one unmatched fighter. Sampson."

"I'll take it."

"Mateo, he outweighs you by forty pounds."

"I'll take it," I repeat and cross my arms, watching everything unfold in my arena. The crowd is fucking *electric* tonight.

"You haven't fought in a few months," Pandora says as she clicks her nails on the keyboard. "Please don't die tonight. I need the fucking money."

I laugh at that and shake my head.

No, I haven't fought in a while because I've been busy. And maybe that's why I'm so on edge lately. I need to sweat it out in the cage.

My eyes skim the area as I listen to the crowd lose their fucking minds, feeling the energy surge through me, and then my gaze stops and I slowly lean forward, plant my hands on the desk, and *stare.*

"Blow this up," I say, nodding at the space on the screen.

"Someone causing trouble?" Pandora asks, doing as I say, but I don't answer her.

Someone's *always* causing some kind of trouble here. I don't police the drugs or the bad attitudes, and I make a fuck ton of money off the booze.

But that's not what I'm looking at.

She doesn't fit in. It's not that she doesn't *blend.* She's tattooed, her red hair in a long braid down her back. She's in a vintage rock-band T-shirt, the sleeves missing, and cutoff denim shorts. Her curves make me salivate. I love a woman who isn't stick thin. I want hips to hold on to and tits I can lose myself in. I can't see her feet, but I'd bet that one-of-a-kind sport bike outside that she's wearing Chucks.

Or sneakers.

She's not dressed to the nines with impeccable makeup and hair styled within an inch of its life.

And her eyes aren't on the cage. They skim the crowd as she works that lower lip between straight teeth, and I instantly want to know *everything* there is to know about her.

Without looking at Pandora, I press a button, and less than a minute later, Snake, my head of security, walks into the office.

"Boss."

"This woman." I point to the screen. "Doesn't leave this building until I have the chance to talk to her."

"Got it."

"Don't approach her. Leave her alone, but if she tries to leave, tell her to wait for me in my private office."

He nods, and then he's gone, and I turn to find Pandora watching me with raised eyebrows.

"What?"

"Do you know her?"

I simply stare at her, and she rolls her eyes.

"You're starting to piss me off, Dora."

"Shocking." She shakes her head and gets back to work. "You'd better go get ready. You're on after the next match."

Without a word, I walk out of the room and down to my private office suite where I take my time changing into my shorts, wrapping my hands, and putting on the open-fingered gloves. I don't wear a helmet.

None of us do.

When there's a knock on my door, I open it and find Snake there, ready for me.

"Status on the girl?" I ask as he follows me down the hallway.

"She's in the same spot. Hasn't moved."

"Let's walk past her on the way to the cage."

"You sure?"

"I didn't fucking stutter."

Natalie Kane is the dark romance pseudonym for Kristen Proby. After publishing more than 85 titles, the majority of which are contemporary romance, Kristen wanted to dive deeper into the morally gray side of things and is enjoying her foray into mafia romance. This is where the swoon of Kristen Proby meets the obsession of dark romance. Kristen Proby after dark, if you will.

Kristen Proby is the New York Times, USA Today, WSJ, and Amazon top 3 bestselling author of more than 85 titles. When not under deadline, Kristen enjoys spending time with her husband and their fur babies, riding her bike, reading in her library, trying her hand at painting, and, of course, enjoying her beautiful home in the mountains of Montana.

Newsletter Sign Up

I hope you enjoyed reading this story as much as I enjoyed writing it! For upcoming book news, be sure to join my newsletter! I promise I will only send you news-filled mail, and none of the spam. You can sign up here.
https://nataliekane.myflodesk.com/newsletter